Dreams
of the
Island

BOOKS BY KATE HEWITT

Kate Hewitt

Dreams
of the
Island

bookouture

Published by Bookouture in 2020

An imprint of Storyfire Ltd.
Carmelite House
50 Victoria Embankment
London EC4Y 0DZ

www.bookouture.com

ISBN: 978-1-80019-110-5
eBook ISBN: 978-1-80019-109-9

Dedicated to my sister Susie, who looked up from reading the first version of this book with a dreamy smile on her face and said "I'm in Ellen's world!" I'll always remember that! I love you!

PART ONE

CHAPTER ONE

Amherst Island, Ontario, 1911

"What do you think of this one, Ellen?"

Ellen Copley watched as her friend Louisa Hopper turned this way and that to see her reflection, the confection of lace, ribbons, and a feather or two that was the latest fashion in millinery perched jauntily on top of her head.

"It's lovely. Quite large, though. I imagine your neck will start to ache."

"Oh, *Ellen*." With a wry smile, Louisa took the hat off and tossed it carelessly onto the bed.

Ellen reached for it, admiring the violet-dyed feathers before putting it back in the box. She'd never worn something so fine, but then she'd never had a need to either. Louisa was intending it as part of her trousseau, for her honeymoon in Toronto next week.

Even though Ellen had had months to get used to the idea of her friend marrying Jed Lyman, an islander and dear family friend, she still felt a little twist of sorrow at the thought. She'd been in love with Jed for years, although no one had known, save for Jed's brother Lucas. He'd guessed after he had declared his love for Ellen at one of Queen's University's "smokers"—the slang term for the dances undergraduates held—that he'd escorted her to last May.

Amidst the loud ragtime music and hazy swirls of cigarette smoke, she'd miserably acknowledged that she was unable to reciprocate his feelings. Lucas had told her he could wait, but Ellen didn't think she'd ever change her mind—or her heart. Lucas was a dear friend, like a brother to her, while once just looking at Jed could have stolen her breath and made her dizzy.

It would have been so much easier, Ellen mused now, if she'd fallen in love with Lucas rather than Jed. Lucas, shy and thoughtful, was surely more her type than Jed, who had never left Amherst Island or his father's farm, and whose taciturn ways bordered on surliness, if you didn't look more deeply to the generous and genuine man underneath.

And it was Jed, with that surprising depth, the sudden glint in his gray eyes, his mouth kicking up in a wry smile, that had made her heart race and her hopes soar, not kind, quiet Lucas.

Sighing, Ellen rose from Louisa's bed and began to pick up the clothes that her friend had carelessly tossed all over the room, despite the fact that they were expensive, newly bought from some of New York City's best boutiques.

Louisa was the only daughter of a banker and his wife, and Ellen had met her when they'd both lived in Seaton, Vermont, and gone to school together. Ellen had been living with her stern Aunt Ruth and genial Uncle Hamish. Neither of them, childless all their days, had ever seemed to know what to do with her, although they'd all come to an understanding in time, just before Ruth's death a few months earlier.

Ellen's mother had died back in Glasgow, when she was just twelve, and she and her father had emigrated to Vermont to join her Uncle Hamish in running the town's general store. Da hadn't warmed to country life and within weeks of arriving in Vermont he'd set out West, leaving Ellen with relatives she barely knew. He was now laying rails all the way to Mexico, and Ellen had only seen him once in seven years, and that only a few months ago.

For a while during those difficult years in Seaton, spoiled Louisa had made Ellen's life a misery, bullying her and turning some of her classmates against her out of sheer spite. Ellen had persevered in being friendly, and eventually the two girls had formed an unlikely and somewhat reluctant friendship that had been, at various times and to varying degrees, both fraught and fun.

Then, several years ago, Louisa had invited herself to Amherst Island, where Ellen spent the summers with her Aunt Rose and Uncle Dyle and their happy brood of five noisy children.

The island was a true home to Ellen, and when Louisa had finagled an invitation, she'd realized she wasn't sure she wanted to share it with her temperamental friend.

Yet Louisa had come on her own insistence, and Jed had fallen in love with her, and now, in two days' time, they would marry.

She'd accepted all that, Ellen told herself firmly as she hung up a nightdress of gossamer silk and fragile lace. She did not like to think of Louisa wearing it. She couldn't be jealous now; it wasn't fair to Louisa or Jed, or even to herself.

She had her own plans now, plans she hadn't yet shared with anyone, intending to reveal them after Jed and Louisa's wedding, when the excitement had died down. Plans that buoyed her spirit and stirred her soul. She didn't need to feel sad simply because Jed and Louisa were together. Besides, she'd mended her broken heart, or so she'd convinced herself.

Louisa tried on another hat, this one with a bunch of grapes on the brim and a wide scarlet ribbon around the crown. She stared at her reflection, her lips pursed, before she took it off and tossed it aside like the others.

"I don't suppose I'll wear it more than once," she said with a sigh and then a toss of her auburn curls. "No one on the island has any sense of fashion."

Even though she was marrying an islander, Louisa could not seem to shake the habit of criticizing the place, Ellen had come to realize. "And they've no need to," she replied. "Hats like these are hardly practical for a farming life." Ellen thought she might topple right over if she tried to wear a hat that ridiculously large.

"Exactly," Louisa answered, and Ellen watched as her friend's face settled into discontented lines, just as it had so often when they were children. She'd thought Louisa had outgrown such sulks, but perhaps she hadn't.

"You knew you'd live on Amherst Island when you agreed to marry Jed," Ellen pointed out, as reasonably as she could. Now was not the time even to think about how unsuited Louisa seemed to farming life in a small community, or to being a farmer's wife. Her parents had accepted the match with grudging reluctance, and only because they had always indulged their spoiled daughter, and Louisa had absolutely set her cap for Jed Lyman. "And you've always loved it here, Louisa."

"It's pretty enough," Louisa agreed, "but I don't intend to molder away here forever." She tossed her head again, burnished curls bouncing against her shoulders, hazel eyes glinting with sudden defiance.

Ellen stared at her with growing unease. "But, Louisa, the Lyman farm is on the island—Jed's *life* is on the island. What can you mean?"

Louisa rose from her dressing table and prowled restlessly around the small bedroom she'd always used in the McCaffertys' farmhouse, now scattered with silk and lace. "I can't imagine being a farmer's wife forever," she said at last. "Surely you see that."

"But—"

"And there's no reason why Jed should shut himself up that way either," she added, spinning away from Ellen to stare out the window.

The sun was just beginning to lower in a deep blue sky, setting the rolling fields and pastures ablaze. In the distance, Lake Ontario twinkled, and Ellen could hear the lowing of the cows in the pasture, her seven-year-old cousin Andrew's distant laughter.

It was a beautiful view, and they were comforting sounds, all of it together making the sweetest and dearest home Ellen had ever known. She'd be sorry to leave it, as she would in just a few weeks, and she couldn't imagine Jed *ever* leaving the island, or even wanting to. He'd been born here, and he'd never left. He was part of its roots and soil as much as the maples arching over Jasper Lane outside.

"Have you spoken to Jed about this?" she asked at last.

The spark of defiance that had lit Louisa's eyes went out suddenly and she sagged onto the bed. "No, not yet. But my father's prepared to offer him a job at the bank in Seaton. He told me when we were in New York—"

"Seaton!" Jed as a banker, in stuffy Seaton! It was an impossible idea, an irreconcilable image. He hadn't even finished high school, for starters, and in any case, he belonged here.

When Jed had proposed a few months ago, Ellen remembered, Louisa had been full of plans about making her home on the island; she'd half-convinced Jed to buy an old homestead near the tiny hamlet of Emerald, although he'd insisted on keeping the Lyman homestead going with his father, next door to the McCaffertys' place.

What had changed? Or had the reality of life here sunk in enough to make Louisa realize she wasn't as enamored with the island as she'd once believed, that she didn't know how to churn butter or make jam or darn her own stockings?

"Louisa," Ellen said gently, laying a hand on her friend's arm, "can you really see Jed as a banker? He didn't even go to high school—"

Louisa shrugged her hand away. "You've always been a snob about that, haven't you?"

"That's not fair," Ellen answered quietly, but her cheeks burned. When she'd discovered that Jed loved Louisa and not her, despite their years of friendship, she'd said some unkind things about

Jed she'd since fiercely regretted—things that he'd unfortunately overheard. Even though she'd long since apologized and he'd forgiven her, the cruelty of her words—calling him an ignorant farmer—still cut deeply, mostly because she hadn't meant them at all. She'd only been speaking out of her own humiliation and heartache. "I only meant that he loves the land," she continued now, "and the Lyman farm has been in the family for decades. How could he leave it to work in a bank?"

Louisa lifted her chin, her eyes sparking once more. "He would if he loved me."

"But you shouldn't even ask it of him—"

"What's it to you?" Louisa shot back, and Ellen recognized the light of malice in her friend's eyes that had been there in childhood, and still occasionally snapped back to life. "You don't have any say in the matter, Ellen, as much as you might have once wanted to."

"Don't," Ellen said quietly. Louisa had suspected Ellen's feelings for Jed last Christmas, but Ellen had thought—or at least hoped—that she'd put her off. And those feelings were buried deep now, best to be forgotten or at least certainly ignored. "I think you should talk to Jed about this," Ellen added firmly, rising from the bed and beginning to tidy up Louisa's discarded hats and fripperies. "Before the wedding, because it's too important to leave to later. Whatever the two of you decide, you need to be honest with each other from the start—"

"Are you hoping he'll break it off?" Louisa interrupted. "So you can have him for yourself? You're perfectly content to stay on this poky island, aren't you, Ellen? Especially if it were with Jed."

Ellen tried not to show how Louisa's fit of temper pierced her, mostly because there was a small, hidden part of her that agreed with that sentiment. Yes, she'd once dreamed of just such a life, and whatever her plans now, it was hard to let go of that dream.

She didn't deign to answer, fearing she'd say something she'd regret. She didn't want to lose her temper with Louisa, not with the wedding so close and her own future shining brightly ahead of her.

"Surely you know me better than that, Louisa," she said finally. "I've been your friend for six years, and Jed's for even longer. Of course I want you both to be happy."

"I know you do." As changeable as ever, Louisa now reached for Ellen's hands, tugging her down beside her on the bed once more. "I'm sorry, Ellen. I'm being awful, I know I am, and you must hate me for it. I must seem like a spoiled I-don't-know-what, but the truth is, I'm so afraid." She bit her lip, a tear sparkling like a diamond droplet on one lash. Even in her obvious misery, Louisa looked lovely, Ellen thought, and always would. No wonder Jed had fallen in love with her.

"Dear Louisa." Ellen patted her friend's hand. "What are you afraid of?"

"I don't know how to bake bread," Louisa blurted.

"Bake bread? What on earth—"

"Or sew, or darn socks, or bottle fruit or—anything. I'm useless, Ellen." Louisa rose from the bed and began to pace the room, wringing her hands like the proverbial maiden in distress. Even though Ellen recognized Louisa's worry was genuine, she suspected her friend was enjoying the moment of drama. "How can I be a good wife to Jed if we live here on the farm?" she demanded. "I can't do any of the things all the farmers' wives do round here, and I won't be able to learn." She whirled around to face Ellen, her tears replaced once more by a blaze of defiance. "I can't do it. I won't, and Jed shouldn't ask it of me."

Ellen suppressed a sigh. Sometimes she forgot how exhausting Louisa could be. And while she recognized that Louisa was afraid, she also suspected she didn't *want* to learn any of the dull things farmers' wives had to do. She hadn't during her summers on the island when they'd been younger. She'd never gone berry picking with the rest of them or helped in the kitchen. One evening she'd informed Aunt Rose that she would have dinner on a tray in her room, to which Rose had replied in her kindly, brisk way, that if Louisa did not wish to eat with the rest of the family, she could fend for herself.

"You need to talk to Jed," Ellen said again wearily. "He knew what you were like when he asked you to marry him, Louisa. He's not expecting you to turn into something else now." Although she doubted Jed was anticipating a call to working in a bank in Vermont.

"I don't think he's even realized, and why should he? He's a man, after all. The bread just appears on the table, the socks darned in his drawer."

"Jed's mother died four years ago," Ellen reminded her. "He's been darning his own socks for quite a while. Talk to him."

She heard Rose calling her from downstairs, and with relief she slipped from the room and hurried to the kitchen.

"And how is dear Louisa?" Rose asked, wry good humor lighting her faded blue eyes as Ellen came into the welcoming room with its scrubbed table and blackened range. She'd spent so many happy afternoons there, with the old brown teapot on the center of the table and sunlight slanting through the wide sashed windows. "Does she even have space to move up there," Rose asked, "with all the things she's bought for her trousseau?"

"A bit," Ellen allowed. "But I think she's rather in a panic."

"Only natural. I imagine poor old Jed's having a bit of a panic as well!"

Ellen just smiled, although again she felt that shaft of pain at the thought of them marrying. Really, she needed to stop thinking about it, and most of all, to stop minding.

"And how are you, Ellen?" Rose asked, laying a hand on her arm, making Ellen wonder if she'd possibly guessed the nature of her thoughts. "It hasn't been so very long since poor Ruth died, and you left nursing school…"

"I'm all right." The last few months had been tumultuous, with her decision to leave nursing school tied to her aunt's sudden death back in Seaton in the summer. Aunt Ruth had been stern and sometimes even cold, and for too many years Ellen had felt her aunt didn't even like her, but the reconciliation on her aunt's deathbed had made Ellen realize life was simply too short to allow such misunderstandings to continue.

After Ruth's death, she'd ended up traveling all the way to New Mexico to visit her father, attempting to heal the hurt his abrupt departure from her life had caused.

She'd succeeded, at least somewhat. Although, in truth, Ellen didn't know what kind of relationship she could have with her father now. His life on the railroad, living in little more than a shack and moving from place to place, was so different to her own, and she wasn't sure if Douglas Copley even knew how to be a father anymore. But at least she was no longer angry or hurt by his abandonment, simply saddened by the way things had turned out.

And now, with all that behind her, she needed to think of her future.

Smiling, Ellen turned away from her aunt, her mind full of what was to come, and all she hoped for.

CHAPTER TWO

Two days later, Ellen sat in the second pew of Stella's Presbyterian church and watched Louisa progress down the aisle, magnificent in white tulle, on the arm of her father. The Hoppers had wanted to have Louisa and Jed's wedding at the Episcopalian church back in Seaton, but Jed's ties to the farm—and the fact that most of the islanders would be unable to travel such a distance—made such a thing impossible.

The Hoppers had conceded the location, and would be hosting the reception afterwards, to take place at the McCaffertys' farm. Louisa had told Ellen they'd shipped the champagne all the way from New York, and hired their own cook to manage the canapés. Ellen had wondered how islanders would take to such fancy fare; she hoped this wouldn't set them against Louisa, for trying to impress them with her hoity-toity ways the minute she'd got here.

Almost reluctantly, Ellen's gaze slid from Louisa to Jed, and her heart gave a familiar and painful twist. He looked so *familiar,* so dear, with his steel-gray eyes and dark hair still unruly despite what appeared to be a generous amount of hair pomade.

A montage of bittersweet memories tumbled through her mind: the first time she'd met Jed, when she'd not quite been thirteen, uncertain and afraid as she stepped from Captain Jonah's boat onto this unfamiliar shore, everything dark around her.

Jed, surly and silent, had fetched her from the station in his old buckboard, and Ellen had not known what to think of this strange, sullen boy with the startling gray eyes. Yet within a few months they'd become unlikely friends, brought together by hardship—Ellen's mother had died when she was only eleven, and Jed's mother was ailing and bedridden.

By the end of that first summer, Ellen had made friends with both Lucas and Jed, as well as all the McCaffertys, from excitable Peter to sensible Caro to feisty Ruth and darling Sarah and Andrew. Rose had felt like a mother to her, and Dyle—dear Dyle—a father. And Amherst Island was the first place where she'd truly felt as if she'd come home.

She recalled lazy days spent in the meadow between the Lyman and McCafferty properties, and a particularly poignant afternoon when Jed had seen her charcoal sketches for the first time. He'd teased her, of course; that's what Jed always did, but there had been affection lurking in his eyes. And when he'd told her, both serious and sincere, that he thought they were good, Ellen's heart had sung.

And then the most poignant memory of all, when she'd thought, for a moment, that Jed might kiss her. Everything between them had felt suspended, transfixed in a moment of breathless yearning, despite Louisa and the attachment that had surely been growing between her and Jed—

But he hadn't kissed her, and the moment had broken, both of them acting as if it hadn't happened at all, and a short while later Jed had asked Louisa to marry him, sealing all their fates. Ellen knew it was better that Jed hadn't kissed her, that she wasn't left with more wondering what-ifs than she already had. Sometimes she thought that perhaps that moment had been all in her mind, no more than her wistful imaginings. She and Jed had never talked about it, although he had, with painful awkwardness, attempted an apology of sorts after his engagement.

There are things I've wanted to say to you, Ellen…

She'd turned away from him then, unable to bear the thought of hearing them when it was too late, when it wouldn't do any good, or worse, hearing some kind of justification or excuse about how he'd never felt that way about her. Better not to say. Better not to know.

Now she forced herself to focus on the ceremony, on the vows being said that would bind Jed and Louisa together forever, for better or worse, for richer or poorer. For their sake, she hoped they found happiness together, and that Louisa could settle to island life, and Jed could see to his wife's happiness. Together they would find their way… and surely that was all anyone could hope for?

"I now pronounce you man and wife!"

To a smattering of applause, Jed and Louisa turned towards the congregation, and Ellen took in their happy smiles, although she suspected Jed felt more relief than anything else in that moment. He'd always hated being in front of a crowd.

Hand in hand, they walked up the aisle towards the doors of the church, and as Ellen watched them go, she felt something in herself lighten and then let go. They were married. Jed was gone to her forever, at least in that way, and to her surprise, she had a sense of peace in that moment. Finally, that chapter of her life had been put to rest.

An hour later, Ellen was standing on the side of the cleanly swept barnyard, tapping her foot in time to the merry tune the best of the island's musicians were making with fiddle, banjo, and bass. Colorful skirts whirled around her as couples took to the floor; despite his self-proclaimed two left feet, Jed had taken Louisa to dance and was moving with careful, cumbersome steps. Louisa, as radiant as ever, didn't seem to mind, her face tilted towards her husband's and filled with joy.

"Care to dance, Ellen?"

Ellen turned to see Lucas smiling at her. They hadn't spoken much since that uncomfortable interview last May, and she couldn't keep from feeling awkward at seeing him now.

"I'm…" she began, and Lucas smiled wryly.

"For old times' sake, if nothing else?"

"Not just old times, Lucas," Ellen answered. Regret rushed through her at the thought of how things had changed between them; before that party at Queen's, they'd been such good friends. "I'm honored to dance with you."

She took his hand and soon they were dancing amidst the other couples, the sawdust sprinkled over the yard flying up in little golden puffs.

"Are you looking forward to going back to Queen's?" Ellen asked as they moved through the other couples in a country dance. "It's not long now."

"No. And I am looking forward to resuming my studies for my last year." He smiled whimsically. "I'll have to start buckling down, you know. Look for a proper job."

"What are you thinking of?"

He shrugged. "Law seems practical."

"Law!" Ellen stared at Lucas in surprise. "But history has always been your first love."

"Yes, but reading dusty, fusty books isn't much of a profession."

"Still…"

"I think I could enjoy the law, if I put my mind to it. And I'll like living in a city… Kingston or Ottawa, perhaps even Toronto. What about you, Ellen? Rose told me you're not returning to your nurse's training. Will you stay on the island? Return to Vermont?"

"Neither." Ellen took a deep breath. She'd been intending to tell the McCaffertys first, but it made sense to speak to Lucas alone. He'd always been the one who had encouraged her love of drawing, and he'd even suggested she exhibit some of her sketches here on the island, and try to sell them to city day-trippers. She hadn't possessed the courage to follow through with his suggestion, but she'd appreciated his enthusiasm. She hoped he'd be happy for her now.

"What, then?" Lucas asked. The dance had ended, and in the lull between numbers, Ellen and Lucas were left standing there, hands still linked as Lucas gazed at her with narrowed eyes. "What are you hiding, Ellen? You look as if you've got a secret."

"It's not meant to be a secret, exactly. I just wanted to wait until Louisa and Jed's wedding was over before I told anyone."

"Wait." Lucas led her across the yard to the back porch of the Lymans' house, the first purple shadows of twilight settling over them.

The wooden boards creaked as Ellen bunched her skirts around her ankles and sat down on the old weathered steps, enjoying a brief moment of privacy.

Lucas sat next to her, and they were both silent as they gazed out at the darkening sky, the first stars glimmering distantly.

"So tell me," he said finally. "What are you planning? Because you're certainly planning something, and I'm very curious to know what it is."

Ellen laughed softly. "You know me too well, Lucas."

"I'd like to think I know you well," Lucas replied, and even in the shadowy darkness, Ellen could see the sincerity in his eyes, hear it in his voice. She was reminded, painfully, of how that same sincerity had throbbed in his voice and shone in his eyes when he'd told her that he loved her.

She swallowed and looked away. "Well, you're right, as usual. I am planning something. I've applied and been accepted to art school."

"Art school!" Lucas reached over and squeezed her hand. "I'm so pleased for you. Where are you going? Ottawa? Montreal?"

"Glasgow, actually."

"Glasgow!" Lucas stared at her in astonishment. "But that's in Scotland."

"Indeed it is," Ellen answered teasingly. "You know your geography, Lucas."

"But… why so far away?"

"I met one of the trustees of the school on the train to Chicago," Ellen explained. "I was working on some sketches, and he happened to see them. We got to talking and he gave me his card… it was all very proper, of course," she added, and Lucas smiled faintly, although she still saw a frown between his eyebrows.

"Of course."

"In any case, when I returned here, I sent him some of my best drawings, and a few weeks ago, I received a reply. I've been accepted to The Glasgow School of Art, on a bursary." She smiled, feeling both the trepidation and excitement course within her. "I'll begin my studies at the school in October."

"So soon…" Lucas still looked shocked, and Ellen felt a rush of sympathy. She knew her news was unexpected, and she suspected Aunt Rose would have a similar reaction to Lucas, pleasure mixed with wariness.

"The school has quite a few lady artists studying there," she said when Lucas had lapsed into a frowning silence. "Some are even teachers. The head, Francis Newbery, has been encouraging ladies to apply to their program." She clutched her knees, trying to imagine this new life that had come her way so unexpectedly. It still felt so vague and hazy, impossible to truly envision. "I'll be boarding with one of the teachers, the Head of Drawing, Miss Gray."

"I see." Lucas finally rallied with a smile. "Well, I'm pleased for you, of course. Very, very pleased. And surprised you're going so far away." He drew a deep breath, his smile turning wry, his eyes shadowed. "You know, of course, that I wanted things to be different for you… for us."

Ellen's cheeks warmed and she looked away, an ache she couldn't properly identify washing through her. "I know," she whispered. "I'm sorry, Lucas…"

"I haven't given up hope, you know," Lucas continued quietly. "Maybe that's foolish of me, but it's the truth."

"Oh, Lucas—" Ellen turned to gaze at him helplessly. How many times had she wished she'd fallen in love with him instead of Jed? And yet… the spark simply wasn't there.

"Never mind," he told her quickly. "I shouldn't have mentioned it. I won't again, and I'll never press you, Ellen, I promise. But… you'll come back, won't you? To the island?" He sounded so sad and uncertain, it made Ellen ache all over again, although she tried to sound light.

"I can't imagine not coming back. The island will always be my home."

"I'm glad to hear that."

They were silent for a few minutes, listening to the faint, tinny strumming of the banjo, the merry fiddling. A burst of laughter sounded from the barnyard and Lucas rose from the porch steps.

"We've been gone long enough, I suppose," he said. "Jed and Louisa will be saying their goodbyes soon. They're spending the night in Ogdensburg before heading to Toronto. Captain Jonah is taking them across specially."

Lucas stretched out his hand to help Ellen from the steps, and as she took it, he pulled her close enough to kiss her cheek. She felt the rasp of faint stubble against her chin and his lips were surprisingly soft as he brushed them against her skin.

"I'll say my goodbye now," he said, his voice rough with emotion. "Godspeed on your journey, Ellen. I know you'll go far." And then he stepped away, and they walked in silence back to the party.

The next morning, over breakfast, Ellen told all of the McCaffertys her plans.

Rose stared at her open-mouthed for a moment, porridge dripping from the wooden spoon she held aloft, before she hurriedly returned it to the pot and pulled Ellen into a tight embrace.

"All the way to Glasgow! Oh, Ellen, we'll miss you so, but how terribly exciting!" She stepped back, her eyes sparkling with tears.

"Oh, Aunt Rose—"

She sniffed quickly and shook her head. "Never mind me. I'm always quick to cry, as Dyle will tell you. But we will miss you so. You'll come back, won't you? At the end of the course, at least?"

"Of course I'll come back," Ellen promised Rose, just as she'd promised Lucas. Truly, she could not imagine doing otherwise.

"When do you leave, then?" Rose asked, all determined briskness now. She dolloped far too much porridge in Ellen's bowl, her hand trembling, and Ellen gave some to Gracie before sprinkling it with maple sugar.

"In a fortnight. I'm going to travel down to New York and take the *S.S. Furnessia* to Glasgow."

"Goodness." Rose's gaze widened. "You've arranged all this without saying a word?"

With a pang of guilt, Ellen nodded, stirring her porridge. "Yes. It wasn't much trouble, and I didn't want to take away from Jed and Louisa's wedding."

Rose shook her head slowly. "I can't even imagine. You've had such experiences, Ellen. First New Mexico and now across the ocean… you're quite the lady adventuress!"

"Are you frightened, Ellen?" Sarah, still dreamy and bookish at thirteen years old, asked. "I would be, going so far away. Do you remember Glasgow?"

"Yes, I do, although not the part I'll be living in." Ellen's memory of Glasgow was the cramped tenement she'd lived in with her father and bedridden mother, grimy with coal dust from the railyard. She remembered working all hours at only ten years old, washing and cooking and sweeping, and then sitting by her mother's bedside while she faded away.

No, this would be much different—school and drawing, living in an elegant neighborhood, having a room of her own.

"And what about meeting all sorts of new people?" Sarah asked. "I'd be scared of that, as well."

"Truth be told, Sarah, I am a bit," Ellen admitted with a laugh.

"Well, I wouldn't be," Caro answered with a toss of her pretty head. Caro was five years younger than Ellen's nineteen, and was in her first year of high school at Glebe Collegiate in Kingston, hoping one day for a place at Queen's. "I think it sounds amazing. Traveling on a steamer by yourself! I wish I could."

Ellen smiled and nodded. She was, in a nervous sort of way, looking forward to the ship passage. Seven years ago, she'd arrived on a steamer with her Da, traveling third-class, a twelve-year-old waif with a thick brogue and tangled hair. Now she was splurging on second-class, and traveling as a young lady of some means, with a future far more certain than she and Da had had when they'd sailed into New York's harbor. She was coming full circle.

Later, when Ellen was alone in her room with a pile of mending, Rose came to find her, several aprons neatly ironed and folded in her arms. "I don't suppose you'll need these in Glasgow," she said wryly as she placed them on top of the bureau.

"I might," Ellen answered. "I'll be trying my hand at pottery and painting as well as drawing. I think most of the students wear smocks."

"Do they?" Rose perched on the edge of the bed. "Well, you ought to buy yourself some nice new dresses, at any rate. Or I could make some up for you. You should have some nice things to start."

"I might do a bit of shopping in New York, before I leave," Ellen said, and then gave a little self-conscious laugh. "That sounds so grand—I can hardly believe it." Uncle Hamish had given her some money after Ruth's death, enough to pay for her passage and some living expenses while she was in Glasgow. If she was careful, it should last all three years.

"I don't like to think of you in New York all by yourself," Rose said. "It's not safe. Perhaps Dyle should take you. You could both go on the train…"

"Uncle Dyle can't be away from the farm for that long, and if I'm going to travel all the way across the Atlantic, I expect I'll be all right in New York City. I've already found a place to stay, a perfectly respectable boarding house for ladies in Gramercy Park." Ellen smiled to soften the refusal. "Besides, I came all the way here from Seaton when I was not quite thirteen. I can manage, Aunt Rose. You know I can."

"I suppose you can." Rose shook her head with a sigh. "I know I'm fussing, but I can't help it. You're like another daughter to me, Ellen. I will miss you terribly."

Ellen blinked hard and swallowed past the thickness in her throat. "And you've been as a mam to me, Aunt Rose."

Rose smiled, and Ellen could see her aunt had more to say. "Ellen…" she began. "I just want to be sure… for my own peace of mind… this is what you want? There's a difference between running to something and running away."

It took a few seconds for her aunt's meaning to be clear, and when it did, Ellen felt her cheeks burn. She knew then that Rose had guessed something of her feelings for Jed. How obvious had she been? Or was her lovely Aunt Rose just so astute?

"I think any journey is a bit of both," she said as lightly as she could, as she picked up her mending once more, unable to look her aunt in the eye and see the compassion there. "But I'm excited about this opportunity, Aunt Rose. I've always loved drawing, and this is the best chance I have to make a go of it. This is the right decision for me, whether I'm running to or away."

Rose sighed and nodded. "As long as you're sure."

"I'm sure."

Yet as Rose left her little bedroom, Ellen wondered just how sure she actually was. Ever since she was a small child she'd wanted a home of her own, a place that would welcome her and never change. Yet her life, she acknowledged wryly, had been one of seemingly constant tumult: first moving from Springburn to Vermont, and then having her Aunt Ruth send her to Amherst Island. That had turned out to be a happy occasion, but for the next seven years, Ellen had traveled between Seaton and the island, her loyalties divided between the home of her heart and the family—Uncle Hamish and Aunt Ruth—who had committed to raising her.

She knew Rose and Dyle would always consider their farm her home; she'd have a place here as long as she wished. So why was she now so determined to leave? *Was* she running away—away from heartbreak and the pain of seeing Jed and Louisa day in and day out?

She hadn't actually spoken to either of them since the wedding; she'd only seen Jed across the barnyard when he and Louisa had been about to drive off from the Lymans'. Their gazes had met across the crowded yard, and for a second Ellen had felt as if the heavy thud of her heart was weighing her down. She thought she saw a storm of emotions in Jed's normally shuttered gaze, but then Louisa spoke to him and he turned away, and they'd left without Ellen having ever said goodbye, or anything at all. She wished she had; she wanted to recapture that settled sense of peace she'd felt in the church. She wanted to be sure.

"I'm not running away," she said aloud now, her voice seeming both small and fierce in the emptiness of her own room. "I'm not. I'm running *to*."

CHAPTER THREE

The day before Ellen was to leave for New York, the McCaffertys had a going-away party for her. It was a small but merry affair, with just the McCaffertys and the Lymans and a few other close friends in attendance, all crowded into the front parlor for games and music, accompanied by apple cider and Aunt Rose's island-famous sugared donuts.

Ellen received the little sending-off gifts with both joy and barely held back tears, as once again she realized how far away she was going, and how unknown her future was compared to the warm and easy familiarity of island life.

There were handkerchiefs embroidered with violets from Rose; a new sketchbook with fresh, crisp paper from Lucas; sachets filled with dried lavender from Caro; and a set of scented soaps bought in Toronto from Louisa and Jed.

Ellen looked around at everyone, her dearest friends and family, and felt her heart swell with love and a strange, sweet sorrow.

"Ellen, you look as if you're going to cry!" Andrew, seven years old and utterly disdainful of all things girlish, sounded appalled by such a prospect.

"Don't cry, Ellen." Eleven-year-old Gracie slid onto her lap with childish ease and hooked one arm around Ellen's neck, burrowing close to her.

Ellen sniffed and blinked back her tears as she cuddled her young cousin. "I won't cry, I promise," she said, her voice wobbling only slightly. "They would be happy tears, in any case, Gracie. I'm just so thankful for all of you." Her gaze moved around the room, resting on each person in turn and yet carefully avoiding Jed.

He and Louisa had returned from Toronto last week and she hadn't spoken to him yet, although Louisa had stopped by the farmhouse to regale all the McCaffertys with the luxurious details of her honeymoon, paid for, Ellen suspected, by Mr. Hopper. Ellen had listened with the right amount of enthusiasm and interest, but when Rose had turned to take the kettle off the stove, she'd caught her eye and given her a sympathetic smile that had made Ellen cringe inside.

Now she forced all that aside as she kissed Gracie's cheek.

"Time for bed," Rose announced. "Before we all turn into pumpkins."

"Yes, we ought to get back, shouldn't we, Jed?" Louisa hooked a proprietorial arm through her husband's. "We're still exhausted from all our travels."

"I'm sure," Ellen murmured. She picked up a tray of tea things to take back to the kitchen, more an attempt to make herself scarce than actually be helpful. Everyone was making to go, collecting hats and coats.

Outside the kitchen window, a harvest moon hung huge and orange in a starlit sky. The night was crisp and still, a harbinger of autumn. Ellen stood there for a moment, savoring the silence and solitude, when she heard footsteps behind her.

"Ellen."

She turned around slowly and saw Jed standing in the doorway, as she knew he would be.

"Hello, Jed." Her voice, thankfully, came out sounding normal. "Thank you for the soaps. They're lovely."

"Louisa picked them out." Jed ducked his head. "You know I don't know anything about things like that."

"I suppose not," Ellen allowed with a small smile. She took a deep breath and set about cleaning up, pumping water into the kettle before plonking it on top of the range. "From the sounds of it, you had quite the time in Toronto—shows and dinners in fancy hotels. I can only imagine."

"It was all right," Jed allowed, and Ellen let out a little laugh.

"High praise indeed, coming from you."

She met his gaze then, and wished she hadn't. His gray eyes were so familiar, that crooked smile so beloved. And she had no business—absolutely no business at all—thinking that way, and so she wouldn't. She turned away, putting cups and saucers in the washing basin as if her very life depended on it.

"Anyway," Jed said, and cleared his throat. "I just wanted to say goodbye. You'll do great things at that art school, Ellen, I'm sure of it."

Ellen blinked, dangerously near tears for the second time that night. It was nothing, and yet it felt so final, in so many ways.

"Thank you, Jed," she said after a moment, her lowered gaze still on the dishes. "I trust you and Louisa will have a good honeymoon year on the farm."

"It will be a lot of hard work." He sounded dubious, and Ellen wondered how well Louisa had turned her hand to the mundane chores and duties of a farmer's wife. It would all be behind her soon. "Anyway…" Jed paused and Ellen dared not look at him. "Goodbye," he said at last, and she listened to him walk away, squeezing her eyes shut and releasing a shuddering breath before the kettle began to whistle.

The next morning, Dyle drove her to the little ferry station, where Captain Jonah waited with his tiny tug. Back when Ellen had been nearly thirteen, Captain Jonah had piloted what amounted to little more than a rowboat, but just like Ellen, he'd moved up in the world.

"Get yourself in, girl," he called, spitting tobacco juice neatly into the blue-green waters of Lake Ontario. "I can't wait forever, you know."

Ellen smiled as she handed her hatbox to him, and Uncle Dyle took her steamer trunk. Captain Jonah was an ornery and eccentric staple of island life, and she'd miss him and his odd ways, along with everyone else.

"Now, Ellen, my girl," Uncle Dyle said, chucking her under her chin as he'd done when she was so much smaller. "You will take care, won't you? And you'll write us, especially your aunt, because you know how she worries."

"Yes, every week, I promise." Ellen's eyes swam with tears and she blinked them back with determination. She was a leaky tap, indeed. She'd already shed buckets when she'd said goodbye to Aunt Rose and her cousins; saying this last farewell felt hardest of all.

"And you also will always remember that you have a home here with us?" Uncle Dyle continued, his eyes that usually twinkled with humor now looking terribly serious. "No matter where you are, or how far you go, whether you become the grandest lady artist there is, or it all goes bust and you feel as if you've got nothing left… you've got us, Ellen, my girl. Always."

"I know." Ellen could barely squeeze the words out through her constricted throat. "I know that, Uncle Dyle. I've always known that."

"Come on, then." He held his arms out, and without a moment's hesitation Ellen walked into them, just as if she were a child. She pressed her cheek against the rough stuff cloth of his work coat, inhaling the familiar scent of hay and pipe tobacco. She thought briefly of her own father, so far away, so distant in so many ways, and Uncle Dyle gave her an extra squeeze.

"Better hurry, I haven't got all day," Captain Jonah called, and with a watery smile Ellen stepped back.

"You take care, Ellen," Uncle Dyle called as she boarded the little boat. "We'll be praying for you."

"And I, you," she called back.

She watched her uncle get smaller and smaller on the dock as the boat made its way for the mainland, the usually placid waters of the lake ruffled up like white lace.

Ellen had taken the train from Ogdensburg to Seaton many times, and it wasn't so different to take it to New York City instead, with a stream of green fields going by for the first few hours, and then giving way to the mills and factories found lower in the state, before pulling in to Grand Central Station in the evening.

Ellen stepped out onto the platform, clutching her hatbox, with a porter fetching her steamer trunk. People hurried by, jostling and chatting, and for a moment she felt completely overwhelmed. It had been a very long time indeed since she'd been in New York, or any city at all. Kingston, where she'd done a year of nurse's training, paled in comparison.

With the help of the porter, Ellen managed to get to the outside of the imposing station and into one of the New York Taxicab Company's new yellow automobiles. Although the price of such a journey was dear indeed, she knew of no other way to get to her boarding house with a trunk in tow.

Outside, the city glowed with electric streetlights, unlike anything Ellen had ever seen, street after street incandescent, the sidewalks full of people, even though it was becoming late.

She craned her head to get a better view as the taxicab rumbled on towards Gramercy Park—doormen standing proudly in their smart uniforms with top hats; elegant ladies and gentlemen coming from the theater or dinners in one of the city's many restaurants. Amidst the glamor were the harsher realities of city life—beggar children with sooty faces and threadbare clothes darting in and out of the well-heeled crowds; factory workers only just finishing a shift walking grimly home, heads lowered against the autumn cold.

Then, finally, the taxicab came to a stop in front of a pleasant townhouse on a tree-lined square.

"Number Eighty-Seven, Gramercy Park," he announced, and walked around to open her door.

After parting with the princely sum of five whole dollars for the journey, Ellen mounted the steps—the driver had, thankfully, already shouldered her trunk up them—and knocked on the door of the boarding house where she intended to spend the next two nights, before boarding the *S.S. Furnessia* for Glasgow.

A stern-faced woman with severe hair and a beaky nose answered the door, making Ellen jump a little at her fierce expression.

"Hello, I'm Ellen Copley…"

"I know who you are. You're awfully late."

"I sent a telegram," Ellen offered hesitantly. "Because of the train…"

"Yes, that's right." The woman looked her up and down once and then gave a brief nod, as if deciding that Ellen did indeed pass muster, if only just. "Come in. You must be half-starved. There's never anything decent to eat on trains, and they're so frightfully dirty."

Ellen was suddenly and poignantly reminded of her Aunt Ruth, saying something very similar when she'd arrived in Vermont from New York with a soot stain on one cheek and her hair in a tangle. Her aunt had made her feel small and unwelcome at first, but later Ellen had learned that that was just her way. Aunt Ruth had been hard but loving, and several months after her death, Ellen still missed her. Perhaps this woman was the same.

"I'm Mrs. Stamm," she said as she led Ellen back towards the kitchen. "I'm not serving dinner any longer, of course, but there's bread and cheese if you'd like it."

"Oh, I would," Ellen exclaimed, deciding to meet Mrs. Stamm's sternness with a friendly gratitude of her own. "Thank you so much, Mrs. Stamm."

Mrs. Stamm nodded, seeming to thaw slightly, and indicated with a nod for Ellen to sit at the oak table in the center of the kitchen while she fetched the promised bread and cheese.

Ellen sank onto a chair, a wave of exhaustion crashing over her. She glanced around the kitchen, everything neat and orderly, a far cry from the comfortable clutter of the kitchen back at Jasper Lane.

For a moment, she let herself picture Aunt Rose by the range, smiling over her shoulder as she poured from the kettle, or Gracie or Sarah at the table, shelling peas or just keeping her company. Jasper Lane always had people in and out and around; Ellen had never felt alone. Lonely. And so she wouldn't now.

She smiled and murmured her thanks as Mrs. Stamm set a plate of bread and cheese and a cup of tea in front of her.

"Get that in you," she ordered. "And then I'll show you your room."

Ellen ate and drank rather quickly under Mrs. Stamm's decidedly beady eye, and then followed her landlady out of the kitchen and up the front stairs with their worn carpet and polished brass runner.

"There are currently four other young ladies residing here," Mrs. Stamm informed her. "One young woman who, like you, is traveling onwards, and two who reside here permanently."

"Permanently?" Ellen couldn't help but be curious. "What do they do?"

Mrs. Stamm sniffed. "One works behind the glove counter at Arnold Constable. The other works in a typing pool at the Metropolitan Life Insurance Company." Her landlady did not sound particularly approving of these pursuits. "But you said in your letter that you were traveling on to Scotland?"

"Yes, to attend art school."

As Ellen had expected, Mrs. Stamm looked startled and then disapproving at this notion.

"Art school," she repeated as she took a brass key from her apron pocket and opened a bedroom door at the top of the house. "I've never heard of such a thing."

"It's quite well renowned," Ellen said with a smile. "It was founded by Charles Rennie Mackintosh, the architect?"

Mrs. Stamm sniffed again. "I've never heard of him."

"He's quite well known in Scotland," Ellen said, although she hadn't actually heard of him until Henry McAvoy, the art school trustee she'd met on the train last spring, had mentioned him. It was thanks to Mr. McAvoy that she was here at all; if he hadn't asked her to send him some sketches, and then arranged a place as well as a bursary…

"Here you are." Mrs. Stamm opened the door and Ellen peeked in to see a modest room with bed, bureau, and chair. "Breakfast is at seven o'clock sharp, and supper at six. If you wish for your laundry to be done, it will be another dollar."

"I'm sure I'll be fine," Ellen murmured. "This is lovely, thank you."

Her trunk had already been brought up by a boy Mrs. Stamm employed for such a purpose, and after lingering for a moment, looking as if she regretted offering bed and board to an aspiring lady artist, Mrs. Stamm said goodnight and shut the door firmly behind her.

Ellen let out a breath as she unpinned her hat and put it carefully on the bureau. She'd only brought two—a serviceable straw boater and a fancier although still modest concoction with a feather and a cluster of berries. Neither could hold a candle to Louisa's creations, but Ellen hoped she might find something a bit more daring when she did her shopping tomorrow.

In addition to a hat, she would need an evening gown for the ship, as well as another dress or two. Her years in Vermont and on the island, as well as nursing school, had not prepared her to become a young woman of some means and style.

For now, she slipped out of her traveling costume and unpinned her hair, grateful to be free from the confines of corset and pins, shirtwaist and pinching shoes.

Clad in her nightgown, her hair in a plait down her back, she pried open the little window and breathed in the damp, coal-scented night air. She felt a pang of loneliness, along with a flicker of excitement. She was alone here as she'd ever been, and yet she had so much to look forward to.

Taking another deep breath, Ellen closed the window and turned towards the bed.

Three days later, Ellen was boarding the *S.S. Furnessia* at Chelsea Piers. The sky above was a bright, hard blue, the sun glinting off the Hudson River. It felt like a lifetime since she'd last been in this harbor, fearing she might be sent all the way back to Scotland, with a white chalk "X" marked on her coat.

Now a far nicer sort of trepidation warred with excitement inside her as she went up the gangplank, carrying her reticule and a new hatbox; she'd bought a slightly smaller hat than the ones Louisa had worn, but it still seemed fancy to Ellen, with three feathers and a band of pink silk.

The last few days in New York had been thrilling but also a little bit lonely, taking her meals with the other four rather dour young ladies; Mrs. Stamm did not, it had seemed, encourage conversation over breakfast or dinner.

Still, Ellen had spent a happy time exploring the grand department stores and elegant boutiques of Manhattan's Ladies' Mile, stretching from 15th to 24th Street on Park Avenue, and she had made some purchases. With her purse considerably lighter and her trunk packed to its gills, she was now ready for the next step in her adventure.

She kept her head held high, her fascinated gaze taking in all the details of the second-class common rooms as a porter led her to her cabin.

The woman she would be sharing with was already in the cabin, having taken the bed by the porthole and arranged most of her things on the bureau and vanity.

"Well, it's not much, is it," the lady sniffed when the porter had left. She'd introduced herself as Florence Worth and she was a broad, bustling matron dressed in bottle-green bombazine, hardly the kindred spirit Ellen had been hoping for. "They're retiring this ship next year," Miss Worth continued. "And I must say I'm not surprised. Some of the furnishings are downright shabby."

Ellen made some meaningless response, not wanting to agree or disagree. After spending her last ship's journey in third-class, she found her accommodation pleasing indeed, and she had no wish for Florence Worth to diminish her pleasure in the second-class offerings: three-course meals in the fancy dining room, the use of a library, and a lounge just for ladies.

As it turned out, it became quickly clear that Miss Worth would be spending most of her time in the cabin, as she suffered from seasickness; Ellen spent as little time there as possible, preferring to explore the ship, although she did return to check on the moaning Miss Worth, and offer to bring her beef broth or tea.

"I don't know how you manage to look so hale and hearty," Miss Worth moaned rather resentfully, on the afternoon of the second day. "You are positively robust." She made it sound like an insult, but Ellen merely smiled. She'd always been resilient, and she'd spent plenty of time on boats, albeit much smaller ones, during her time on the island.

"Do let me know if you need anything, Miss Worth," she said solicitously. "Anything at all."

With Miss Worth insisting she could not stomach so much as a dry biscuit, Ellen headed back out to explore the parts of the ship she hadn't seen yet. She walked along the second-class deck, enjoying the brisk, salty breeze and the endless stretch of gray-blue that led to a distant shore. It had been seven years since she'd been on a ship, crossing the sea, starting another life, and it gave her a pang to think of her younger self, afraid and excited in turns, just as she was now, with so much uncertain.

She watched a few children cavort around the deck before a nanny chivvied them back inside; they didn't look much older than she had been, back then.

The sky had darkened to pewter and the wind needled her with cold.

"The wind is picking up, miss," one of the ship stewards said to her as he walked by. "And it looks to rain. You'd best go inside, to keep warm."

Ellen smiled her thanks and headed back to the second-class library, which was an oasis of quiet calm, with only one other young woman present, sitting at a desk, writing a letter. She glanced up as Ellen entered, her gaze alert and interested.

"I say, are you traveling alone?" she asked and, a bit hesitantly, Ellen confirmed that she was. Young women traveling on their own were still eyed a bit askance; Ellen suspected that was why she'd been paired with the indomitable Miss Worth, to act as an informal chaperone. "As am I," the young woman exclaimed. "My name is Letitia Portman."

"Ellen Copley. Pleased to meet you, Miss Portman."

"Oh, but you must call me Letitia, and allow me to call you Ellen. I hope I'm not being terribly impertinent to suggest such a thing? It's just I can't stand on formality. It's *such* a terrible bore."

"I don't mind at all," Ellen answered with a laugh. After the rather turgid conversation of her cabin mate, Letitia's candor was refreshing. They shook hands, and then Letitia subjected Ellen to a frank stare.

"We're a strange species, aren't we," she said as she sat back in her chair, and beckoned Ellen to sit as well. "The fearsome young lady, traveling alone! Are we courageous or foolish, a scandal or the future? No one knows what to do with us."

Ellen gave a small smile, for she was slightly intimidated by Letitia's confident and worldly air, the humor and intelligence sparkling in her brown eyes. She was a handsome woman, perhaps a few years older than Ellen, with light brown hair loosely dressed and a spattering of freckles across the bridge of her aquiline nose.

"Where are you bound?" she asked after Ellen had sat down on a settee across from her.

"Glasgow." Ellen knew the ship was going on to London after it stopped in Glasgow. "Well," she amended, "the Glasgow School of Art."

"Oh, so you're an artist! How marvelous. I do admire any kind of ability in that direction. I'm utterly hopeless. Stick figures are quite, quite beyond me."

"I don't know if I'd call myself an artist," Ellen said with a little laugh. "Not yet, at any rate…"

"You're going to art school, aren't you?"

"Yes—but to learn. I've never even had a proper lesson before."

"Entirely self-taught! That's even better." Letitia smiled, her eyes sparkling. "Besides, artists are born, not made, I suspect."

"Perhaps," Ellen agreed. She wished she had half the confidence of Letitia, who seemed set to sail through life—first on this ship, and certainly afterward. Ellen felt as if she were inching along in retrospect, overawed and intimidated by so many things. Last night, she'd eaten in her room because she'd been too nervous to face the dining room with its tables of eight, sparkling chandeliers, and respectably middle-class patrons.

And the truth was, whatever Letitia insisted, she didn't feel like a proper artist at all, and she wondered if she ever would. Her worst fear was that someone—Henry McAvoy, perhaps, or even Francis Newbery, the director of the school—would tell her they'd made a mistake and there wasn't a place for her after all. What would she do then? She didn't have the means for the fare back, and she could hardly stay in Glasgow, a single woman alone with no occupation or support.

"What about you?" she asked Letitia. "You're American, by the sounds of it. Why are you traveling to Scotland?"

"I'm taking a place at the University of Edinburgh's Medical School," Letitia answered and Ellen was suitably impressed. Of course someone as confident and worldly as Letitia Portman would be doing something so weighty and admirable.

"You're studying to be a doctor?"

"That's the hope," Letitia answered cheerfully. "I had the dev—the dickens of a time finding a school that would accept a woman, of course."

Ellen had never actually met a lady doctor before, not even during her time at nursing school, yet she could certainly believe this vibrant, self-assured woman capable of anything. "But Edinburgh did?"

"Yes, they have been accepting women students since 1889. Very forward-thinking of them."

"Indeed."

"Are you on your own for the voyage? Because we must band together. I'm sharing a room with a fearful old bat—she's always wafting smelling salts about and talking about her nerves."

"Oh, dear." At least Miss Worth had not resorted to smelling salts yet.

"I've come here to escape, and to write my family."

"Do they approve of your ambitions?"

"My father did. I've no brothers, you see, and he's a medical man himself. He wanted to keep it in the family. My mother, however, had a fit." Letitia grinned. "She told me I was a veritable bluestocking, and would never find a man willing to marry me, which is probably true." She made a face. "Still, I'm not so enamored with marriage and babies and all that. What about you?"

"Oh, I don't know," Ellen replied, a bit taken aback. An image of Jed flashed in her mind and then was thankfully gone. "I haven't thought too much about it yet. I'm only nineteen."

"Nineteen! A babe in arms. I'm twenty-four." Letitia sighed. "And I'll be nearing thirty before I finish my studies, but it took this long to persuade my mother to let me apply, and then to be accepted. I'm lucky to have the opportunity, I know. But do say you'll eat luncheon with me today? I can't bear having it in my room, and people do look at me askance when I'm on my own."

"I wouldn't think you'd mind," Ellen said with a laugh.

"Oh, I don't, but I'm dreadfully bored. Honestly, I have the attention span of a gnat. You'll have to tell me stories to keep me entertained."

"I'm not very good at those." Ellen could not imagine entertaining someone like Letitia. She was dull indeed by comparison.

"Then you shall simply have to draw me," Letitia answered gaily, and rising from her chair, she ushered Ellen from the library towards the second-class dining room.

For the rest of the voyage, Letitia took Ellen under her wing, arranging for them to have meals together, take turns around the deck, and even teaching her how to play bridge—a terribly complex card game that Ellen felt she was quite hopeless at, much to the despair of her fellow players.

By the time they were nearing Glasgow, Ellen felt she'd made a firm friend, and it was a great relief after the lonely days she'd spent in New York.

"Are you nervous about starting university?" she asked the morning they were to depart. Ellen had worn her new hat, which hadn't seemed all that grand in the shop but now felt ridiculous with its feather and ribbon band, next to Letitia's practical, efficient plainness, dressed as she was in a dark serge skirt and no-nonsense shirtwaist, a small straw boater crammed flat onto her head.

"Nervous? No," Letitia said firmly. "I'm looking forward to it—I've been applying to medical schools for two years, and I'm ready finally to begin." She turned to Ellen with one of her frank smiles. "What about you?"

"I suppose I am, a little." Actually, she was quite terrified, although she didn't feel she could admit that to Letitia.

"Well, you shouldn't be," Letitia said briskly. "You've been away from home before, when you went to nursing school."

Ellen had told her new friend the basic version of her life— from Springburn to Seaton to Amherst Island. "Yes," she agreed, "but that was only to Kingston."

"And you're from Glasgow originally," Letitia continued. "You know where you're going."

"But Springburn is worlds away from art school," Ellen protested. "And anyway, I'm not nervous about being in Glasgow, or being so far away from home."

Letitia raised her eyebrows. "What, then?"

"Just… school, I suppose." She was finally pursuing her dream, her passion, and that terrified her more than anything else. What if she failed? What if she wasn't any good at all? What if it didn't satisfy her the way she longed for it to?

"I'm sure it will all go splendidly," Letitia assured her. "It's natural to feel nervous, I suppose," she added generously, even though she didn't. "But we really ought to go, otherwise it'll be ages before we can get off this tub!" She clapped a hand on Ellen's shoulder. "You'll be fine. And the first free day we both have, I'll take the train over to Glasgow. It's not all that far, or so I've been told."

Ellen smiled in relief at the thought of seeing someone familiar again. "That would be lovely."

"Well, then. Off we go!"

At first, as Ellen stepped onto the gangplank that led down to Glasgow's dock, she was conscious only of the smell of Scotland: sea and soot, a smell that seemed both achingly familiar and now terribly strange. Then, as she came down, her hat, unfortunately, falling forward to cover one eye, she was conscious of something else. Henry McAvoy, the trustee she'd met on the train to Chicago, was waiting for her with a smart carriage, an expectant look on his face.

He was the last person Ellen had expected to see; in fact, she hadn't expected to see him at all except perhaps in relation to the school, since he was a gentleman of such great means. Yet here he was, clearly waiting for her, beaming from ear to ear.

"Mr. McAvoy," she said faintly as she came down to meet him.

Henry McAvoy swept his hat from his head and executed a courtly bow, his eyes twinkling. "Miss Copley! You don't know how pleased I am that you're finally here."

CHAPTER FOUR

Ellen gazed at Henry McAvoy in both surprise and concern. "I'm pleased to be here," she said, executing a little bob of a curtsey. She had no idea how to treat him; he was by far her social superior, and while those lines had been blurred when they'd been two strangers on a train in the middle of America, they were starkly clear now.

She was glad to see him, but she also felt uncertain. What *was* he doing here? She doubted that one of the school's trustees routinely met new students individually off the ship, and she could feel Letitia's curiosity like a palpable thing, as she craned her neck to peer at the gentleman and his smart carriage.

"Please let me introduce my friend from the passage," she said, willing her flush to fade as she struggled to make sense of the situation. "Miss Letitia Portman. Letitia, Mr. McAvoy."

Mr. McAvoy swept an overly gallant bow. "Charmed, I'm sure."

"Miss Portman is about to start medical school," Ellen continued, determined to bring a normality to this strange meeting. In her wildest imaginings, not that she'd had many, of her arrival in Glasgow, she'd never once considered anyone—much less a trustee of the school—would meet her by the ship! And yet as she half-listened to Mr. McAvoy asking Letitia about medical school, she acknowledged that such behavior shouldn't really surprise her. Henry McAvoy had, after all, broken with convention by inviting her to dine alone in his hotel restaurant when they'd met in Chicago—and she'd broken convention by agreeing.

Meeting her here today was, she supposed, true to his nature, and yet it still left her feeling uneasy.

"So, ladies," Mr. McAvoy said, turning to smile at Ellen, "may I offer you a ride in my carriage? Miss Copley, I was intending to take you to Miss Gray's house and, Miss Portman, I will gladly take you to whatever your destination may be."

"Even Edinburgh?" Letitia asked with an arch of her eyebrow. She looked amused by Henry's courtly exuberance, and Ellen blushed again as her new friend slid her a speculative look, clearly wondering as much as she was why Mr. McAvoy was here.

"Perhaps not quite that far," Henry admitted with a laugh. "I fear my horses would tire! If only I'd brought my smart new motorcar, but I am afraid I am still learning the mechanics of it, and I didn't wish to alarm Miss Copley." He turned to Ellen with a warm smile, which she returned uncertainly before looking away. Was he being too familiar, or was she simply being oversensitive about the matter?

"I am only having fun with you, Mr. McAvoy," Letitia assured him. "In truth, I am staying the night at Armstrong's Hotel, on Sauchiehall Street."

"Then I shall take you there," he declared, and went to call a porter for their cases.

As soon as he'd departed, Letitia leaned closer to Ellen, her eyes sparkling. "You never mentioned the dashing Mr. McAvoy to me while we were on the ship!"

"I did," Ellen answered just a little too quickly. "I told you how one of the trustees saw my drawings while I was on the train out to New Mexico—"

"And I thought you meant some stuffy old suit!" She raised her eyebrows in delicate query. "Mr. McAvoy is a trustee? How thoughtful of him to greet all the school's new students in such a fashion. Quite, quite considerate, not to mention time-consuming."

"Letitia," Ellen muttered, for she knew her friend was teasing her, and she was too disconcerted to take it in the spirit it was meant. "I don't know whether he greets all the students," she said after a moment, when she'd managed to recover her composure. "But he was certainly kind to me while I was in Chicago, and has always encouraged my studies here." She drew herself up and looked her friend in the eye. "I'm grateful for his concern, that's all."

"As am I," Letitia answered, her eyes still glinting teasingly. "I was planning to take the tram to the hotel. Mr. McAvoy's carriage will be far nicer."

"I've arranged for a porter," Mr. McAvoy said as he returned to them with a bounce in his step. "We should be on our way shortly, I'm sure you'll be glad to know. Travel can be so exhausting."

"I am quite invigorated," Letitia countered with a smile. "There is so much to look forward to!"

"Indeed there is," he answered Letitia, but he was looking at Ellen.

The porter loaded their cases onto his carriage, and then, gallant as ever, Mr. McAvoy waved his driver aside and helped both Ellen and Letitia into the enclosed carriage himself.

Ellen sat back against the velvet cushions, hardly able to believe that she had actually arrived in Glasgow and would be beginning her tutelage in just a few days. She leaned forward to draw back the curtain and peer out of the carriage window as they left the docks for the city proper.

It was strange to be back in the city of her birth, although the busy, broad streets of Glasgow's center were a far cry from the narrow streets and cramped tenements she'd known in Springburn, by the railyards. Her life in Springburn, Ellen reflected, seemed almost to belong to someone else, and yet she knew, despite her new clothes from the Ladies' Mile and the pompadour hairstyle she'd spent far too long arranging this morning, the little girl from Springburn with the sad eyes and tangled hair still lurked inside her, and always would. She would never be rid of her, and she wasn't sure she wanted to be.

"How does it feel to return to Glasgow, Miss Copley?" Mr. McAvoy asked, and Ellen turned from the window.

"Strange," she admitted with a little smile. "Very strange."

She didn't say anything else, for she was suddenly seized with an unexpected homesickness and loneliness that seemed to catch her by the throat and bring tears to her eyes.

Quickly, to hide her sudden emotion, she leaned forward and looked out the window, determined not to succumb to that sudden sorrow. She had everything ahead of her, just as Letitia had said.

And yet returning to Glasgow reminded her of her mother, dead now for eight years, and her Da, just as lost to her out in New Mexico. The three of them had once had such grand dreams of emigrating to America; Ellen could still picture her father's broad smile as he told her about the fish that would fair jump into her hand.

But there hadn't been any fish, and her Da hadn't liked the New World he'd been so excited to join. Her mother had never even made it that far, dying in the kitchen of the only house she'd known in her married life, when Ellen was just ten.

Now Ellen swallowed down the tears she didn't want to shed, not when she was finally starting this bright new chapter of her life, not when she'd finally found the courage to pursue her own dreams. She might never be able to leave that little girl behind her, but she could leave Springburn.

"Ah, here we are, Armstrong's Hotel," Mr. McAvoy said cheerfully. He jumped out of the carriage and then helped Letitia to the pavement. "Miss Portman, it has been a pleasure."

"Indeed," Letitia murmured. She said her goodbyes to Ellen, who had also alighted from the carriage, hugging her fiercely as she whispered in her ear, "You must write me and tell me everything that happens. This is quite the exciting adventure for you, Ellen. And I hope to see you soon. I'll write as soon as I can, with a date."

"Yes, please do," Ellen said fervently. "I know I will enjoy having a friend close by, and I can't wait to hear about all your adventures, Letitia."

Waving merrily, Letitia went into the hotel, leaving Ellen feeling even more alone, despite Henry McAvoy's presence.

"Are you ready to continue on to Miss Gray's, Miss Copley?" Henry McAvoy asked after a moment, and Ellen turned to him with as bright a smile as she could manage.

"Yes, of course. I am quite looking forward to meeting Miss Gray. Are there any other art students boarding with her, do you know, Mr. McAvoy?"

"I hope you might call me Henry," he replied lightly once they were settled back in the carriage, and heading towards Renfrew Street where the School of Art was located, along with many of the instructors' homes.

"I…" Ellen's mind spun as she tried to think of a way to respond. Although Henry McAvoy had been friendly and solicitous in Chicago, she had assumed the difference in their social positions would make any kind of friendship beyond an acquaintance impossible, as well as deeply inappropriate. Refusing his request now, however, when he was a trustee of the school she was about to start, seemed churlish in the extreme, as well as foolish. "I'm honored," she said finally, and Henry's smile widened.

"And I would also hope," he said, still smiling, "that I might call you Ellen."

Wordlessly, Ellen nodded. What else could she do? Yet she wondered what the other students, or even the professors, would think, to know she was on such familiar terms with a trustee, and a young gentleman at that. She didn't think Henry was much more than thirty.

"I am looking forward to showing you some of Glasgow's sights, if you will allow me the privilege," Henry continued. "When you have a moment to spare."

"I'm sure," Ellen murmured noncommittally. Was she crazy to wonder at the nature of Henry's intentions? Perhaps he was simply being friendly, knowing how at sea she must feel. It felt wildly presumptuous to think he was being anything other than merely solicitous.

"Ah, here we are," Henry said. The carriage rumbled up in front of a neat, narrow home in the middle of a row of respectable terraced houses. "Let me help you down from the carriage, Ellen."

Ellen blushed at the use of her Christian name, even though she knew she'd just, albeit mutely, given him permission to use it. It still felt strange, as well as inappropriate.

"And now I shall introduce you to Miss Gray," Henry said, and he drew her to the front step of the house and rapped smartly on the door.

Ellen didn't think Henry was aware he was still holding her hand. He might be unconventional, but holding hands in public was surely a step too far, even for him. As discreetly as she could, she tugged her hand from his and waited, her heart thumping, her hands clasped together, for the door to open.

Seconds later, it was opened by a tall, elegant woman with dark hair and soulful eyes, wearing a loose dress covered by what looked like a man's overcoat. Ellen had never seen an outfit like it, yet Norah Neilson Gray wore it with glamorous ease.

"Mr. McAvoy!" she exclaimed, her eyes sparkling with a knowing sort of humor. "How charming to see you. And this must be Ellen Copley."

Ellen bobbed an awkward curtsey and Norah let out a light laugh.

"Oh my dear, we do not stand on formalities here. You may call me Norah, if I may call you Ellen." She held out one slender hand, which Ellen took as awkwardly as she had curtseyed.

Despite Norah Gray's easy manner, she continued to feel disconcerted—and rather conservative and even prudish in the dress she'd been so proud of when she'd purchased it in New York.

"Come, we'll have tea in the sitting room," Norah said. "Henry, you must join us."

Ellen followed Norah into a room that was, at first glance, both overcrowded and interesting. Canvases cluttered the walls, done in a variety of styles, some with thick splodges of oil paint, others delicate watercolors.

Fascinated, Ellen stepped closer to a painting of young girls playing in a garden, the colors muted and haunting.

"Do you like that one?" Norah asked as she poured tea from a Chinese-painted teapot. "It was inspired by my childhood in Helensburgh. We had such a lovely garden."

"You did this?" Ellen exclaimed, and then let out an apologetic laugh because she sounded so incredulous. She was, in fact, quite overwhelmed; she'd never even used paint of any kind before. All of her artwork was in charcoal pencil, often on the back of butcher's paper, the only medium she'd ever had the opportunity to work with.

Norah seemed to guess the nature of her thoughts for she said, "I am sure you will find so many opportunities here to explore and develop your talent, Ellen. Mr. Newbery encourages his art students to try all manner of classes—painting, sculpture, drawing, embroidery, metalwork... but, of course, you must find your true calling. Every artist, I think, has a medium in which she is the happiest and most creative."

"And what is yours?" Ellen asked as she sat down on a horsehair sofa and accepted a cup of tea from Norah. The cup had Chinese characters painted in indigo on its side, and no handle. Ellen had never seen anything like it, and she cradled it between her hands uncertainly.

"Oils, I think," Norah answered after a moment's reflection. Her gaze drifted towards the pale painting of the children in the garden. "But I do like watercolors on occasion. They give things a rather ghostly feel." She turned to Henry, who was sitting on the edge of an ottoman, balancing his cup on his knee. "And what about you, Henry? What medium do you prefer?"

Henry smiled ruefully. "As you know, I am no artist, merely a connoisseur."

"As an observer, then. You have seen most all of the works that have come out of the School. What do you prefer?" Norah's eyes twinkled and she gave Ellen a laughing glance, making her wonder what her landlady thought of Henry bringing her here.

Henry reflected for a moment, his blue eyes thoughtful above his teacup as he lifted it to his mouth. "I do have a fondness for charcoal pencil," he said, and Ellen quickly took a sip of tea to hide yet another blush.

Nora's mouth had curved in a knowing smile and Ellen could feel the older woman's gaze upon her before she said, "Well, I look forward to seeing what you are capable of, Ellen. Henry has certainly vouched for you, and I have seen a few of your charcoal drawings myself. But it will be interesting to see what you are able to do in other mediums, and how you can stretch yourself. As artists, we must never be content to remain comfortable."

"I've never used paint before," Ellen admitted. "I'm afraid I am quite inexperienced, Miss Gray."

"Norah, remember," she reminded her. "And inexperience means little, in my opinion. You will get plenty of experience here. It is dedication and creativity, courage and boldness, that count." She put her cup down and rose from her chair. "But, Henry, you really ought to leave us now. Ellen is no doubt exhausted from her voyage, and I am sure she wishes to settle into her room and rest." She turned to Ellen with a smile. "Later we can walk to Renfrew Street, and you can see the school building. Charles Mackintosh completed the new addition only a year ago; it is quite remarkable. And perhaps we shall finish the day with tea at Miss Cranston's tearoom, which is just as remarkable."

"I can see that I am being dismissed," Henry said lightly as he rose from the ottoman. "I hope to see both of you ladies again soon."

"I am sure we will be far too busy," Norah answered lightly. "An artist cannot be distracted from her work, Henry." Although her tone was still light, her gaze rested seriously and even sternly on the charming trustee. "You must remember that, you know."

Ellen watched as color touched Henry's cheekbones.

"I shall bear it in mind," he answered and, with a gallant bow, he took his leave.

Norah closed the door behind him and turned to Ellen, her eyebrows raised. "It seems you have an admirer there."

"Oh, no, I don't think…" Ellen began, mumbling in her embarrassment. "Surely not…"

"Never mind, it is of no account. You have come all this way to study, Ellen, and I meant what I said about not being distracted, and certainly not by the likes of Henry McAvoy. He is charming, I know, and a devotee of the arts, which suits the school very well, but it would not do at all for you to set your cap at him."

"Oh, I wouldn't," Ellen assured her, her face fiery now.

"Good. His parents are quite snobbish, and his mother is insistent that he marry a gently reared society miss, you know the sort?"

Ellen did not know the sort at all, but she supposed she could imagine, and it was a far cry from who she was. "Honestly, Miss Gray, you needn't worry. I didn't even know Hen—Mr. McAvoy was going to meet me at the docks."

"Ah, then you shall have to be careful, because he can be quite insistent, and he's used to getting what he wants." She raised elegant eyebrows. "You are aiming for a diploma, are you not?"

"Yes…"

"Then you will have to work hard indeed. Only half of the candidates last year were granted a diploma. It is not a thing to undertake lightly, I warn you."

"Oh, I assure you, I won't," Ellen said quickly. "I wish to devote all my time to studies. I didn't intend to have a friendship or even an acquaintance with Mr. McAvoy at all!" She bit her lip, embarrassed again at revealing too much.

Norah's mouth twitched in a small smile. "Henry has always been too impulsive for his own good," she said with a sigh. "It is, at least in part, why he is a trustee and not an artist. He simply hasn't the patient or forbearance to work hard at something. His family is in banking, and he's been handed a vice-presidency, although heaven knows what he'll do with it. He prefers to gallivant around the world on behalf of the school. Now, come, I will show you your room."

CHAPTER FIVE

Three days later, Ellen stood in front of the cheval mirror in her bedroom at Norah's house, gazing at her reflection. Today was the first day of term, and she was incredibly nervous. Butterflies swooped and swarmed in her stomach, and she smoothed the front of her plain dark skirt that she'd chosen to wear along with a white shirtwaist. She knew her clothes would be covered during lessons with a large smock, and Norah had told her that sensible, plain clothing was best.

"We create art, we don't wear it," she said with a smile, and Ellen thought of the dresses she'd splurged on in New York that would never likely see the light of day in Glasgow. How foolish and ignorant she'd been, but she supposed it was a lesson she'd had to learn.

The last few days with Norah Gray had been illuminating—as well as nerve-wracking. After Ellen had rested, they'd walked the few blocks to the School of Art's home on Renfrew Street, an impressive building with huge windows that Charles Rennie Mackintosh had designed.

Norah had shown Ellen the library, the studios with their strange smells of paint and turpentine, and the long, sashed windows letting in streams of September sunlight. Ellen had tried to imagine herself standing in front of one of the large easels, listening to one of the instructors and actually putting paint to canvas, but it had felt like nothing more than a dream.

"Fra Newbery has insisted that women be allowed to attend life drawing classes," Norah had told her, referring to the school's head by his nickname. "You will not find us backward here, I assure you."

"Life drawing?" Ellen had repeated blankly. She didn't even know what it was.

"Of nudes, my dear," Norah had said, almost gently, as if she expected Ellen to be embarrassed, which of course she was. She'd fought a flush, striving to keep her expression composed, and feared she failed miserably. "How else can you draw the human form with any accuracy?" Norah had asked, to which Ellen had no real answer.

After they'd toured the art school, Norah had taken her to a tearoom run by the formidable Miss Cranston on Buchanan Street, an institution as venerable as the school itself.

Ellen had never been in such a place, and she could not keep from staring at everything. The walls were hung with paintings done by the "Glasgow Boys"—a group of painters that had come out of the school—and she was fascinated by their colorful depictions of various subjects, almost all of them from around Glasgow. While some were realistic, others gave no more than an impression of color and light, a hint of emotion, and yet they were powerful all the same. Ellen had never seen such artwork before; the walls of Jasper Lane, as well as her aunt and uncle's house in Seaton, were hung with samplers and the Farmer's Almanac calendar, perhaps the odd print of a famous painting, something by Monet or Degas. The paintings in the tearoom were something else entirely, with their focus on simple, rural subjects, their stark lines and poignant realism.

"Aren't they marvelous?" Norah came to stand beside her as they both surveyed a painting by James Guthrie of a girl herding geese. "'To Pastures New'," she'd said, with a nod towards the painting. "Apropos, don't you think?"

The tearoom itself was decorated in the latest Arts and Crafts style; the separate Ladies Room was large and comfortable and there were plates of cakes and scones that customers could help themselves to without the need of a server. It felt like someone's home, and reminded Ellen a bit of Jasper Lane, the kind of place you could simply stroll into and be made welcome. She was enchanted.

"Miss Cranston is a patron of the school, and of Charles Mackintosh," Norah had explained. "These Ladies Rooms have provided places for women artists to meet together for years now. She is really a most remarkable woman."

Ellen was fast getting the sense that everyone in Glasgow's art world was remarkable—except for herself. Norah had told her about the artistic vision of various instructors and pupils, the exhibitions they had put on and the awards and commendations they had received.

She'd listened while Norah had described the visionaries and luminaries that made up the art community of Glasgow, considered the second city of the Empire—men and women who had been bold enough to see something different, and then to paint or sculpt or work it out of cloth or iron.

Ellen felt rather ridiculous with her little portfolio of pencil drawings, some of them on butcher's paper, made with nothing more than a nub of charcoal. Now that her first day was actually here, she was terribly afraid she would humiliate herself in front of all the other students, or be told she wasn't School of Art material, after all.

Norah rapped on the door of her bedroom. "Come, Ellen. We don't want to be late on your first day!"

Slowly, Ellen opened the door. "I feel like a fraud," she admitted, and Norah's eyebrows drew together.

"My dear, you must never admit it. We're all frauds, and we're all genuine. There is no separating one from the other." She tapped Ellen's temple. "What you have that is unique is up here. It is your vision of the world, what you are able to bring to the table, and to this community. That, my dear, does not make you a fraud." Ellen managed a small smile, and Norah turned briskly away. "But I'm afraid I have neither the time nor the patience for such shilly-shallying. You have been granted an enormous opportunity, Ellen Copley. Use it."

Suitably chastened, Ellen could only nod as she followed Norah out of the house.

An hour later, she stood by an easel in her first painting class; there was a jug of daisies and a few oranges on a table in the center of the room, with a draped and rumpled rust-colored cloth. The instructor, Maurice Grieffenhagen, had lectured them for over a quarter of an hour on the importance of composition, most of which had gone right over Ellen's head.

There were a dozen pupils in the class, both men and women, all of them very serious-looking in their voluminous smocks. Ellen stared at her blank canvas and tried not to panic. She felt as if she'd never so much as picked up a pencil.

"Miss… Copley, is it?" Ellen tensed as Maurice Grieffenhagen came to stand by her, his eyes shrewd above his pointed gray beard. "Most of the others have made a start, Miss Copley. Is there a reason why you are staring at a blank canvas as if a painting will magically appear upon its pristine surface?" He smiled slightly to take some of the sting from his words, but Ellen still felt scorched by humiliation.

"I—I was just considering how best to start," she said, trying not to stammer, and Mr. Grieffenhagen nodded in understanding.

"The muse is fickle, Miss Copley. Perhaps, for the sake of our lesson, you could at least pick up your brush." He handed her a paintbrush and moved on to the next student, leaving Ellen cringing in mortification. Was this how it was always going to be?

She stared at the blank canvas in terror, afraid to spoil its so-called pristine surface. Nothing she could paint would compare to that perfect whiteness.

She glanced up and saw a woman across the room with a plain, freckled face and a ginger pompadour make a funny face, followed by an encouraging smile. Heartened, Ellen picked up her brush. The paint felt thick, the brush unwieldy, as she made her first wavering line across the canvas. She looked up once more, and the woman caught her eye and winked. Smiling back, Ellen painted another line.

By the end of the class, she had, she hoped, managed to make a decent start; the oranges were apparent, at least, and Mr. Grieffenhagen had given her a grudging nod, which, compared to before, had felt like the highest praise. His mocking criticism still stung, but she told herself to shrug it off. As Norah had told her, she had no time for faint-hearted histrionics. She was here to learn, and, God willing, get better.

Ellen gathered up her things as students streamed from the classroom; she stilled when she felt a hand placed on her arm.

"Don't take what Mr. Grieffenhagen says to heart." The woman from across the room was smiling at her. She was dressed exceedingly well under her smock, in a satin-striped skirt and matching jacket, and Ellen guessed she was a woman of some means.

"I fear I am meant to take it to heart," she answered. "It seems very serious here. I am trying to match it."

"Oh it is," the woman assured her. "Fra Newbery has tried to roust all the dilettantes from the school, but he hasn't managed to get rid of me yet." She tossed her head with a little laugh, and Ellen smiled.

The woman's open friendliness and lack of pretension was refreshing, especially as some of the other students, with their paint-smeared smocks and grubby fingernails, seemed serious indeed.

"And would you really call yourself a dilettante?" Ellen asked and the woman laughed again.

"Oh, indeed. I am Francis Newbery's nemesis. The socialite who dabbles in art. He can't stand anyone who isn't a 'Serious

Artist,' but he allows me to attend classes because my father gives a large amount of money to the school." She raised her eyebrows. "It proves to be quite an incentive to allow at least one dilettante amidst all these melancholy *artistes,* like a cat among the pigeons. And it suits me, because I do like to dabble." She held out a hand, which Ellen took. "Amy McPhee."

"Ellen Copley."

"Well then, Ellen, if you don't mind me calling you that, that's an odd accent I hear. You sound both Scottish and American."

"I suppose I am," Ellen answered, and with a lighter heart she walked out of the studio, explaining to Amy just how she'd come to arrive at the Glasgow School of Art.

A fortnight into term, Ellen was both exhausted and invigorated. She'd been exposed to so many different artistic styles and mediums, and in just two short weeks had learned and experienced more than she'd ever dreamed of. But she still felt, on occasion, unsettlingly out of place; so much of what the instructors said, while seeming to resonate with the other students, went right over Ellen's head. Composition, contrast, convention… they blurred in her mind until she didn't know which was which. In the end, all she could do was paint or draw as best as she knew how, but sometimes it seemed like lamentably little.

In between lectures and studio sessions, the other students often argued about this style or that, tossing around terms such as Impressionism or Cubism that Ellen had barely a passing acquaintance with. No matter what Norah had said, she felt like a fraud, and she suspected some of the other students felt it as well.

Her friendship with Amy was, at times, her only saving grace—down-to-earth and dismissive of any artistic pretensions, Amy was always happy to talk fashion rather than composition, and she regaled Ellen with stories of Glasgow society that made her laugh. As well as being down-to-earth, Amy was exceedingly pragmatic about her own fortunes—she was to marry a man of suitable standing and wealth, most likely in the next year or two.

"We just need to find him first," she told Ellen cheerfully. "Mama is getting rather desperate. I'm twenty-three, you know. Positively ancient."

Tucked up in her little room at Norah's, Ellen poured her fears and frustrations into the letters she wrote to Lucas, knowing that he, more than anyone else from the island, would understand what she was feeling.

> *I always thought it would be invigorating to be among so many like-minded people, and yet I fear we are not as like-minded as I had hoped to be! I suppose, even as a child, I knew I was not an Artist; I simply liked to draw. Perhaps that is what kept me from pursuing that path all these years, and now that I have, I fear the distinction is all the more obvious.*

When her first letter from Canada arrived, Ellen was overjoyed. It was from dear Aunt Rose, and Ellen sat curled up in the armchair in her room, savoring her aunt's descriptions of her beloved Amherst Island. In her mind's eye, she could picture the way the maples lining the shore were turning russet and gold, or how the waters of Lake Ontario would be slate-colored under an autumn sky. She could smell the hint of frost in the air, along with woodsmoke and the fruity, mulchy scent of apples being pressed into cider.

Sitting there with Glasgow's sea of chimneys and slate roofs visible from her windows, her fingers ink-stained from a drawing class and one of the new smocks she'd purchased hanging on her door, she felt an almost unbearable wave of homesickness—not just for the island, which she missed dearly, but for a life that was familiar and comfortable, instead of so new and strange. She was tired of dour-faced Serious Artists, and even Norah's stern companionship. She liked Amy, but her friend was happily frivolous, and sometimes Ellen longed for a deeper companionship, but with whom? She was, as she'd so often been, a stranger to her own life, a stranger to herself.

Sighing, Ellen continued to read Aunt Rose's letters, tensing a little when she came to the last paragraph.

> *Jed and Louisa seem to have settled into married life. They are living, of course, in the Lymans' farmhouse, but Louisa has hopes, I believe, to build a new place on the other side of the pond. I am not sure Jed sees the need; as you know, Lucas has left for Toronto, and there is plenty of space for just the three of them there. However, as you also know, Louisa most often has her way! She has made quite an effort, I am happy to report, of being a good wife to Jed; she asked me the other day how to churn butter—but when I showed her the calluses on my hands, she was quite horrified! Still, I wish them happy, and I know you do as well.*

Ellen put the letter down once more, gazing out the window unseeingly as she pictured Jed and Louisa together, turning the farmhouse into their marital home. She tried to picture Louise churning butter, and failed. Louisa had never lifted a finger unless she had to.

Aunt Rose believed the best in everybody, Ellen knew; it was one of the things she loved most about her. Yet how much would Louisa really try to fit into island life, especially if she still nurtured hopes of moving to Seaton, where Jed would work for her father at the bank?

Ellen reminded herself it was none of her concern where Jed and Louisa lived, or how their married life progressed. Her life was here now. Yet even though she knew she could never allow herself to entertain tender feelings for Jed in the slightest, she still cared about him and she suspected he wouldn't be happy in Seaton, working behind a desk. She couldn't imagine it, and she doubted he could, either.

"But he's happy with Louisa," she reminded herself quietly as she stared out at the twilight settling softly over the chimneys and slates of the city. "He chose her, not you."

And even now, over a year since he'd made that choice, the knowledge stung, if only a little. Jed and Louisa were, on some fundamental level, completely unsuited to one another. Yet, according to Aunt Rose, they were making a go of it. She needed to, as well.

With a determined nod, Ellen set the letter aside. She was going to embrace her new life in Glasgow, and try harder to make friends with the other students. Perhaps with time Glasgow and her life at the art school would become familiar and even beloved to her. She'd made a good friend in Amy McPhee, but then Amy was not the typical art student, as she'd explained herself. Still, Ellen hoped that with a bit of effort and determination, she would start to feel more settled. The other art students were serious-minded, but some of them had made friendly overtures; a young gentleman in her drawing class had admired her sketch of a hand, claiming she had managed to capture the wrinkles on the palm very well.

Her mouth twitched in a smile as she imagined writing such a thing to anyone from the island: *I have drawn a remarkable hand, and another pupil says the wrinkles in the skin are quite accurate.* Everyone would think she was mad, and Ellen half-wondered if she was. Yes, life at the art school, the intense focus on something that she'd never dare think of as more than a pleasant pastime, was both fearsome and wonderful.

A rap on the door startled Ellen from her thoughts.

"Ellen?" Norah called. "You have a visitor."

"A visitor?" Ellen rose from her chair, opening the door of her bedroom to see Norah gazing at her with something close to disapproval. Her stomach swooped nervously; as kind as Norah was, Ellen was still intimidated by her. "Who is it?"

"Who do you think it is?" Norah asked, her eyebrows raised. "Your admirer, of course." She turned to go back downstairs, and quickly tidying her hair, Ellen followed her.

Henry McAvoy was waiting in the drawing room, one hand braced against the mantelpiece as he studied a small oil painting hung above it, a river landscape done in oils.

"Ellen!" He turned with a smile at the sound of the door, his hands outstretched. "I couldn't stay away another day. I've so desperately wanted to know how you are getting on."

"Well enough, I hope," Ellen answered. She'd left the door to the sitting room open, and she was conscious of Norah bustling about in the hallway. There was something both vibrant and alarming about Henry's presence in the little sitting room, smiling at her in such a delighted, familiar way. "Thank you for enquiring. It's very kind of you."

"My motives are entirely selfish, I assure you," Henry said, and he came forward to take Ellen's hands in his own, which she thought a bit forward. "I want to hear all about your first few days at the school. I've come to take you out to tea at the Willow Rooms, another fine establishment owned by the lovely Miss Cranston."

"That's—that's very kind of you, Henry," Ellen began, stammering slightly, "but…"

"But what?" He raised his eyebrows, his smile gentle and playful. "I consider myself your champion, Ellen. And since I put your name forward to be accepted by the school, it is my God-given duty to make sure you are settling in. I brought the motorcar today as well, since I know you've never ridden in one."

Ellen stared at him helplessly, her hands still encased in his. How could she refuse him? She'd felt in her bones, and certainly in Norah's disapproving stare, that a friendship with Henry McAvoy was not a wise idea. And yet, remembering her resolve of a few moments ago to make more of an effort, she wondered why she was so reluctant.

Although Henry had been effusive in his kindness and praise, Ellen didn't think he could possibly consider her a romantic prospect. Their stations in life were surely too different for that. Perhaps she was reading too much into Henry's naturally friendly ways, and in truth she would like to talk with someone who had no pretensions to art, even if he had an obvious interest in the subject as a trustee.

Feeling reckless and a bit daring, she slipped her hands from his. "Let me just get my coat."

CHAPTER SIX

Half an hour later, Ellen and Henry were settled in the Willow Rooms on Sauchiehall Street, the building and interior designed by Charles Mackintosh and hung with paintings, as the tearoom on Buchanan Street had been.

"So what did you think of your first ride in the motorcar?" Henry asked as he poured them both tea.

"Bumpy," Ellen answered with a laugh. "And alarmingly fast. But I enjoyed it." She'd never experienced anything like it, with the wind rushing past her and the world streaming by in a colorful blur. "Where I come from, there's only one motorcar, and it had to be driven across the ice in winter to get there." She smiled at the memory of how everyone had gathered by the shore to see the motorcar come across to the island, looking incongruous in the middle of a flat field of white.

"How charmingly parochial," Henry said with a laugh. "That's one thing I like about you, Ellen. You've had such quaint experiences."

Ellen wasn't sure she liked the sound of "quaint"; it seemed a bit patronizing. Still, she held her tongue and merely smiled, because she supposed life on Amherst Island would seem quaint indeed to a man of the world such as Henry.

"I'm so glad you enjoyed it, at any rate," Henry continued. "I hope to introduce you to all sorts of new experiences."

"You make me sound like a pet project," Ellen said tartly, before she could think better of it.

Henry's face fell almost comically. "Not at all, not at all," he assured her. "Quite the opposite." What, Ellen wondered, *was* the opposite? "Please don't take offense. I would dread for you to do that."

"I'm not offended." Being insulted by Henry felt like kicking a puppy; he so wanted to please and be liked.

"Then you've put my mind at ease." Henry gave his usual charming smile as he added cream to his tea and stirred it. "But now you must tell me how you are finding art school."

"It is all very new and strange," Ellen answered after a moment. "At times, I admit, I feel quite intimidated. But I hope with the passage of time I shall become more accustomed, and, of course, I am immensely grateful for the opportunity." She added this as a matter of duty, because Henry had already reminded her once how it was thanks to him that she was here at all. While she didn't enjoy the idea of being beholden to him, she accepted it as part of his due.

"It is understandable," Henry answered with a nod, "that it would be overwhelming at first. You've never been around so many artists before, I expect."

"Or any at all," Ellen answered with a laugh. She found she could be candid with Henry in a way that she had not yet found the courage to with her fellow students.

"But just because you are a young woman from a small place, Ellen," Henry continued seriously, "do not think that you have less ability than anyone else at the school. I have seen your work, and Francis Newbery himself said you had great talent, if unschooled." He smiled wryly. "That is why you are here, of course. To learn. But the raw ability is something you have always had. Don't ever doubt it."

"Thank you," Ellen murmured, touched by his praise, as well as a little discomfited. She was not used to such flattery; her teachers certainly didn't give it to her, and her art had always been such a private thing. She'd only shown her sketches to a few people—Jed and Lucas, Aunt Rose and Uncle Dyle. "It is very kind of you to say so," she told Henry.

"It is not mere kindness," Henry answered. "I believe it right down to my toes! But now let us talk of something more pleasant."

"Is art not pleasant?" Ellen teased. She realized, somewhat to her surprise, that she was enjoying herself more than she had since she'd arrived in Glasgow, and she felt more comfortable with Henry than she had with anyone here, save perhaps Amy. She was glad he had asked her to tea.

"I must admit, I am a shallow enough creature to prefer parties to art," Henry said and Ellen stared at him, confused by the sudden change of direction in the conversation.

"Parties…" she repeated blankly.

"Yes, my mother is having a ball on the Friday night after next. It is, I fear, a somewhat tedious social occasion, with far too many young ladies swanning about in ball gowns, looking for both marriage and dance partners. As her only son, I must of course attend, and I was hoping you would consider making this burden easier to bear."

"I'm afraid I don't…" Ellen began, still genuinely at a loss, stopping when Henry leaned towards her, his eyes bright as he took her hand in his own.

"I am asking, Ellen, if you will accompany me to the ball as my special guest."

For a second, Ellen could only stare at him. "A ball…" she repeated, her hands still clasped in Henry's. She slipped them out of his and reached for her cup of tea, needing a moment to gather her thoughts, as well as her composure. She gazed down into the milky depths of her cup, feeling a disconcerting mixture of confusion and fury. Was Henry asking her out of *pity*? Surely he realized how impossible her attendance at such an event would be. She could certainly not go to the ball as his special guest. She could not go at all.

And no matter how carefree and insouciant he could seem, a man of his stature in society would know that. He would know it very well indeed. To attend a ball as his guest would be social suicide for Ellen, if she had any pretensions to society. She would be labeled brazen, grasping, a harlot or worse. Her mind raced, trying to think of a way out of this predicament.

"Ellen?" Henry prompted, and she looked up to see him smiling rather whimsically at her.

"I'm sorry, Henry, but I cannot go to a ball," Ellen said, trying to pitch her voice between kind and firm. "It's quite impossible, as I'm sure you realize."

"Impossible?" He raised his eyebrows, still holding onto his whimsy, although now Ellen suspected it was with some effort. "I realize no such thing! Especially if I call for you in my motorcar—"

"Don't," Eleanor cut him off, her voice turning sharp. She pressed one hand to her hot cheek; she most certainly was blushing. "Please, *please* don't."

Henry frowned. "I don't understand."

"Don't you?" Ellen asked, her voice low. "Surely you see the impossibility of it… of our different positions… would you make me a laughing stock?"

Henry stared at her for a moment, his forehead furrowed, and then he sat back in his chair and shook his head slowly. "Ellen Copley," he said, "I didn't take you for a snob."

"A snob!" She drew back, stung. "I'm hardly that. I'll have you know I grew up by the railyards of Springburn—" Something she hadn't actually wanted to mention, but she wore it as a badge of honor now.

"There are many forms of snobbery," Henry informed her. "And believing a lass from Springburn can't come to a ball held in a villa in Dowanhill is snobbery, whether you think it or not."

Ellen shook her head helplessly. Henry had a way with words, it was true, but she knew in her bones, in her very soul, that she was right. "It seems like common sense to me."

Henry leaned forward, and Ellen thought he might reach for her hands again, and so she quickly put her teacup down and clenched them together in her lap. "Ellen," he asked earnestly, "why do you think it's so impossible for you to attend this ball? Plenty of young ladies will be there—"

"Young ladies I have no acquaintance with," Ellen returned. "Ladies of society, who, as you said, will be arrayed in their finest and looking for husbands, who have been invited by your mother and are not your *special guest*."

"Then don't come as my special guest," Henry said with a smile and a shrug. "Just come. All that matters to me is that you're there."

"Why?" Ellen asked, although she almost didn't want to know the answer.

"Why do you think?" Henry countered. A stubborn gleam had entered his eye that Ellen wasn't sure she liked. The implication of his question seemed obvious, even if she didn't want it to be.

"I wouldn't fit in," she argued. "I don't even have the right clothes."

"Is all that stands between you and this ball—a gown?" Henry asked and Ellen fought down the fury she'd felt when he'd first invited her. Why couldn't Henry see the awkward and untenable position he was putting her in? Why did he make it all sound so obvious and easy? Because, Ellen realized, it was for him.

"It's not just about the gown," she said a bit impatiently, "although I certainly don't have a gown that would be suitable for such an occasion."

"That is easily remedied—"

"Don't you dare," Ellen warned him, properly angry now with how deliberately obtuse Henry was being. "I cannot accept any gifts from you, Henry, and certainly not a gown. Surely you see that."

"I see that it's priggish nonsense," Henry returned with spirit.

"To you, perhaps, as a man of some standing and means," Ellen returned with just as much spirit. "But not to someone like me."

"Someone like you? See, you are a snob. A reverse snob."

"That is nonsense and you know it. I am being practical, not snobbish. If I came to your ball, I would be reviled, Henry, or at least ignored—"

"So you think. But the world is moving on, Ellen, especially in a modern city such as Glasgow. You must move with it—"

"Well, I'm afraid I've never been very good at that," Ellen cut him off with finality. "I don't like change."

"And yet you moved all the way across the Atlantic," Henry returned. "Twice."

"Yes." Briefly, Ellen thought of the girl she'd been, standing on deck with her Da as they sailed past the Statue of Liberty eight years ago. Things had changed so much since then, and some of that change had not been welcome. Her father leaving… Aunt Ruth dying… being sent from Seaton to Amherst Island and back again… There had been many joys along the way, but it still hadn't been easy. And, truth be told, she wasn't sure just how much she'd actually changed on the inside.

"Even so, I must be firm on this," she said to Henry. "It would not be appropriate for me to attend this ball in any capacity, and certainly not as your guest. I'm quite sure your parents would not approve."

Henry's eyes flashed with ire. "I am a grown man, and not beholden to my parents," he answered. "I don't care what they think."

"But perhaps I do."

His eyebrows shot up. "You care about the opinions of people you've never met?"

"Oh, Henry, are you trying to be difficult?" Ellen exclaimed.

He smiled a bit at that, but she could still tell he was both hurt and irritated by her insistent refusal.

"I do not wish to embarrass myself, or be an embarrassment to a bunch of strangers. I certainly don't want to be made a mockery of, or gain a reputation—"

"What kind of reputation?"

"I don't even like to say!" Ellen's cheeks warmed. She was not about to mention terms such as gold-digger or harlot to Henry. "I don't even know why you want to ask me to such a thing—"

"Don't you?" he said quietly, and Ellen felt as if her heart was suddenly suspended in her chest.

She looked away, not wanting to answer, and perhaps make Henry declare himself even more. She could hardly believe how quickly the conversation had moved, how his *intentions* had moved—or had they? Had Henry felt something for her since the beginning, back in Chicago? Ellen could not credit it. They barely knew each other.

"It's quite, quite impossible," she said quietly. "And by speaking to me in such a manner, you are compromising my integrity at the school. If anyone thought you had recommended my acceptance because of some... some feeling on your part..." She blushed to say the words.

"I recommended your acceptance because of your natural talent," Henry returned with a hint of ire. "How could you ever think otherwise?"

"I don't know what to think," Ellen cried. She felt entirely out of sorts, the bonhomie of the pleasant afternoon quite spoiled.

"I think this has all got out of hand," Henry said after an uncomfortable moment of silence. "I meant the invitation as a gesture of friendship, and nothing more. Please forgive me if I seemed... forward. And if it helps, you wouldn't be the only art student there." He lounged back in his chair, speaking lightly, those awful moments of unexpected intensity thankfully passed.

"I won't?" Ellen asked cautiously. She still couldn't conceive of going to the ball, but she was curious that another art student would be in attendance. Perhaps things were more modern in Glasgow than she'd realized.

"No, of course you won't," Henry said with a smile. "My parents support the school, as you know I do. So it's not nearly as inappropriate as you think."

She felt unsettled by that, and wished he'd been forthcoming about such details when he'd first asked. Had she just embarrassed herself in front of Henry, by coming over so prissily, and implying he had romantic feelings for her, when he may have been intimating no such thing? She'd certainly got such things wrong before, thinking Jed harbored gentler feelings when he hadn't, and then assuming Lucas didn't, when he had. Perhaps she simply couldn't understand men at all.

"I… I don't know, Henry," she said hesitantly. "It still seems…" She could not quite put it into words.

"Think on it," he said easily, and leaned forward to pour her more tea. "You don't need to give me an answer now. I wanted only to mention it."

She was no nearer an answer an hour later when Henry dropped her back off at Norah's, having been the epitome of easy friendliness for the rest of their afternoon together.

The house was quiet as Ellen came in; Norah was no doubt in her studio, a surprisingly comfortable shed in the back garden that afforded the artist plenty of light. Ellen tiptoed upstairs and closed the door, grateful for a moment's peaceful solitude.

Except she did not feel very peaceful, with Henry's invitation still rattling around in her mind like a marble. *Should* she accept? What if it wasn't as wildly inappropriate as she'd first thought? The artist community, funded by local industrialists, was not bound by the same social mores and constraints that Ellen had known all her life, and yet…

Her gaze fell on the letter she'd been reading earlier, from Aunt Rose. She thought of how Louisa was adjusting to island life, even learning to churn butter. Couldn't she, then, adapt as well? If Louisa could become a farmer's wife, then perhaps she could become, if not a Serious Artist, then at least a little more bold and carefree, embracing this strange and wonderful new life. She could embrace all of the opportunities Glasgow gave her, instead of remaining mired in the past, wondering *what if* or *if only*.

Quickly, before she could change her mind, she dashed off a letter to Henry, accepting his invitation to the ball, and put it downstairs on the hall table, to be taken out with the morning post.

All night long, Ellen tossed and turned, unable to sleep for the thought of the letter she'd left downstairs. She wondered if Henry would read more into it than she meant, and if she were being dangerously forward in agreeing to attend the ball, even if not as his guest.

A *ball*... what on earth would she wear? Even her best dress, the one she'd bought in New York for dinner on the *S.S. Furnessia*, was not the sort of thing one wore to a society ball, surely.

Sometime near dawn, she fell into an uneasy, dreamless sleep, only to wake suddenly to a rapping on her door.

"Ellen?" Norah called. "Breakfast is on the table. You'll be late if you don't hurry."

Blearily, Ellen rose from the bed and quickly washed and dressed. The sun was streaming through the window and a glance at the timepiece she wore pinned to her shirtwaist showed her that she was indeed very late.

She hurried downstairs, resolving to take the letter from the hall table and consign it to the fire. She'd accepted Henry's invitation in a moment of foolish pique and reckless daring, but in the cold, bright light of morning, she knew it wasn't sensible to attend. She wasn't that sort of person, no matter how hard she tried or wished for it.

As she came into the hall, however, she saw the silver salver that held the post was empty. The letter was gone.

"Has the post already gone?" she asked Norah as she came into the breakfast room, trying to sound light. Norah, of course, wasn't fooled.

"Yes, Elsa took it out a short while ago." Elsa was Norah's cook and maid of all work, who seemed to turn her hand to anything, and then melt into the background. Her gaze narrowed as she took in Ellen's discomfiture. "If you did not want to send the letter, Ellen, perhaps you should not have put it out on the hall table."

Ellen tried not to squirm under Norah's knowing gaze. "It's fine," she said airily as she stirred jam into her porridge, trying to ignore the curdling sense of trepidation in the pit of her stomach. "I was just wondering, that was all."

All morning, Ellen could not settle to anything in her lessons, and was given a dressing-down by the intimidating Mr. Grieffenhagen in her painting class, which left her burning with shame.

"You must commit to your subject, Miss Copley," he said, his voice ringing out through the classroom so all the other pupils perched on their stools could hear.

Ellen stared down at her lap, her cheeks flaming, as Mr. Grieffenhagen continued his diatribe.

"An artist feels and believes in what he—or she—is doing. We are not making pretty pictures. We are breathing life."

She bit her lip and managed to murmur her apology and, with a huff, Mr. Grieffenhagen moved on. Ellen stared at her half-finished painting of a copper jug and a few oranges and sighed inwardly. Such a bland scene hardly seemed as if she were *breathing life*. And yet even though she hated being humiliated in a class, she knew Mr. Grieffenhagen had a point. She was not entering fully into the spirit of the school because she was afraid. Afraid she didn't fit in; afraid she was in the wrong place. Afraid she'd be exposed as a fraud.

She'd spent so much of her life in fear, Ellen reflected morosely during the afternoon tea break. Most of the other students were chatting in little knots of people, but Ellen had chosen to sit alone; Amy was chatting with another "dilettante", a young society lady with artistic pretensions.

Sipping her tea alone, Ellen felt almost as she had when she'd first moved to Seaton, and had stood by herself in the schoolyard while all the other pupils walked smugly past her, ignoring the new girl who had the wrong accent and too much hair.

"Why so glum?" Amy McPhee plopped herself down next to Ellen, adjusting her voluminous skirts. Unlike many of the female students at the school, who preferred the new, less formal and uncorseted style of dressing, Amy McPhee was a regular Gibson Girl, with her hair pinned up in an elaborate style and her dress, underneath her smock, trimmed with ribbon and lace and far from practical.

"Do I look as glum as all that?" Ellen asked and Amy inspected her, her lips pursed.

"You have an expression like curdled milk. You aren't taking old Griffy to heart, are you?"

"Griffy?" Ellen repeated with a choked laugh. "Amy, how do you dare…?"

"He can't hear," Amy replied with a wink and a grin. "And, in any case, I'm not studying for a certificate. What can they do to me? Fra Newbery wants my money, or rather my father's money, and so he'll let me stay and sit in on lessons."

"You sound terribly cynical."

Amy smiled. "Merely pragmatic, my dear. But what's wrong, really?"

Ellen sighed. "I just wonder if I really belong here."

"Because you're not taking yourself seriously all the time?" Amy answered, her hazel eyes glinting with humor, and Ellen let out another reluctant laugh and shook her head.

"You really are irreverent."

"Look, Ellen, I've seen some of your drawings and paintings, and I wish I had that kind of talent. You've got more raw talent in your little finger than I'll ever have in my whole body. Maybe you don't swan about and consider yourself an artist with a capital A, but you have the real thing and that's what matters."

"You're kind to say so."

"What do you want out of life?" Amy asked frankly, and Ellen blinked, surprised and rather discomfited by the blunt question.

"What do you mean?" she asked, mainly to stall for time.

"I mean, what are you here for? To get the certificate and be a professional artist? To better your skill? To make friends? Decide why you're here and go after that ambition. Then perhaps you'll start to feel as if you fit in."

Why *was* she here? Because she'd wanted to leave Amherst Island. Because her life had been at a crossroads and she'd thought it was time to pursue her dream. But she wasn't pursuing her dream, even though she'd come this far. She was still holding back, hiding in the shadows. She had done so for so long that she wasn't sure she knew how to be any different. But she knew she wanted to be.

"Thank you," she said to Amy. "That's sound advice. I will think on it."

"Good. And in the meantime, you can join the Glasgow Society of Lady Artists. They have a house on Blythewood Square, and plenty of the female pupils here are members. They do exhibitions and parties and all sorts of things—you'd be most welcome, and you might make some friends as well."

"That's very kind—"

Amy held up a hand. "I warn you, I won't take no for an answer. We have a meeting next week."

"All right, I'll come," Ellen said, smiling, her heart lightening, and Amy smiled back.

CHAPTER SEVEN

The Society of Lady Artists was housed in an impressive building on Blythewood Square, with a door of square glass panes designed by Charles Rennie Macintosh himself. Inside there was a large room for lectures, studio space, and a long gallery with sofas and chairs where women came to mingle, chat, and laugh together.

On a blustery Wednesday evening in early October, Amy swept in with Ellen, and after listening to a lecture by an imposing lady sculptress from Edinburgh, she moved around the gallery with Ellen, introducing her to everyone. Ellen was surprised to see Norah there, chatting with a few other artists she recognized: Jessie King and De Courcy Lewthwaite Dewar. Veritable icons in the Glasgow art world, but Ellen's initial sense of intimidation soon dissolved in the face of all the easy conversation and laughter.

Norah introduced her to some of her friends, and Ellen glowed when she mentioned that she was her boarder, and "a student of considerable talent." Amy, overhearing, raised her eyebrows as if to say "see?" and Ellen couldn't keep from smiling. "Considerable talent" was high praise indeed, coming from Norah.

By the end of the evening, she actually felt a part of things, shyly offering a few of her own opinions, for the women were forthright, expostulating on everything from the Scottish Exhibition of National History, Art, and Industry that had just finished, to the recent news of two shipbrokers who had been arrested for defrauding the Union Bank of Scotland.

As she and Amy were leaving, far later than Ellen had antici-
pated, she worked up the courage to tell her friend about Henry's
invitation. She had received a short yet warm note back in reply,
confirming her attendance, which had sent her into even more
of a spin.

Now Amy raised her eyebrows, impressed. "The McAvoy ball?
It's a splendid event. My family goes every year."

"You'll be there?" Ellen felt a ripple of relief at the thought. "I'm
glad I'll know at least one person. Henry, that is, Mr. McAvoy,
said there would be a few lady artists in attendance, but I wasn't
entirely sure…"

"I suspect so," Amy said after a moment, but her expression
had turned gleefully shrewd and Ellen could feel herself starting
to blush. "I have heard a rumor," she continued, her voice light
although her eyes were narrowed, "that Mr. McAvoy called for
you for tea on Saturday."

"We're friends," Ellen said. Her face felt fiery now. "We met in
Chicago, you know, last year. How did you hear that, anyway?"

"You can't go to Miss Cranston's tearooms and not be noticed!
Just be careful, Ellen. Mr. McAvoy is a gentleman, but he's
always been one to defy convention. Whether he should or not
is another matter." Amy rested one gloved hand on Ellen's arm,
her expression compassionate and a little worried. "Please forgive
me if I am speaking out of turn, but it's just that I wouldn't want
you to get hurt."

"I have no intention of getting hurt, or encouraging Hen—Mr.
McAvoy in any way," Ellen said, her voice sounding stiff. She felt
wrong-footed again, thinking one moment that her appearance
at the ball was not as risqué as she feared, and the next certain
that it was.

Amy nodded, her lips pursed. "And yet you accepted his
invitation."

Ellen tried not to bristle. "Do you think I shouldn't have?"

"I don't know." Amy sighed, a frown now furrowing her forehead. "I think you could have a lovely time at the ball, and I shall certainly be glad to have you there. But if… if Mr. McAvoy has developed an affection for you, you must be sure his intentions are honorable."

Ellen drew back, horrified. "I wouldn't return Mr. McAvoy's affections in any case," she answered. "I do not hold him in that kind of regard, and I cannot imagine ever doing so." She shook her head. "In any case, he has asked me as a gesture of friendship, nothing more."

Amy cocked her head, her gaze sweeping over her thoughtfully. "You do protest quite vociferously! He's a handsome man, and more than charming. And, of course, he has his family fortune to inherit."

"I'm not of his class, Amy," Ellen said, her voice coming out more stiffly than ever. "Surely you realize that."

"If Mr. McAvoy does not find that an impediment, why should you?"

Ellen shook her head. "You were warning me off him a moment ago."

"As I said, I don't want to see you hurt. But if Mr. McAvoy's intentions are honorable…"

"I don't want him to have any intentions at all. And in any case, I'm not…" Ellen took a deep breath, realizing why Henry's possible interest held no excitement or appeal for her, only alarm. "I'm in love with someone else," she admitted, her voice flat now. "Back in Canada."

"Oh, are you?" Amy's gaze brightened with curiosity. "And yet you came all the way here? Will he wait for you?"

"Certainly not." Too late, Ellen realized how it sounded, like some romantic love affair. "He's married to someone else."

"Oh." Amy sat back, clearly scandalized, and Ellen hurried to explain.

"Nothing ever happened between us, of course. He was—is—a family friend. But I fell in love with him, and he fell in love with someone else."

"Well, if nothing happened, I hardly think you should keep a candle burning for him!" Amy shook her head. "No, no languishing allowed. Go to the ball, Ellen, and see if it can't distract you from moping after this Yankee." Her eyes danced and she leaned forward. "Now onto far more important matters. Have you got a dress?"

A few days before the McAvoy Ball, Ellen called on Amy at her home in Dowanhill, a neighborhood of impressive villas and private homes that was as far from Springburn as could possibly be. Ellen had worn her Sunday dress and her best hat, and she nearly curtsied to the parlormaid who opened the door before remembering herself.

Amy flew down the stairs, her arms outstretched. "Ellen! I'm so glad you've come. Now, I've got the best gowns out. Come have a look at Madame Amy's Couture!" She laughed merrily and led Ellen up the stairs; the carpet was thick and plush, the brass stair rods gleaming. The air smelled of expensive leather and lemon furniture polish. It made Ellen's head spin. She'd never been in such a posh house before, and it made her regard Amy in a whole new light. Louisa's family home back in Seaton, elegant as it had seemed, positively paled in comparison.

Amy's bedroom was enormous, with a separate seating area, and a fire burning merrily in the grate. A lady's maid was smoothing the flounces of one of the gowns laid across the canopied bed, but she stepped back smartly as Amy entered.

"Oh, Metcalfe, you can go now. Miss Copley and I will fend for ourselves most admirably, I assure you."

The maid bobbed a curtsey. "Very good, miss."

"But do tell Cook to make us a plate of something delicious, and a pot of tea as well. Fashion is thirsty work. You may bring it up in a few minutes."

"Very good, miss," the maid said again, and left the room.

Ellen stared at Amy in amazement. "You sounded like such a grand lady! I feel as if I should start to bow and scrape."

"Not a bit of it!" Amy cried. "Anyway, it was just the maid. Now, onto important things. Your dress!"

Ellen shook her head slowly, amazed all over again at how easily Amy dismissed the young woman who had served her. In her former life, she might have had aspirations to a lady's maid position, and not even in a house as grand as this. She would have been the one curtseying and fetching tea, wearing Amy's castoffs if she was lucky, instead of one of her best gowns. It made Ellen feel disconcerted, that things could change so much, even as she doubted that they really could.

"Now, how about this one?" Carelessly, Amy searched through the rainbow of satins and silks spread out on the counterpane. "It's a lovely shade of golden-brown… just like your eyes." She glanced at Ellen, narrowing her eyes. "Don't tell me you're having second thoughts!"

"I can't imagine wearing one of these gowns," Ellen blurted. "They're far too nice for me, Amy." She knotted her fingers together as she shook her head. "And I don't even know what I'd do at a ball. I can barely manage a waltz…"

"Then we'll have some dancing lessons," Amy proclaimed. "Really, there are only a few you need to learn. The McAvoys will only have waltzes and country dances. They abhor ragtime."

"Ragtime is one I know," Ellen answered, thinking of the "smoker" dance at Queen's University she'd gone to with Lucas. They'd done all sorts of funny dances, from the Grizzly Bear to the Turkey Trot. Learning those silly steps wouldn't serve her well now, clearly.

"Why don't you try this one on?" Amy asked, thrusting the golden-brown gown towards Ellen. She took it reverently, the sheen of the silk finer than any dress she'd ever laid eyes on before.

"Are you sure about letting me borrow something like this, Amy?" she asked. She knew the dress must have cost a fortune, along with the others laid carelessly on the bed, and she trembled inside to think of spilling something on it and ruining it.

"Of course!" Amy answered gaily. "I won't wear most of them again anyway. They're all last season, but I think they're still fashionable, don't you?"

"I have no idea," Ellen replied with a laugh. "I wouldn't know one year's fashions from the next. But I think they're all lovely."

"Well, go on, then, try it on. I can't wait to see you in it."

Amy directed her to a screen in the corner of the room, painted with garden scenes that were quite exquisite.

Ellen spent a moment examining them before Amy said, laughing, "Now's not the time to study art, Ellen. We're all about fashion now."

Laughing a little herself, Ellen retreated behind the screen and carefully changed into the ball gown, trimmed with silk rosettes with a lace underskirt in pale gold. Amy helped her with the tiny buttons that went up the back, and then turned her around to face the cheval mirror.

"What do you think?"

"Oh…" Ellen gazed at herself in wonder. "I've never seen anything so fine."

"You do look beautiful," Amy agreed cheerfully.

"I meant the dress, not me," Ellen exclaimed, embarrassed, and Amy raised her eyebrows.

"Why shouldn't you be proud and confident in the way you look? You're always trying to hide yourself, Ellen, and you really are lovely."

"Don't you think it's a bit… revealing… in the front?" Gently, Ellen tugged up the bodice, but with a laugh, Amy batted her hands away.

"Not at all. It's perfectly respectable to show a hint of bosom. Now." She clapped her hands together and nodded towards the other gowns spread out on the bed. "I do like this one you've got on, but I wonder if that dark green with gold trim might bring out the hazel in your eyes? Shall you try it on?"

An hour later, Ellen had tried on more dresses than she could even remember, and had finally settled on a gown of emerald green satin. It was deceptively simple, and the low neckline and short sleeves were more daring than anything Ellen had ever worn before. When she said as much to Amy, her friend had just clucked her tongue.

"You can't dress like a nun or a schoolgirl when you're going to a ball. Everyone will have similar necklines, and some even more daring than yours!"

"I know, but—"

"You must embrace it, Ellen," Amy told her severely. "And hold your head up high. You don't want a bunch of prissy society girls turning their noses up at you."

"I'm sure they will no matter what I wear," Ellen said with a wry smile even though inside she hated the thought.

"No, they won't, because I won't let them, and neither will you. You have as much right to be there as they do."

"But I don't, not really—"

"You've been invited, haven't you? Now, I'll call for Metcalfe to box this up, and our driver can take it round. You can't possibly carry it yourself."

"Thank you, Amy," Ellen said, the words heartfelt even as she felt a distinct unease at the thought of attending the ball in just a few days.

"You know it's my pleasure. I'll add a dance card as well, since I don't think you have one?"

Ellen managed a laugh. "Of course I don't."

"You shall be the belle of the ball, Ellen," Amy said as she kissed her cheek in farewell. "Glasgow's Cinderella!"

Which was rather apt, Ellen reflected as she started walking back towards Renfrew Street and Norah's house. The question was, when would she turn back into the rag-wearing skivvy that Cinderella had been?

The air was crisp and smelled of coal fires and woodsmoke, and the leaves of the trees that lined the street were a bold yellow. Humming under her breath, Ellen felt her spirits lift a little, and for the first time since arriving in Glasgow she actually felt a flicker of excitement for what lay ahead. She would dance and drink champagne and talk about art—who could have ever dreamed that the little waif from Springburn would be received at one of Glasgow's best houses? It terrified her, even as it made her smile.

Back at Norah's house, there were two letters for her on the hall table, one from Letitia in Edinburgh, and one from Lucas. Ellen took them both upstairs; she removed her hat, coat, and shoes, and curled up in the chair by the window and read them both by the last of the afternoon's sunlight.

She read Letitia's first, enjoying her new friend's description of medical lectures and dissections at Edinburgh University, even as she shuddered at the thought of having to dissect a human body. She'd have to paint one soon enough, and she knew she'd find that challenging. Letitia promised to visit soon, and laying that letter aside, Ellen opened Lucas's.

She felt a bittersweet pang of nostalgia and longing as she saw his familiar scrawl across the page, the ink smeared in places. It seemed a long time ago now that she'd danced with Lucas at Jed and Louisa's wedding, and they'd told each other their plans. Now she read about his hopes to work as a law clerk in Toronto after graduation, marveling at how far they'd both come.

> *I went for an interview a few weeks ago and felt like quite the wet-behind-the-ears yokel who has just come up to town, but I suppose that was always likely to be the case. Four years in Kingston won't prepare me as much as I would like for Toronto city life, I expect. But I do hope to enjoy it. I'm managing to finish my studies in December, and I shall start as a clerk in January. Needs must when it comes to earning a wage! I've arranged to take rooms near King Street, and have already met a few lads who are in the same position as I am. I expect it will all not be as dull as I've feared, nor as interesting as I've hoped. But worthwhile, I think, even if sitting in an office reading briefs all day is not what I'd envisioned my life's work to be.*
>
> *After a summer back home I miss the island more than I expected to, but, in truth, I think I just miss you. I know that's not what you want to read, and you are no doubt enjoying life as a Lady Artist, but I will write it the same, because it is true and I can't bear you not knowing. Think of me what you will.*
>
> *As ever, Lucas*

Tears stung her eyes as she finished the letter and she blinked them back, knowing that she had no cause to miss Lucas the way he missed her. She'd given him her answer months ago, when she'd told him she saw him as a brother rather than as anything more. She couldn't change her mind now, simply because she was feeling a little homesick and lost. It would be unfair to both her and Lucas.

Sighing, Ellen stared out at the darkening sky, a few crimson and yellow leaves fluttering to the pavement below. For a moment, she could imagine those trees were the stand of birches that separated the Lymans' property from the McCaffertys' on Amherst Island. She could picture herself beneath them, a sketchbook open on her lap, and Lucas next to her, sprawled out lazily, talking about science and history and all of his wonderful ideas. He'd never finished cataloguing all the flora and fauna of the island, although he'd made it his life's work as a child. Ellen wondered if he ever would.

For a second, she ached with homesickness, with the loss of knowing that a moment like that one would never happen again. She and Lucas had chosen different paths, and it seemed far too likely that they would intersect rarely, if at all. The thought brought her a regret more bitter than she liked to acknowledge, because his friendship had always been dear to her, and she feared now it might be lost forever.

CHAPTER EIGHT

The night of the McAvoy ball, Ellen stood in front of the small, cloudy-looking glass in her bedroom and tried to do her hair in the loose pompadour style that Amy wore, with little success. She'd used more than a dozen pins and it seemed likely it would all fall into hopeless tangles as soon as she stepped outside, into the wind.

It was a filthy night, raining steadily and gusting wind, and Ellen's plan to walk to Dowanhill did not seem such a good one. She almost wished she'd taken Henry up on his offer to collect her in his motorcar, scandalous as that might have been.

Carefully, she smoothed down the front of the emerald-green gown, still half-amazed that she was wearing such a lovely thing. She'd never bared her shoulders or bosom so much before, and she was half tempted to tuck a lace handkerchief in the neckline of her gown, just to cover a bit of skin. Amy, she thought ruefully, would no doubt pluck it out again as soon as she saw her.

A knock sounded on the door, and Ellen called for Norah to come in.

Norah wore a shapeless dress of brown muslin with a velvet wrap over her shoulders. She wore no corset and yet managed to look elegant and in command despite her typically unconventional dress. Ellen had told Norah she was attending the ball several days ago, and her landlady had not looked pleased. She hadn't said anything, however, just pressed her lips together and gave one swift nod.

Now she gazed at Ellen in all her finery and said, "You certainly look the part. I've arranged for a hansom cab for you. You can hardly walk in this weather."

"Thank you, Norah," Ellen said, touched by the older woman's thoughtfulness, especially considering her disapproval of Ellen's attendance at the ball. "That's very kind. I'll repay you, of course."

"There's no need. It's simply practical," Norah answered briskly. "I thought of sending for one of the new motorized taxicabs, but they always seem as if they break down. People are forever standing by the roadside while the driver turns the crank, looking hopelessly annoyed. A horse-drawn conveyance is more reliable, I think."

"I've only been in a motorcar once," Ellen confessed, and then quickly looked away as she saw the understanding gleam in Norah's shrewd eyes. It had, of course, been Henry's motorcar.

"Well, I hope you enjoy yourself at such an occasion," she said after a pause, "and that you're not too distracted from the real reason you came to Glasgow." She arched an imperious eyebrow. "If studying art and honing your craft is the real reason, and not to snare a rich husband?"

Ellen flushed as she kept her eyes on the looking glass, unwilling to meet Norah's knowing gaze. "I am here to study art," she said firmly. "That is all."

Norah left with a swish of her skirts, and knowing she could delay the moment no longer, Ellen gave one last pat to her hair and then reached for the silk wrap that went with the dress; it hardly seemed likely to keep her warm, but she couldn't wear her old brown coat buttoned up over the top. Forcing her shoulders back and her chin up, she stepped out into the night.

The driver leapt down from his perch to help her into the hansom cab, and Ellen settled against the seat as nerves leaped and writhed in her belly like a landed fish.

It was a short drive to Dowanhill, and the McAvoys' villa was lit up like a beacon against the night sky. Guests were mounting the steps: men in tall hats and tails, women in ball gowns dripping with jewels and furs. Despite Amy's emerald gown and wrap, Ellen felt decidedly underdressed. She wore no jewels or furs, and her slippers, thankfully hidden by her dress, were her own, worn and old, as Amy's feet were far smaller than hers. She wished in this moment that she had an escort—a mama or papa, a friend or chaperone, or even a maid. Anyone to stand by her side, so she didn't have to mount those steps all by herself, and be subject to everyone's speculative looks.

Murmuring her thanks to the driver, she alighted from the carriage and, taking a deep breath, she squared her shoulders and climbed the steps to the McAvoys' villa.

The foyer of the house was huge, with a floor of black and white checkered marble and a huge electric chandelier above. Guests swarmed the space, and servants in elegant livery circulated with trays of champagne.

Ellen felt completely out of her depth.

A servant stepped forward to take her wrap and another offered her champagne. She'd never drunk it before, and she had to keep from making a face as the fizzy bubbles tickled her throat and nose. She looked around a bit desperately for someone she knew, trying not to notice the curious looks of strangers who could undoubtedly sense that she was not one of them.

"Ellen!"

She didn't know whether she felt relief or dismay at the sight of Henry coming towards her, dressed in a white tie and tails. He looked dashing in his evening wear with his dark hair slicked back with pomade, his blue eyes sparkling, but his obvious ease in such fancy clothes made Ellen feel even more like an impostor. She wished she really had put a bit of lace along the neckline of her gown.

"I'm so pleased you've come," Henry said, taking her hands in his. Even through the white elbow-length gloves Amy had lent her, she could feel the warmth of his hands. She could also feel the curious stares of the guests around her; they were no doubt wondering just who she was, and why their hosts' son was greeting her in such a familiar fashion.

"I'm pleased to be here," she said, and slipped her hand from his. "Your house is lovely."

Henry gave the impressive foyer an indifferent glance. "I suppose it is, although I prefer less ostentation. Come, let me introduce you to some friends."

And before she could protest, he took her hand once more and led her into the villa's ballroom.

The room was huge, filled with people, and even though she knew they were not, Ellen felt as if every single one of the McAvoys' guests was staring at her. She shouldn't have come, she thought. She should have cried off, said she was ill, anything but endure all this open curiosity and even hostility, all the sneering speculation she could see in narrowed eyes and pursed lips, although Henry seemed blithely unaware of it.

"Mama, this is the lady artist I was telling you about. Ellen Copley, the school's most promising new student."

A tall, elegant woman with Henry's dark hair and blue eyes turned to survey Ellen, who only just kept herself from dropping a curtsey.

"Pleased to meet you, ma'am," she murmured, and Mrs. McAvoy's eyebrows rose, at her words or her accent or something else entirely, Ellen didn't know.

"Likewise," she said, and she sounded condescendingly amused, which made Ellen cringe. Was everyone at this wretched ball laughing at her, thinking how appallingly obvious it was that she didn't fit in? Did they know where she came from? Could they guess?

Henry was talking to his mother about Ellen's art, but she could barely take in a word. Mrs. McAvoy did not look particularly impressed by her alleged talent, and was certainly not pleased by her son's enthusiasm, her narrowed gaze moving from Henry to Ellen and back again as her mouth drew tighter and tighter.

"Really, Henry," she said when there was a tiny lull in the conversation, her tone laughingly dry, "you are too kind, taking in the school's strays like puppies. Sometimes it's better just to put them out of their misery." She met Ellen's gaze with glinting challenge, while Ellen stood rooted to the spot, hardly able to believe the woman had issued such a direct and terrible insult as if she were making a light joke at which everyone would politely titter.

"It's not like that at all, Mother," Henry said, sounding annoyed, but Ellen couldn't stand there and listen to any more. Several people nearby had heard Mrs. McAvoy's comment, and were now laughing behind their hands as they whispered to their neighbors. She felt a desperate, dire need to escape the conversation, the room, the whole ball. "You ought to see her sketches," Henry said, and Ellen couldn't bear for him to stick up for her for another second. He was only making it all worse.

"I'm sure Mrs. McAvoy has no interest in my sketches," she said, managing a strangled laugh. "Really, I'm a complete amateur. I have so much to learn." She paused as she met Mrs. McAvoy's gaze directly even as she quailed inside. "Fortunately, I am a quick learner." She held the older woman's gaze for another unbearable second, seeing the knowledge and satisfaction enter her steely gaze. "Now, I must excuse myself. I've taken up too much of your time already."

"You haven't," Henry protested, but Ellen just shook her head, murmuring her apologies, and then walked as quickly away as she could manage in her narrow-skirted gown.

It took her a few moments, but she finally found the retiring room for ladies, off the house's main corridor, which was bigger than the whole downstairs of Jasper Lane. A few young women were chatting as they powdered their noses, and they glanced speculatively at Ellen, falling silent as she hurried past them and sat down on a chaise in the corner, her hands pressed to her cheeks.

Mrs. McAvoy's insult had cut her to the core, because it had played on every fear she'd had. She didn't belong; she *was* a stray. And now everyone knew it, although, of course, they'd guessed before. She couldn't bear to stay at the wretched ball for another moment. Could she sneak out without saying goodbye to Henry? She'd have to. The last thing Ellen wanted to do was go back into that room and face everyone's sneering stares.

She'd plead a headache when she saw him again, or perhaps she'd just tell him the truth. She shouldn't have come here. He shouldn't have invited her. She should have known what she was capable of, where she belonged… and so should have Henry. *Wherever that actually was.*

Two young women dressed as brightly as peacocks came into the room with a swish of silk and a toss of their elegantly coiffed heads, strings of pearls gleaming against their white bosoms.

"Who on earth is that country bumpkin in the green gown?" one of them asked in a carrying voice, and Ellen shrank into the corner of the chaise, wishing the shadows would shroud her.

A few of the women already in the room shared knowing glances, clearly aware that the country bumpkin was only a few feet away.

"That dress is at least two years old," the other young lady contributed with gleeful malice. "Although Henry McAvoy certainly seems fond enough of her! He always had queer taste."

"But loads of money," someone else said, and they all giggled.

"Do you think that's why she's here?" the first woman asked with a sniff as she examined her reflection in the gilt-edged mirror and clearly found it satisfying. "To set her cap at him and his money? What do you suppose she's offering, to make him look at her twice?"

One of the women tutted. "Don't be common, Rosemary—"

"Well, why else would he be interested in her?" Rosemary demanded. "She's a complete nobody. She must be enticing him with *something*."

With every word they'd uttered, Ellen had shrunk farther back into the chaise, wishing she could disappear. But as the querulous Rosemary's voice rang out for everyone to hear, she felt something inside her snap. She wouldn't apologize for who she was anymore. She wouldn't hang her head in shame simply because she didn't have the clothes or the money, the opportunities or the sense of privilege, that these young women did. Poor lass from Springburn she might be, but she still had more breeding and class than to gossip like fishwives as these young women were doing, and impugn an innocent woman's character on no basis at all.

She rose from the chaise, shaking out her skirts with deliberation, her fingers trembling against the silk. The movement caught the women's eyes, and Ellen saw how their eyes widened as they realized who she was. Not one of them had the grace so much as to blush, and Rosemary merely lifted her chin in smirking challenge.

"I'm not here for Mr. McAvoy's money," Ellen said clearly, meeting each of their shocked gazes in turn, although it cost her. She was caught between an empowering rage and a deep, terrible sadness. "But I can assure you, I'm not here for the company either," she added. She raked them with as much dignified contempt as she could, even as she fought the urge to cry. "I'm afraid I find it sadly lacking," she finished, and with her head held high and her heart beating hard, she sailed out of the room.

She walked directly to the foyer, which had emptied out, and asked one of the footmen to fetch her wrap. Her face was still flaming, tears far too close, and she had to keep herself from trembling, but she was glad she'd said what she had. No doubt she'd feed society's gossip mill for a year, but it didn't matter. She would never attend another ball again, because no matter whether she belonged or not, she didn't want to.

"Ellen!" Henry's voice rang out behind her. "Surely you're not going already?"

"Yes, I am. I should never have come, Henry." Ellen didn't look at him as she thanked the footman for her wrap and put it around her shoulders.

"You're not going because of what my mother said, are you? She didn't mean it unkindly, I assure you—"

"She most certainly did," Ellen snapped. "You can't have it both ways, Henry. You can't say I'm a snob, and then pretend your mother isn't. She was warning me off, and I am heeding it. I knew I didn't belong here, and the truth is, I don't even want to. I never should have allowed you to coax me into coming."

"But we haven't even danced yet," Henry protested, with a nod towards the empty card dangling from her wrist by a silk ribbon.

In one vicious movement, Ellen ripped it from her wrist and thrust it at him. "As far as I am concerned, you may waltz alone," she said, and she started to turn away.

Henry caught her hand in his, staying her. "Ellen, please. I'm sorry my mother upset you. She thinks she's being humorous—"

"No, she doesn't," Ellen said fiercely as she pulled her hand away. "Country bumpkin I may be, but I know that much. She was trying to insult me, and she succeeded, although I think less of her, and everyone else here, for it. You're all a bunch of parasites, feeding off people's pain and difficulties, laughing behind your hands. Do you know how hard your servants work?" she demanded. "The tweenies were most likely up before four in the morning to prepare for this ridiculous ball."

Henry stared at her in amazement. "Why on earth are we talking about the tweenies?" he asked in genuine befuddlement, and Ellen let out a ragged laugh.

"Because they matter, and they were most likely born into better circumstances than I was."

"Surely not," Henry protested. "Ellen, you are exaggerating, because you are cross. I understand it—"

"But I'm not," she said quietly. "Perhaps you didn't realize that." How could he? How could someone of Henry's wealth and status understand where she'd come from?

"That doesn't matter to me," he said at last, reaching for her hands once more.

"But it matters to me." She took a step away. "I'm sorry, Henry. I've enjoyed being your friend. But this was a step too far. I… I don't think we should see each other again, in any capacity."

"Ellen, you don't mean that." Henry looked crestfallen, but Ellen hardened her heart.

"I do," she said, and then turning away from him, she strode out of the grand house, into the night.

CHAPTER NINE

January 1912

"Well done, Miss Copley. Your most recent painting is quite…
competent."

Ellen suppressed a smile as Mr. Grieffenhagen moved past her.
Competent was, she knew, high praise indeed from her demanding
instructor, and the biggest compliment he'd paid her in the four
months she'd been at the school.

"Clearly you're coming on," Amy told her after the painting
lesson was over and they were walking towards the refectory. "*I've*
certainly never been called competent."

"You can dream," Ellen teased back and Amy grinned.

They settled at one of the tables with cups of tea and pieces
of ginger cake. Ellen glanced around at all the pupils chatting
and eating and felt contentment settle deep in her bones. She'd
worked hard these last few months, not just to improve her artistic
ability, but to increase her confidence, and to, as Norah liked to
say, "suck the marrow out of life" here in Glasgow.

Besides her days at school, she'd started taking an active part
in the Glasgow Society of Lady Artists, and had attended dinners
and lectures there regularly. She'd made a few more friends among
the female pupils at both the art school and the Society, and she
nourished a secret hope that she might be chosen to take part in
the Society's winter exhibition.

She had not seen Henry since that disastrous evening back in October, at the ball. He'd written her a formal letter of apology afterwards, and promised not to seek her out. Ellen found she missed his company, but she knew she'd made the right decision. Their worlds were simply too far apart, and she needed to focus on why she'd come to Glasgow in the first place—for her art.

Amy had been sympathetic when Ellen had told, albeit briefly, what had happened at the ball.

"Oh, Mrs. McAvoy is dreadfully catty. No one gets on the right side of her, as far as I can see. I wish I'd seen you first, Ellen, and I would have warned you off her."

"It was better this way," Ellen had reassured her. "I had my doubts about attending that ball in the first place, and they were proved right. I shan't be borrowing any more gowns, I promise!"

"You act as if you've been put in your place," Amy had argued, "but it doesn't have to be that way. Glasgow society really is very enlightened."

Ellen had thought of Amy's casual dismissal of her maid, whose first name she did not even know, and simply shook her head. "As I said, it's better this way."

And so it was—without the distraction of a friendship with Henry, she had far more time and mental energy to focus on improving her skills, and she spent the evenings sketching in her room, or sometimes in the parlor with Norah, listening to music as they read or sketched. Although her landlady had not said anything about the matter, Ellen knew she approved of her friendship with Henry ending.

"It's a shame you can't be friends with Mr. McAvoy," Amy remarked now as they sipped their tea.

Ellen rolled her eyes. "Not this again, Amy…" Her friend had a romantic streak and seemed intent on casting Ellen and Henry as star-crossed lovers, while Ellen kept insisting that they were nothing of the sort.

"It's only that he doesn't visit the school as much as he used to. He's positively *avoiding* you, Ellen."

"He's respecting my wishes."

"It's so tragic of him, don't you think? He hasn't escorted any ladies anywhere since October, you know. He's obviously pining."

"I think you read too many story papers, Amy," Ellen said tartly.

"And I don't think you read enough. Do you have any romance in your heart at all? You could at least renew your acquaintance—"

"I don't wish to." Although, Ellen acknowledged, that wasn't quite true. Henry had been an easy companion, and she'd enjoyed his company. Still, she knew she would not change her mind. "Why don't we talk about something else? Are you submitting something for the winter exhibition?"

Amy wrinkled her nose. "Certainly not. I'm a dilettante, remember?"

"Your work is still accomplished," Ellen protested. Amy made fun of her artistic ambitions, but she had a raw talent for capturing still lifes in all their peaceful beauty. "Why don't you try, at least?"

"I will, if you will renew your acquaintance with Mr. McAvoy."

"Amy! I can do no such thing. It would be far too forward."

"Then at least allow him to think of approaching you," Amy argued. "Word could get to him…"

"I'm sure it could." Amy, of course, moved in the same exalted circle as the McAvoys. "No, thank you. Suit yourself if you won't submit to the exhibition."

"You will, I suppose?"

"Yes, I might as well try." She was choosing between a still life in oils, a medium she still struggled with, and a pencil sketch of a flower seller on Renfrew Street.

Amy sighed and shook her head. "Very well, I shan't mention Mr. McAvoy again. But, Ellen… don't you want to be with someone, someday? You can't pine for this mysterious man back in Canada forever."

"I'm not pining," Ellen replied, and meant it. Mostly. Rose continued to give her news of Jed and Louisa, and how they were both settling into married life on the island. It didn't hurt her nearly as much now as it had a few months ago.

"But surely you want to marry?" Amy pressed. Her own engagement was imminent; she'd been escorted to several balls by a local gentleman named Charlie Whittaker for a few weeks now, and blushed whenever she spoke of him, although Ellen had yet to meet the fine fellow. "Besides," Amy continued, "there is no reason why you can't be a Lady Artist and a respectable married woman. A society matron, even. Look at Frances or Margaret Macdonald, or Jessie King. They all married, and continued their careers. We're far more forward-thinking than you seem to believe."

"Amy," Ellen retorted tartly, "I'm not looking to marry."

"Not now, perhaps," Amy allowed. "But eventually, surely."

Ellen just shook her head. The pain of loving Jed and losing him to Louisa had certainly diminished, but that didn't mean she was ready to consider someone else. Just the thought of giving herself to a man, body and soul, made her shrink inside. The risk of being hurt, of becoming heartbroken, was simply too great. She'd always been a quiet, self-contained sort of person, and she supposed she always would be, even if the idea of a soulmate somewhere held a distant, dreamy appeal. "I have more important things to consider now," she told Amy firmly. "And I like my life just as it is."

Yet on her way back to Norah's cozy house, Ellen's mind drifted once more to the past, and what had and hadn't happened between her and Henry, as well as between her and Jed. Yes, she liked her life now, but something vital still felt as if it were missing. She cherished her letters from Lucas, yet they were a poor substitute for a friendship with someone living and breathing in the same city as she was.

While she'd made friends with some of the other artists, and could, rather cautiously, call Norah her friend, she still felt she lacked a kindred spirit, someone who understood her truly—her artistic ambitions as well as where she came from, what she missed. Perhaps she would never find that person. Perhaps they didn't exist.

Still, there was nothing to complain about, Ellen told herself. She had spent a quiet and pleasant Christmas at home with Norah; they'd enjoyed many conversations about art and philosophy. She had even taken to wearing dresses in Norah's loose, uncorseted style, although only when she was at home. She did not quite possess the daring to go out in the streets of Glasgow without the comforting armor of a corset and fitted gown.

Her friend Letitia had come to visit over Hogmanay, and Ellen had been entertained with her many anecdotes about life as a female medical student at Edinburgh.

"I had my first Anatomy lesson right before Christmas," she'd told Ellen over cups of tea at Mrs. Cranston's tearooms. "And I didn't turn a hair! I admit it did make me a bit queasy, seeing the poor dead man laid out on a table, his skin as white as a fish's belly. And when the scalpel first went in…! The *sound* of it, Ellen… I may have swayed a little. But another student—a man, I hasten to add—fell to the floor in a dead faint. No one was giving him smelling salts, I warrant, and telling him he did not possess the constitution for such endeavors."

"Oh, Letitia, it all sounds perfectly dreadful," Ellen had said, laughing as she shook her head.

"You ought to be used to it," Letitia had answered with a sniff. "Leonardo da Vinci used to study corpses to improve his understanding of human anatomy."

"Thankfully we have live models now," Ellen had replied. Although she had blushed mightily when they'd had their first nude model in the classroom, back in November. At least she hadn't burst into fits of giggles like some of the other lady pupils, and she'd managed to keep her eyes firmly on her canvas when not actually looking at the model, whose expression had been a perfect study of boredom.

Now, as dusk settled in the late afternoon in the iron-hard cold of winter, she arrived home to find a letter from Louisa for her on the hall table—the first she'd ever sent.

Ellen picked up the envelope with Louisa's untidy, childish scrawl on the front rather apprehensively, wondering what her erstwhile friend and occasional enemy might have to say to her, to write after all this time. She feared that hearing Louisa's undoubtedly blissful descriptions of married life with Jed still held the power to sting.

Slowly, Ellen mounted the stairs to her bedroom. Amherst Island felt more and more distant with each passing day she spent in Glasgow, immersing herself in school as well as the Society of Lady Artists. She'd become used to city life, and even to the consuming attitude of most artists, as if nothing mattered but paint and charcoal, oils and clay.

For a moment, she let herself linger on the world she used to know—the lake would be frozen now, the trees stark and bare, the fields and meadows long stretches of white, drifted with snow. Ellen gazed out her bedroom window at the slate roofs and soot-stained chimneys of Glasgow and felt as if she were another person entirely from the young woman who had walked across those fields in dusk, and knocked on the door of the Lyman farm.

She glanced once more at the letter. She knew from Aunt Rose that Louisa and Jed had settled into a new farmhouse on the other side of the Lyman property. Jed had built it specially for her, even though there was plenty of room in the old farmhouse. It seemed a waste to Ellen, but Rose had been more accepting; a newlywed couple, she'd written, needed their space. Ellen hadn't liked to think too much about why.

At least it seemed Louisa had dropped her aspirations to move back to Seaton and have Jed work in a bank; Ellen was grateful for that. But why had Louisa written? What news did she have to share?

Carefully, Ellen slit the envelope and read what Louisa had written; her friend's loopy handwriting filled up an entire page.

> *Dear Ellen, I do apologize for not being a better correspondent, although, truth be told, I've never been good with letters, as you probably have guessed.*
>
> *It's hard to imagine you all the way in Glasgow, which I've heard is quite a dreary city. Rose assures me you don't find it so, but I'd rather not be stuck among the railyards and chimney stacks! If I had to go anywhere, I suppose I'd like Paris well enough.*

Ellen sank into the chair by the window, mentally rolling her eyes at Louisa's barbed comments and blatant self-absorption. She knew Louisa was pretty and she could be charming when she chose, but, not for the first time, Ellen wondered what Jed had seen in the woman he'd chosen to be his wife, and why she had deigned to be Louisa's friend in the first place.

Breathing in deeply, Ellen continued reading.

> *In any case, life here on Amherst Island continues on the same. I always did envy you your precious island, but it's more mine now than yours, I should think! Especially now, with my exciting news, and I'm sure you can guess what it is. Jed and I have been married for nearly six months, after all!*

Ellen stilled, her gaze resting blindly on those chimney stacks Louisa had disdained. She was not so naïve or innocent that she couldn't guess what news Louisa had to share. Resolutely, she turned back to the letter.

*As I'm sure you've guessed, I'm expecting! The baby is due in
midsummer, I think. I feel dreadfully tired, but Jed says I'm
blooming, and so I must be. You know how sparse he can
be with compliments, although of course when it matters
he says quite the right thing…*

Ellen could read no more. She tossed the letter aside, dropping her head into her hands as her stomach roiled. Louisa was
expecting Jed's child, and while Ellen knew she should hardly
be surprised, she was all the same. Yet even more hurtful than
that news was the casual, easy intimacy Louisa obviously shared
with Jed. Ellen had seen it at the wedding too, and yet still
she'd resisted believing it. Jed and Louisa genuinely loved one
another. *How?* Her heart cried out, even as her mind insisted,
Let it be.

"Ellen?" Norah called, tapping once on her door. "Supper is
ready."

Taking another deep breath, Ellen lifted her head from her
hands. "Coming, Norah," she called, and she rose from her chair.

She poured some ice-cold water from the pitcher into the
basin on her bureau, and quickly washed her face and hands.
When she looked in the mirror, her eyes still seemed dazed, but
otherwise she presented the image she needed: a quiet, composed
Lady Artist.

Downstairs, Norah was dishing out a warming beef stew in
the small dining room at the back of the house. Besides the cook
and a boy to do some of the hard work, Norah did not hire any
servants. She sent the washing out and managed the rest for
herself, and Ellen helped.

Now Ellen hurried to set the table, setting glasses and fetching
water.

Norah raised her eyebrows as Ellen took her seat. "You've had
news from home, I take it?"

"Yes, of some neighbors, old childhood friends. They're expecting a baby, which is of course tremendously exciting." Ellen smoothed her napkin on her lap and then took a plate of stew with murmured thanks.

"I suppose such things make you wonder about what you may have missed," Norah said as she sat down opposite Ellen.

Ellen looked up sharply, but her landlady's face was bland. She had no idea how much the older woman might have guessed of the heartbreak she'd left behind. "I wish them well," she said firmly, more firmly than she actually felt. "I am perfectly content here, I assure you, and I have no aspirations towards marriage or babies at the moment." She hoped she'd convinced Norah, as well as herself, with her firm tone.

"I am glad to hear it," Norah answered. "There was a matter I wished to discuss with you," she continued as she poured them both water. "Regarding the Society's winter exhibition."

Ellen's heart skipped a beat as she composed her expression into one of polite, professional interest. "Oh, yes?"

"You most certainly possess the talent to take part in it," Norah said and Ellen felt the beginnings of a smile curve her mouth. She was going to be included in the exhibition! It felt like a validation of all her choices to come here, to pursue art, to leave her beloved Amherst Island behind.

"Thank you, Norah."

"But while you have the ability," Norah continued, "you still lack the focus and passion. Everything you've done for the school has been executed well, even flawlessly at times. You are a most competent artist."

Ellen stared at her, the meaning of her words penetrating slowly. *Competent.* This time it was not the praise she'd thought it had been coming from Mr. Grieffenhagen.

"Thank you," she finally said when she had found her voice. "I think."

Norah's features had softened with compassion, and perhaps even pity, that Ellen could not bear to see. After all her effort, was she still not good enough? Not passionate enough?

"Ellen, you have not yet found your way," she said gently. "Or perhaps I should say, your calling."

Ellen opened her mouth to reply, although she wasn't even sure what she was going to say, but Norah held up a hand to forestall her.

"Art is so much more than putting a brush to paint or a needle to thread, or whatever medium you choose. It's about communicating something real, something true, that you feel deep inside you. It needs to be important." Norah's eyes were alight, her expression earnest and yet still compassionate.

Ellen could not quite keep the hurt from her voice as she stated flatly, "You mean it's not just about painting pretty pictures."

Norah smiled faintly. "That sounds like something you heard in a lesson."

"Mr. Grieffenhagen," Ellen acknowledged. "He also said I was competent. At the time I thought he was complimenting me, but now I see he was not." Her voice trembled and she looked down at her hands, mortified that she was betraying so much childish emotion to Norah, and yet unable to keep herself from it. She thought she'd come so far in both confidence and ability since arriving in Glasgow, but she could see now that the Lady Artist she'd been trying to be was no more than a façade, a part she'd played in the hopes that she'd inhabit it, or at least fool those around her that she had. Clearly she'd fooled no one. *Competent.* Now it sounded like the worst insult.

"Ellen, I am not trying to insult or hurt you," Norah said, her voice sharpening slightly. "You must not take it so. I want you to improve, to grow. That is why I am saying what I am. Any artist must learn to accept criticism, to take it and learn from it."

Ellen looked up, blinking rapidly. She took a sip of water to clear the lump that had formed in her throat. "And how I am to improve in this way, Norah? How can I gain a *calling*?" She couldn't keep the very slightest sneer from her voice, for in truth she despaired of ever finding such a thing. She'd learned how to mix paints, how to solder metal, how to grind her own colors, even. But a calling? It wasn't something that was taught. It couldn't be learned.

"It is something you will have to discover for yourself," Norah said. "You need to ask yourself why you like to create art. Look deep inside for the answer. What are you trying to accomplish—"

"I don't know," Ellen said, her voice rising in frustration. "It's just something I always did, ever since I was a child. I never *questioned* it—"

"But now perhaps you should," Norah returned. "If that is something you have never done. Every artist needs to understand her purpose, and then live for it."

Which sounded rather high-minded, Ellen thought a bit sourly, too high-minded for her, perhaps. For much of her life, she'd been trying only to survive, and drawing had offered her a little happiness amidst the uncertainty and lack. There had been no higher calling, no *purpose,* other than that, but that obviously wasn't enough for the likes of Norah.

Ellen tried to suppress the sudden surge of bitterness welling up inside her. Did Norah know what it was like to be hungry, to be orphaned and alone, to feel so hopeless? With all this talk of calling and purpose, could she imagine being a child like that?

"But enough of this talk for now," Norah said quietly. "Our meal is becoming cold. Think on what I said, Ellen. That is all I ask."

For the next few weeks, Ellen thought of little else. As much as Norah's well-meaning and high-minded advice had rubbed her raw, she would rather think about art and her apparent lack of focus or calling than wonder how Jed and Louisa fared back on Amherst Island. She couldn't bear to acknowledge how envious she felt of Louisa, preparing to welcome a child into this world, moving on with her life, her marriage.

"You've seemed preoccupied lately," Amy said one morning as they cleaned their paintbrushes in the large stone sink in the studio. "Could it be because of the dashing Mr. McAvoy?"

"Oh, *Amy*." Ellen shook her head. "He preoccupies you far more than he does me. No, I haven't thought of him at all. It's something Norah said."

"Norah Neilson Gray?" Amy's eyes widened; she was not on the familiar terms Ellen was with one of the school's professors.

"Yes, she spoke to me a few weeks ago, about the winter exhibition." Ellen glanced down at the brushes, the water turning cloudy from the paint. "Norah has said she won't include me in it, because I lack a *calling*."

"A calling?" Amy wrinkled her pert nose. "I certainly don't have one of those."

"And I don't either," Ellen said glumly. "Even though I'm hoping to obtain my certificate, I doubt I will, if I don't have this great sense of purpose."

"Goodness, I thought we were just painting pictures." Amy raised her eyebrows comically. "What do you think she meant, exactly?"

"It seems I need to communicate something true and real with my art. Something important, from deep down inside."

Amy let out a most inelegant guffaw. "And what's important about a couple of moldy oranges and an old felt hat?" She nodded towards the still life display they'd been working on that morning.

Ellen gave a small smile. "Nothing, perhaps, but I think I do understand what she means, at least a bit." Amy cocked an eyebrow, waiting for more, and Ellen continued slowly, "Since coming to the school, I haven't done any art that's just for me. It's all been about form and style and being *competent*, which is a word I now loathe, but sometimes I wonder why I'm here. I feel like the passion I had for art has been sucked out of me by learning all the methods and forms."

"But you're doing so well," Amy protested. "And surely anyone becomes tired of lessons, especially when someone like old Griffy is teaching them—"

"Really, Amy, you shouldn't call him that," Ellen admonished in a whispered hiss. "But yes, I suppose that's true. And I do enjoy many things about being here." She liked being independent, and her time spent at the Society's building on Blythewood Square, and her conversations with Norah. She'd been doing all she could to make the most of her life in Glasgow, and yet something was still missing at its center. "I need to remember why I started drawing in the first place," she said, feeling the words deep inside her as she said them, and Amy looked at her in open-mouthed curiosity.

"And how are you going to do that?"

The answer, when it came to her, was blindingly simple. She was in Glasgow already; she needed to return to her roots. She needed to go to Springburn.

The following Saturday, Ellen dressed in a plain skirt and shirtwaist, buttoned up her wool coat, and put on her sturdiest boots. Then she took the number four tram to the north of Glasgow, past the railway works she remembered from long ago, down Atlas Road and then Vulcan Street, to her old stomping ground on Keppochhill Road.

It was strange to see the soot-stained buildings again, the grocer's cart leaning against a runty tree, the lines of washing waving in the chilly winter wind, sheets that would be grimed with soot before they dried.

Ellen felt as if she'd catapulted back in time; she almost felt as if she were ten years old again, a wicker basket over one arm, as she spent her Da's meager earnings haggling over moldy potatoes leftover at the end of the day.

She spent several hours wandering the streets, feeling like a ghost, invisible to this world of hard work and endless graft, the twins of despair and sorrow blunted by sudden, surprising joys. She drifted along the streets, listening to the familiar sounds of women gossiping and bartering with shopkeepers, children playing with hoops and balls in the street, dodging in and out of the steady stream of humanity, all of it conducted to the distant clatter of the railway works, busy even on a Saturday afternoon, the metallic orchestra of her childhood.

Finally, when her feet were aching and she felt blisters on both heels, she bought a tin mug of tea and a paper-wrapped sandwich from a peddler with a pushcart and retreated to a low brick wall where she could watch the world go by.

Memories assaulted her at every turn, bittersweet and poignant, and then, as she watched all the activity, her gaze was caught by a young woman selecting apples from another peddler. She was about the same age as Ellen, her clothes worn and carefully darned several times over, and she examined each apple carefully, inspecting it for dents or bruises, before she put it in her basket. The peddler watched her with folded arms, a mingling look of exasperation and pity on his face.

Ellen remembered being in exactly the same place. Like this woman, she had taken her time to examine the wares of every peddler, and to make sure she got the most for her hard-won pennies.

The memory made her fingers twitch with sudden longing, because she knew how it felt, deep down, just where Norah had said she needed to feel. It felt urgent, the desire to capture the moment and commit it paper.

She had a lovely sketchbook of her own now, with a calfskin cover, but she had not thought to bring it to Springburn. So, just as in the days of her childhood, she reached for what was on hand: the paper her sandwich had been wrapped in and a stub of pencil gathering lint in the bottom of her coat pocket.

As soon as she began sketching, she felt as if everything inside her had both settled into place and caught on fire. She'd missed this so much, the simplicity of lines drawn on paper, the stark elegance and *truth* of it, communicating honestly with the world as she knew it.

She had no use for fancy oil paints and canvases stretched on wooden frames, or embroidery hoops or looms or potters' wheels and kilns for clay. She just wanted this: a scrap of paper and a bit of lead. That was all she'd ever wanted.

Her pencil seemed to fly over the paper, and with just a few bold strokes she had sketched the scene, or at least the beginning of it: the woman's sorrowful wistfulness, the peddler's exasperation, the hint of a deeper story within the simple, everyday transaction. She was gazing down at the creased paper with a glow of satisfaction when a hand reddened and callused by work suddenly grabbed the sheet.

"Excuse me, but is that me you're drawing?"

Ellen's head jerked up and, with shock, she found herself staring straight into the face of the young woman she'd been sketching; she had crossed the street and was now looking at her with both anger and suspicion, her brows drawn together as she scowled.

"Wh—why, yes," Ellen stammered. "It is."

"And what gave you the right to go putting me to paper?" the young woman demanded. "Coming here with your fancy clothes, gawping at all of us—"

"Fancy clothes!" Ellen almost laughed, but then quickly reined it in. "My clothes aren't fancy—"

"They are to me."

"But…" Ellen looked down at herself, the plain skirt and shirtwaist she'd chosen, and realized that eight years ago, when she'd been a Springburn lass, she would have thought these clothes fancy as well. "I didn't come here to stare or make fun," she said quietly. "I came because I used to live here, right on Keppochhill Road." She pointed to the shabby building across the street, washing strung from its windows, the once-red brick now black with decades of soot. "Right there."

The woman looked disbelieving, her lip curling scornfully, and Ellen hurried to continue.

"Please, you must believe me. I would never come here to gawp. I came to remember who I used to be, who I really am. I'm at the School of Art now and I realized I'd forgotten why I started to draw in the first place." She was speaking faster and faster, the words tripping over each other as she hastened to explain. "I saw you buying apples and you reminded me so much of myself. My mother was ill when I was young, and I used to buy her fruit to help her feel better, and I always made sure she didn't get a bruised apple. Sometimes it felt like the only thing I could control."

Finally the woman's face softened, and she glanced down at her basket of apples. "I bought these for my brother. He's got a terrible cough. I wanted to buy oranges, but they're too dear."

Ellen nodded, sympathy rushing through her. "I'm sorry. I know how hard it can be, truly I do."

"May I…" Shyly, the woman gestured to the scrap of paper clenched in Ellen's hand. "May I see it? If you don't mind?"

"Of course," Ellen said, and showed her the sketch. "I've only just started…"

"No one's ever drawn me before," the woman said wonderingly. "Do I really look like that?"

"I think so, but, of course, you should be the judge."

"Dougie would like to look at that," the woman said, and Ellen surmised Dougie was her brother. "He's always drawing things, he is."

"Why don't you keep it?" she said, and held the paper out.

"Oh, I couldn't…"

"Please, I want you to have it." She realized she meant it, even though part of her longed to keep working on the sketch. "I can make another, if I need to. It's in my head now, anyway."

"You just keep it in your head?" The woman laughed and shook her head. "Well, I never." But she took the drawing with a murmur of thanks.

"What's your name?" Ellen asked. "I'm Ellen Copley."

The woman smiled shyly, all animosity gone from her expression. "Ruby," she said. "Ruby McCallister."

*

As winter began its melt into spring, Ellen traveled to Springburn as often as she could and made sketches of various scenes she saw enacted on the busy streets: two boys scuffling over a tin can they were kicking; a skinny cat glaring suspiciously from a window ledge; several men coming from the railway works, their faces soot-stained, their arms around each other's shoulders, their teeth startlingly white in their faces as they shared a laugh.

She did them all in pencil, on paper, because she wanted to show life in Springburn, with all of its joys and sorrows, in the simplest and purest form, without the pretension of paint or clay.

She also spent time with Ruby during her visits, and met her new friend's younger brother Dougie, who was ill indeed with what Ellen sadly suspected was consumption. Once she brought a net bag of oranges, to the young boy's delight and Ruby's silent gratitude.

Sitting in the kitchen of their two-room flat, the coal fire sending out its scant warmth and oily smoke, Ellen felt more at home than she suspected she ever would in the ballrooms of Dowanhill, or perhaps even the studios on Renfrew Street.

She'd been afraid she hadn't changed from her Springburn days, and then she'd tried to convince herself she had. But perhaps true confidence, true *calling,* came from knowing where you'd come from and who you now were, and realizing they weren't all that different.

When she had a dozen drawings she was happy with, she intended to show them to Norah for inclusion in the winter exhibition, a prospect which made her heart tremble inside her. Showing Norah—or anyone—these drawings felt far more frightening, more revealing, than displaying one of the still lifes from her lessons. This would be showing someone her heart, and then letting them judge it.

And yet she knew she would do it, because this was why she had come to Glasgow; *this* was her calling. She'd found it, felt it resonate deep within her. She just hoped her professors agreed.

One evening after supper, she drew Norah aside and asked if she could show her something.

"Of course, my dear," Norah said, and silently, her heart pounding with both anticipation and nervousness, Ellen handed her the sketchbook of drawings. "Sketches, in pencil?" Norah asked, skepticism in her voice, but she opened the book and began to riffle through the drawings, her fingers slowing as she turned the pages, studying each drawing in turn, her face drawn in stern lines of concentration.

Ellen waited, her heart thudding sickly. If Norah told her they were no good, she wouldn't know what she would do, or even if she could continue at the school. If this wasn't enough, then nothing she possessed, or did, would be. But perhaps there would be some peace in knowing that, and in giving up this dream forever.

Finally Norah looked up. "These are really quite good, Ellen," she said quietly. "They possess both heart and honesty, a compelling combination. They are the only things you've done where I feel as if I've seen a glimpse of your soul."

"Thank you," Ellen whispered, swallowing hard. She felt, strangely, almost as if she could burst into tears.

Norah closed the book. "I think these are really quite good enough to be included in the winter exhibition. I'll show them to the Committee tomorrow." She paused, a smile softening her features. "Thank you for showing them to me, Ellen."

CHAPTER TEN

A month later, in the beginning of March, Ellen donned her smartest gown for the Glasgow Society of Lady Artists' winter exhibition. Her sketches had been framed and displayed together in the back of the building's long gallery, titled simply *Sketches from Springburn*, and while their placement was far from prominent, Ellen was beyond proud to be included.

Many of the pupils from the School of Art came to the exhibition, along with several professors and trustees. Ellen saw Henry circulating amidst the guests, and the sight of him after so long, with his sweep of dark hair and bright blue eyes, his smile as charming as ever, even from across the room, gave her a surprising pang of something like homesickness. She'd missed him, she realized, even though she hadn't meant to.

Life had been so busy; she hadn't been aware of the lack until now. She had been spending her Saturdays in Springburn, away from the world of school and art; either sketching scenes she came across in the street or sitting in Ruby and Dougie's humble kitchen, with a big brown pot of tea strong enough to stand a spoon in, reminding her of her childhood.

Now, in the midst of all the circulating artists and guests, Henry caught her eyes and after a second's hesitation he started towards her with a small smile.

"Hello, Ellen."

"Hello, Henry." She gave a brief of nod of acknowledgment, feeling strangely formal. She recalled her harshly spoken words in the foyer of his family home in Dowanhill, and felt the need to bridge the chasm that had yawned between them since then. "You're well?"

"Well enough." He nodded towards the sketches hung on the wall behind them. "Those are truly brilliant, the best you've ever done."

"Thank you."

"So deceptively simple," he continued, his voice roughened with sincerity. "And yet with such depth. It is the genius I saw in you back on that train to Chicago."

"That's very kind of you to say," Ellen answered, and then impulsively continued, "I think I lost some of my spark when I came to Glasgow. I was so intimidated by everything—the professors, the pupils, the whole atmosphere. It took going back to Springburn to remember who I am, and why I love to draw."

"And also perhaps an unfortunate experience at a ball?" he added with a wry smile. "Ellen, I still feel I need to apologize—"

"No, you don't. I was rude to you then, Henry, and I'm sorry. But I hope you can see now what I meant."

"I can," Henry answered slowly, "but I still don't agree with you."

"Henry—"

"My grandfather was a coal miner," Henry cut across her. "Did you know that?"

"He—what?" Ellen looked at him in befuddlement.

"A coal miner. Not a coal mine owner, but one of the poor, soot-faced souls who spend sixteen hours out of twenty-four down a dark mine. He bettered himself, took some risks, had a healthy dose of good fortune, and here we are." Henry's whimsical smile was touched by sadness. "We're not so different, you and I, Ellen, no matter what you've chosen to believe."

"Why didn't you tell me before?"

"I didn't think it mattered."

Ellen shook her head. "You know it does, at least to me, but it also doesn't, because our stations *are* different now, Henry. Too different for your mother."

"And if I don't care about my mother's opinion?"

"Perhaps you should." Ellen felt as if she'd waded into deep water without realizing, and now had completely lost her footing. "None of this matters anymore, anyway—"

"It does to me." He took a meaningful step towards her, and Ellen saw a few speculative looks from the people around them. As gently as she could, she stepped away.

"I should go speak to the other guests…"

Henry held one hand out in supplication. "Wait. I wanted to speak with you privately, Ellen, just for a moment. If I may."

Ellen swallowed. "There isn't anything to say in private—"

"There is. I've kept my distance as you requested, but now that I've seen you again I need to say what I have been wanting to say for some time. Please, Ellen?"

She shook her head, knowing she didn't want to hear what he wanted to say, and yet feeling it was unfair to refuse him outright. "Very well," she finally relented, against her better judgment. "But only a moment."

She moved to a private alcove off the gallery, sheltered enough from the milling crowds, while not being too secluded.

"I can't tell you how good it is to see you again," Henry said in a low voice that was filled with warmth. "May I be so bold as to ask if you missed me at all?"

It seemed cruel to lie, although perhaps it was crueler to tell the truth. "I have missed our friendship," Ellen said carefully. "But, as you know, I've been busy."

"Yes, I know. And I am very proud of you, Ellen." He held up a hand to forestall the protest she hadn't been going to make. "I don't mean to condescend, but I feel as if I played some small part in your success."

"You played a large part, Henry. Of course you have. And I am so grateful—"

"It is not your gratitude I desire." He took a step closer to her, his eyes now full of intent, his easy humor changing into something alarmingly serious.

"Henry…" Ellen began weakly. She had no idea what to say.

"I recognize this is neither the time nor place for a declaration," Henry said as he nervously ran a hand over his pomaded hair. "But I fear I may never be granted the opportunity otherwise, all things considered."

Ellen just shook her head, her mouth too dry for her to speak.

"Ellen, I'm in love with you."

Ellen blinked, astonished, even though everything about this moment had been leading to this declaration. The simply stated fact still possessed the power to leave her speechless. "You barely know me…" she began, but he shook his head.

"I know you. I feel as if I've always known you. And what I don't know, I wish to. I know you don't feel the same, not yet. But I feel I must make my intentions known, because you seem so sure they are not honorable."

"I never—"

"You think the difference in our stations, a difference I do not agree with, would keep me from proposing marriage."

Marriage? Ellen's mind swam as she tried again. "This is not—"

"Ellen, please. Let me have my say. After that you can walk away, reject me out of hand, slap my face if you like. But I must say what has been in my heart for so long. You must grant me that, at least."

Numbly, Ellen nodded. She had never expected such an avowal of affection from Henry, not after such a short acquaintance, and yet Amy was about to be engaged to a man she'd only seen a handful of times. Why was she so surprised? Simply because she'd never imagined that a man such as Henry would be interested in a girl like her?

"So what I wish to say is this." Henry's mouth quirked up at the corner, but his eyes were full of earnest sincerity. "I love you, Ellen. Perhaps I fell in love with you back in Chicago, when I saw you on that train. It started then, at least, and it has grown with the more time I've spent with you, and the more I've come to know you. Nothing would make me happier than having you for my wife. I accept that you don't love me in the same way, so all I ask is that you think about it. About us. The possibility that in time we might make a good partnership, because I think we could, Ellen. I know you'll protest that you're from Springburn and I'm from Dowanhill and all that nonsense, but I promise you, Ellen, I don't care a fig about that, it's not true anyway, and in any case, it's the twentieth century. These things matter less and less to people."

"Maybe so," Ellen allowed. Her head was spinning, and she pressed one hand to her flushed cheek.

Henry cupped her other cheek with his palm, the contact making Ellen's skin tingle, his eyes blazing with sincerity.

"Will you promise me that you'll at least think about my suit?" he asked, his voice low. "We have time. I'm not in a rush, although I'd marry you tomorrow if I could."

"Henry…"

"But just keep your heart open to me, a little, if you can. Or even just *think* about opening it." He smiled whimsically as he dropped his hand from her face. "Do you think you could do that, Ellen?"

Ellen stared at him, amazed at how conflicted she felt. She'd assured herself, as well as others, that she had no romantic interest in Henry McAvoy. She'd been sure she'd made the right decision in severing their friendship back at the ball. Yet when he'd touched her face so gently, love shining in his eyes, she'd known that wasn't quite true. She didn't know what she felt for Henry, but it was something.

"I…"

"All I'm asking is for you to think, and to wait."

"I… I suppose I could do that," Ellen whispered, feeling as if she were committing to far more than she should, and Henry beamed with relief.

"Thank you, Ellen." He took her hand in his own and kissed it. "Thank you. That's all I ask, truly."

Ellen nodded wordlessly, her mind still spinning. She could hardly believe she'd agreed… and to what, exactly?

"I'm going to America for several months," Henry continued, "so you will have plenty of time to think."

"America? But why?"

"I'm helping to curate an exhibition at the Metropolitan Museum, on Scottish artists." Henry smiled, real enthusiasm glinting in his eyes. "I sail next month for New York, on that wonderful new ship, the *Titanic*."

CHAPTER ELEVEN

April 1912

Ellen hunched her shoulders against the chilly spring breeze as she stood with Amy in front of the offices of *The Glasgow Herald*, waiting for the latest issue of the newspaper to be distributed. It was the nineteenth of April, and four days ago the newspaper had published a special edition, with the terrible headline blazing *Liner Disaster. Feared Great Loss of Life.*

Ellen had read the story in dawning horror, her stomach hollowing out as she'd taken in each word. It was unthinkable that the great *Titanic* had actually hit an iceberg and sunk. At first, the reports had said all lives had been saved, and Ellen had breathed a trembling sigh of relief. Henry was alive.

Then, three days ago, the newspaper put out another special report: *An appalling disaster has occurred. The White Star officials admit that it is very probable that only 675 out of the 2250 passengers and crew on board the* Titanic *were saved.*

Yesterday, the *Carpathia* had finally arrived in New York City with the survivors, and today that all too short list would be printed in the newspaper. Ellen prayed she would see Henry's name.

In the six weeks since Henry had declared himself, Ellen had seen him several times, for tea or a drive. She had decided that if she were to consider his proposal seriously, she needed to get to know him better, and in truth she'd enjoyed their outings together.

Henry had always been easy company, ready for a laugh or a chat, ever solicitous of her comfort and well-being.

Once, he'd even come with her to Springburn, and met Ruby and Dougie; Ellen had been both surprised and gratified to see how at ease he was in their little kitchen, drinking coffee from a tin mug and chatting to Dougie, whose cough had worsened in the wet spring, about his favorite artists.

"Did I pass?" he'd asked, his eyes alight with humor, as they'd traveled back to Renfrew Street by tram.

"Pass?" Ellen had blushed a little at the shrewd understanding in Henry's gaze. "What do you mean?"

"Come now, Ellen. You are still holding onto a bit of that silly snobbery. You brought me to Springburn to see if I would turn my nose up at your friends. My grandfather might have been a coal miner, but I was born with the proverbial silver spoon. I see it in your eyes every time I look at you."

Ellen couldn't help but laugh. "Silver-plated perhaps," she'd teased. "I suppose there is some truth to what you say, but I really brought you to Springburn because it's an important part of who I am," Ellen had answered. "So yes, I wanted to see if you could accept it."

"And so, I ask again, did I pass?"

Ellen shook her head, laughing again as she touched his arm lightly. "Yes, you passed," she'd assured him. "With flying colors."

Standing in front of the newspaper office now, the raw April wind buffeting her and Amy, Ellen had a horrible feeling that none of it mattered anymore. The night before Henry had left for Queenstown to board the Titanic, which had already sailed from Southampton to Cherbourg, he'd kissed Ellen for the first time.

He'd come to Norah's house to say goodbye, taking her hands in his, and telling her again that he loved her. He never seemed to tire of saying it, and Ellen felt her defenses, such as they were, beginning to crumble.

There, alone in the little sitting room with the fire flickering brightly in the grate, he'd ducked his head shyly and asked, "May I kiss you?"

Wordlessly, Ellen had nodded.

Henry's kiss had been brief and yet so very sweet, and after he'd left, Ellen had decided what her answer was going to be. She would marry him, and she would tell him so upon his return. She didn't love him with the consuming emotion she'd felt with Jed, but she felt a deep affection, and surely that was a better foundation for marriage than anything else. Besides, although their past experiences were worlds apart, their lives now were entwined through living in Glasgow and being involved in the School of Art. Marrying him made sense, and it also made her happy.

Now Amy slid her gloved hand in Ellen's and held on tightly as the doors to *The Glasgow Herald*'s offices opened, and several grim-faced men came out with stacks of freshly printed newspapers. Ellen's heart seemed to leap right into her throat and she squeezed Amy's hand hard.

"I almost don't want to look," she admitted in a shaky whisper. "Is that cowardly? I don't want to know, because at least in the not knowing…"

"I'll look for you," Amy said, and went forward to take one of the newspapers. She came back a minute later, the newspaper clutched in one hand, the fresh ink smeared on her gloves. "All right," she said, her voice croaky, her face pale. Ellen squeezed her eyes shut as Amy started reading the list out loud. "Following is the list of first- and second-class passengers rescued from the Titanic as received by wireless…" Quickly, she scanned the list. "They're in alphabetical order."

"Oh, just look, Amy, look," Ellen implored. "I can't bear it a second longer."

"Madill, Miss Georgietta A.," Amy read. "Marschall, Pierce. Marvin, Mrs. D.W." Amy hesitated and Ellen opened her eyes, her heart, which had moments ago seemed to be in her throat, now plummeting towards her feet as heavy as a stone. "Minnahan, Mrs. W.E.," Amy read heavily. "I'm sorry, Ellen. He's not there."

"Let me see it," Ellen demanded, and nearly ripped the paper from Amy's hands while her friend watched miserably. She scanned the list for herself, and saw the names in black and white. Then she flung the paper to the ground and turned away from Amy, pressing her trembling lips together, desperate to compose herself.

Amy laid a hand on her shoulder, but Ellen barely felt it. She felt numb and so very cold inside, as cold as Henry must have been as he sank beneath the icy waves… Oh, she couldn't think of it. She couldn't bear thinking of it, of his terrible last moments, whether he'd been afraid or resigned or brave. He must have been brave.

She closed her eyes, fighting against the relentless images that flashed in her mind, of darkened hulks of iceberg, the cries of people begging to be saved…

"The lists might not be complete, Ellen," Amy offered quietly. "There is still so much confusion around the whole thing. If we wait, there might be more news tomorrow. More survivors. Surely they didn't get them all in the first go. Everything's been in such a state—"

Ellen shook her head. "No," she said flatly. "I know he's dead. I can feel it." It was as if there was an emptiness inside her, where there had once been hope. She turned around, resolute now, thankfully cloaked in numbness, which was better than the grief she knew yawned beneath, like the dark, swirling water beneath the ice. "I must go back to Norah's. She will want to know."

Norah took the news stoically, her lips compressing as she gave one brief nod. "I suspected as much. It is a terrible, terrible tragedy," she said, and left the room.

The whole city seemed to be in mourning as the news rolled in. Only seven hundred and six survivors, and over fifteen hundred dead, many of them Glaswegians who had been part of the great ship's crew.

Ellen felt as if she were traveling in a fog; everything felt muted and distant, even irrelevant. She had not realized she cared for Henry until recently, and she'd only known him a short while, but the fact that she hadn't even been able to tell him made the pain of his loss all the harder to bear.

Her grief was a private burden, because no one, not even Amy, had known the depth of her feelings for Henry. She'd barely known it herself! She hadn't yet written any of her friends or family to tell them of the news, and the letters she had received were full of an ignorant cheer that she couldn't help but resent, even though she knew it wasn't fair.

For while she'd been intending to accept his proposal, the truth was she hadn't, and so she had no status as the fiancée she felt in her heart she was. She was nothing more than Henry's acquaintance, perhaps his friend, and people would only look askance at her if she admitted how grief-stricken she was. Ellen wondered if anyone would even believe her, if she spoke about Henry's proposal. In any case, she did not.

Two weeks after she'd first heard the dreadful news, Ellen returned to Norah's house to discover, much to her surprise, a letter from Edith McAvoy, asking her to call on her the next day at the villa in Dowanhill.

With trepidation, Ellen mounted the villa's steps the next afternoon. The weather had finally started to warm, and in the square's garden, the cherry trees' pink blossoms were starting to unfurl. Nerves leapt in her belly as she remembered the last time she'd climbed these steps, to attend the McAvoys' ball. That evening had been terrible in so many ways, and yet she was still glad she'd stood up for herself. But she had no idea why she was climbing the steps now, or what awaited her inside the imposing villa.

A parlormaid showed Ellen into a comfortable drawing room; a fire burned in the grate, even though the day was warm. A few minutes later, Edith McAvoy entered, dressed all in black. Her hair, as dark as Henry's, was drawn back severely, and her face looked bloodless. She was an entirely different woman from the one Ellen had encountered at the ball; that woman had been glittering with both life and malice, but this woman looked drained of all her spirit.

"Miss Copley," she greeted her rather flatly. "It is kind of you to see me."

"I am honored to be asked, Mrs. McAvoy," Ellen answered stiltedly. She had no idea why the grieving woman had called her to the villa, or if she even knew about Henry's proposal. She doubted she did, but then why was she here?

"I know you were very important to Henry," Mrs. McAvoy said as she sat down and arranged her stiff skirts. She gestured for Ellen to sit as well, and she did so. "When he told me he had asked you to marry him, I must admit, I was not pleased."

What on earth, Ellen wondered, was she to say to that? She merely nodded.

A maid brought a tea tray in and Mrs. McAvoy gestured for Ellen to pour. As she did so, the older woman resumed.

"I don't think you can blame me for that, Miss Copley. Henry told me how you did not initially welcome his suit, and that you felt the two of you were ill-matched. I think we were in agreement on these matters."

Ellen swallowed, unsure how to reply. Yes, she had thought that way, but she'd changed her mind. She did not think Edith McAvoy would welcome the news now.

"You know they have found his body?" she asked bleakly.

Ellen's hands shook and hot tea splattered onto her fingers. With effort, she kept them steady as she finished pouring them both cups of tea. "I didn't know that," she said quietly.

Edith McAvoy accepted a cup of tea, her pale face somber as she explained. "Yes, the White Star Line chartered a ship from Nova Scotia to retrieve as many bodies as they could. I think over three hundred were found. Henry had his passport on him, the poor lad. I suppose he held a hope of being rescued." She retrieved a lace-edged handkerchief from her sleeve and dabbed at her eyes. "So they were able to identify him. We're having his body shipped back. I couldn't stand the thought of him being buried in some strange cemetery in Halifax, with no one ever to visit his grave."

"I see," Ellen managed numbly. The older woman's words made Henry's death all the more real and horrible. She stared down at her tea, and after a moment Edith McAvoy continued.

"The funeral will be in a fortnight, after his… well, when things are settled."

"Yes."

"You are welcome to attend," she stated, her manner turning rather stiff. "I know Henry held you in great affection, and it seems… appropriate for you to be there."

Ellen could tell this cost the woman a great deal. She suspected that if Edith McAvoy had her way, she would not have any part in her son's life, or her current situation. And she knew that she had no right to attend the funeral, or even be here speaking to Henry's mother. Their relationship had not been official or recognized. Edith McAvoy was being generous.

"That's very kind of you, ma'am," she said quietly. "Thank you. I will be sure to be there."

Ten days later Ellen stood in the shadow of the tall, needle-like spire of the Dowanhill Church on Hyndland Street and watched, still numb inside, as Henry's body was laid into the earth.

She stood apart from Henry's family, knowing she had no right to include herself in their number, yet feeling closer to him than the other mourners who stood back from the gravesite to give his family a bit of privacy in this difficult moment.

Amy had accompanied her to the funeral, as had Norah, although her landlady now stood with a few of the art professors who had known and liked Henry. Amy stood next to her, and as Ellen watched Henry's casket lowered into the ground, she linked arms with her. Ellen leaned into her friend's embrace, suddenly feeling so weary, she could barely stand. How could she be grieving so much, when she'd known Henry so little? Or was she grieving more than Henry? Was she grieving the end of a dream, of the life she'd begun to imagine for herself, as a wife, a mother, mistress of her home?

Afterwards, she went back to Amy's rather than the reception at the McAvoy home. Edith McAvoy's welcome, it seemed, did not extend that far. She wondered what would have happened if Henry had survived and she had married him. Would his parents have thawed and accepted her eventually, or would she and Henry have always been navigating that precarious social divide, torn between familial duty and love?

The answer no longer mattered.

"You look as if a breath could blow you over," Amy said once they were settled in a small sitting room with cups of tea and slices of cake.

Ellen took a small sip of tea and picked at her cake before pushing it away.

"I feel as if I could blow right over," she said. "I wish I would."

"Oh, Ellen." Amy eyed her friend with sympathy. "I thought," she said after a moment, "you didn't care for him that way?"

"I thought that as well." A lump formed in Ellen's throat as she remembered how firmly she'd declared to Amy that she had no intention of setting her cap at Henry. She hadn't told her friend about Henry's offer or her decision; it had been too private a matter, and she would hardly tell her friend she'd accepted a proposal before she told the man himself. Now she swallowed past that lump, her voice coming out thickly. "The trouble is, I discovered that I did."

"Oh, Ellen." Pushing aside the tea tray, Amy went and took Ellen in her arms. "I'm so very sorry."

And then, after weeks of numbness, Ellen finally thawed. It was painful, excruciating even, but necessary. She pressed her head into Amy's shoulder and wept.

The next few weeks drifted by in a sea of indifference for Ellen. She attended lectures, but she heard not a word; she painted and sketched and sculpted, but none of it mattered. When Mr. Grieffenhagen raged at her, she merely stared at him, unmoved. He shook his head in exasperation before moving on, which was, Ellen supposed, as much of a reprieve as she could expect.

Amy tried to rouse her out of her lethargic state, inviting her to tea and to a lecture at the house in Blythewood Square; Ellen went, but she felt as if she were a ghost, drifting among the living. She wished she were a ghost. She'd known loss in her life, and disappointment, and grief, many times over, but this struck a deeper chord.

"I don't even know how I can miss him so much," she confessed to Amy one spring afternoon. "I shouldn't. I didn't know him that well, and yet… he loved me, Amy, and I cared for him. I think I would have loved him, if I'd been given the chance, and it tears me apart inside to know that I wasn't, and that he'll never know. He died not knowing how I felt, or that I would have married him."

*

A month after Henry's funeral, Norah finally took her aside. It was mid-June, and spring was on the cusp of summer, the air warm and fragrant, the nights wonderfully long and light.

"Ellen, you cannot go on like this," she said sternly, as Ellen sat in her little sitting room and picked at a loose thread on her skirt. She did not answer and Norah let out an impatient sigh.

"Do you think you are the only one who has ever grieved?" she demanded and Ellen looked up in surprise.

"No, of course not."

"Don't you think other people found the will to go on, Ellen? Learned how to join in with the living?"

Ellen's eyes filled with tears and she blinked them back. "It has been less than two months, Norah, and Henry was very dear to me."

Norah's gaze narrowed. "How dear?"

"If you must know, he had asked me to marry him. And when he returned from America, I intended to accept." Ellen's voice trembled and she pressed her lips together in an effort to regain her composure before continuing, "Now a whole life I might have had is lost to me. I grieve that, along with the loss of Henry."

Norah was silent for a long moment. Ellen stared down at the floor, longing only for this wretched interview to be over.

"I want to show you something," Norah finally said and, to Ellen's surprise, she turned and left the room. After a moment's hesitation, Ellen followed her.

Norah was in the foyer, buttoning up her coat. Ellen gaped. "Where—where are you going?"

"To my studio. And you're coming with me."

"Your studio—" Ellen exclaimed. She had never been allowed in that inner sanctum, and she had no idea why she was being summoned now. Wordlessly, she reached for her own coat.

Norah walked briskly through the back garden, down to the old brick outbuilding that she'd fashioned into an art studio, and used to paint portraits.

Ellen felt a little stirring of curiosity as Norah unlocked the door and ushered her into one large room with long sashed windows letting in the June sunlight. Canvases lay stacked against a wall, and a few were propped on easels and shrouded with sheets. Ellen breathed in the scents of turpentine and linseed oil.

She stood in the doorway while Norah riffled through some canvases in the back of the studio, clearly looking for one in particular.

"Here we are." She pulled out a small canvas and wordlessly handed it to Ellen.

She took a moment to study it, her gaze resting on the dark oil paint. It was classic Norah, a portrait of a mother with a boy; the woman wore a white dress that slid from her shoulders, with a loose bouquet of yellow flowers in her lap. The boy, in a yellow smock, leaned against her; she had her arm around him as she gazed at him, her mouth turned down in what Ellen wasn't sure was a frown of resignation or simply an expression of her devotion.

"What do you see when you look at this?" Norah demanded, sounding almost angry, and Ellen's startled gaze flew up to meet her landlady's.

"You mean beyond a mother and her son?"

"What emotion do you see, Ellen?" Norah pressed. "What do you *feel* when you look at this painting?"

"I…" Ellen licked her lips. "Sorrow, I suppose, although I'm not sure why. The mother… she looks almost as if she is afraid she's going to lose her son. Or even…" She paused, and Norah raised her eyebrows.

"Or even?" Norah prompted. There was a fierce light in her eyes that took Ellen aback.

"Or even… as if she's already lost him."

"Yes." Norah lowered the painting, and the fierce light in her eyes had dimmed, replaced by something that looked like grief as her shoulders slumped and her eyes briefly closed. "Yes, exactly."

"Norah, I don't understand…"

"The people in this painting are models," Norah stated flatly. "They're not even related. I scoured the streets before I found what I was looking for, and brought them into the studio."

Ellen felt a flicker of surprise and even disappointment. She'd assumed there was a story behind the painting, because she had felt the emotion in it.

Norah must have guessed what she was thinking, because she nodded, as if agreeing with something Ellen had said, and continued, "The truth of this painting is not who the people are. It's the feeling that went into capturing them on canvas." She let out a long, low breath. "I've never been a mother, Ellen, and I never will be."

"You might," Ellen protested. Although her sophistication and success made her seem older, Norah was in fact only thirty years old.

"No, it is a decision I made a long time ago. I knew if I married, my dedication to painting would be compromised. But it doesn't mean I have not grieved the children I will never have." She rested her gaze meaningfully on Ellen. "The life I will never have. That is what I have communicated with this painting. The loss I have felt, in the choices I have made."

Ellen swallowed uncomfortably. "I never meant to presume that you hadn't…" she began and Norah shook her head impatiently.

"I am not telling you all this so you feel sorry for me, far from it. I am telling you this because I want you to do what I did. Pour your emotion, all your grief, into your work. It will help you and perhaps it will help others." She gave a small, sad smile. "And perhaps, better still, it will produce a great work of art."

*

Several weeks later, Norah's charge was still reverberating through her as Ellen went about her lessons. She felt a desire, and even a need, building inside her to paint something of what she'd felt in losing Henry, and yet also of the surprising joy she'd had in knowing him so briefly. She'd started something in pencil, but the medium she'd loved for her *Sketches of Springburn* seemed insipid for the message she wanted to communicate now, the emotions she longed to pour out, like a maelstrom inside her, battering at her defenses.

Then, one night, as she sat curled up in her armchair and gazed out at the summer night sky, the first stars just beginning to appear like pinpricks on a dark velvet cloth, an idea came to her. An idea that was enormous and frightening and yet wonderfully right.

The next day, she asked Norah if she could use some of her studio space, and her landlady gave a satisfied smile as she nodded.

"Yes, of course. Just let me know what you need."

Alone in the sunlit space, armed with oils and brushes, Ellen began a work the likes of which she'd never even dreamed of before.

At the end of June, Ellen received another summons to Dowanhill. She mounted the steps of the McAvoys' villa with the same wary trepidation as before; Edith McAvoy had not reached out to her since Henry's funeral and, in truth, Ellen hadn't expected ever to see the woman again.

Ellen had barely stepped across the threshold before Edith McAvoy came to the point. She bustled into the small sitting room where Ellen had been directed by the parlormaid; it was not the spacious drawing room of before and Ellen wondered if the change of room was meant as a slight, and if so, why.

"It seems," Edith said in a strained voice, without any greeting, "that our son has left you a bequest in his will."

Ellen blinked, too stunned to reply.

Edith's mouth compressed. "Did you know about this?"

"No, of course not." Ellen's mind whirled. Clearly Edith thought she was a gold-digger who had sunk her greedy talons into her son. Ellen shook her head slowly. "I never asked for anything from Henry. And if you feel it is… inappropriate, then of course I will refuse…"

"I do not know whether to believe you," Edith returned coolly. "But it was my son's wish that you be provided for, and I will honor his request, for his sake, I must make clear, and not yours."

Ellen flushed at the intended insult. "I do not need provision, ma'am."

Edith arched an imperious eyebrow. "That, I believe, is open to debate. My solicitor will deliver the details of the bequest to your residence. I thought I should see you in person to inform you of my son's wishes. I do not expect we shall meet again, Miss Copley. In fact, I rather hope we do not."

Ellen swallowed the sting, determined to be dignified. "As you wish, Mrs. McAvoy." Something in the woman's chilly expression, the grief Ellen thought she saw behind the coldness in her eyes, made her step forward. She reached out with one hand to touch Edith's hand before she thought better of it and dropped it. "I miss him too, Mrs. McAvoy," she said quietly. "Terribly."

Edith's face contorted and for a moment Ellen thought she might cry. Then her eyes sparked with rage. "How dare you compare your infantile emotion to what I, his own mother, feel. Good day to you, Miss Copley. You will not be asked back here again. The maid will show you out."

The next day, a letter arrived from the McAvoys' solicitor. When Ellen opened it and read its contents, she gasped aloud. The amount Henry had left her was more than enough, if she were careful, to see her established comfortably for the rest of her life.

PART TWO

CHAPTER TWELVE

June 1914, two years later

"Are you nervous?" Ruby asked in a whisper as the guests began circulating through the gallery of the Society of Lady Artists' house on Blythewood Square. "An exhibition all on your own, Ellen! You're practically famous!"

"Not quite, Ruby," Ellen answered with a little smile. "All the women pupils who are getting a certificate are exhibiting. I'm one of several."

"Yes, but even I know it's yours they're talking about," Ruby answered. "And how can they not, when you look at the size of it?" Grinning, she nodded towards the shrouded canvas that took up nearly a whole wall.

Ellen smiled back even as she tried to suppress the nerves fluttering through her stomach. It had taken her nearly two years to complete the canvas inspired by Henry's death and the sinking of the *Titanic*. Tonight was the first time it would be revealed to the public.

The last two years had held both joys and sorrows; Ellen still mourned Henry, but it was a softer emotion, and one she lived with companionably day in and day out. Using her grief constructively, through painting, had helped.

She'd become closer to Ruby and Dougie, too, spending many happy afternoons in their little flat in Springburn, drinking tea and chatting, and also teaching Dougie, whose health had improved a little. He was interested in art, and Ellen enjoyed showing him the rudiments of drawing.

Then, just a few months ago, Ruby and Dougie's father had died in an accident at the railway works. At the same time, Ellen had, much to her amazement, been offered a position at the School of Art, as a drawing instructor, upon the completion of her certificate. Few students were offered such an opportunity, and Ellen accepted gladly.

The events together had led her to leaving Norah's, and with the bequest Henry had given her, purchasing her own little terraced house near the school. She'd invited Ruby and Dougie to live with her; as she'd expected, Ruby had at first declined, claiming she could not accept such charity.

"Ruby," Ellen had persisted, "if it is simply a matter of pride that is keeping you from joining me, then please, please cast it aside! I'd so much rather not be on my own, and you know the fresher air will do Dougie good. He could go to the local school, a good school, and eat and drink good, fresh food. It will be miles better for him, and it's not charity, because the money isn't even mine, not really." She'd never felt comfortable having the money from Henry's bequest, and she was glad to use it for this end.

Ruby had stared at her for a moment, her lips pressed together, her eyes full of tears. "You're too good to us, Ellen," she had finally said. "Truly you are."

"I'm really rather selfish," Ellen had answered. "This is as much for my sake as it is for yours or Dougie's."

A week later, Ruby and her brother had moved in, and it had all felt wonderfully congenial, almost as if Ellen were living with family again—evening meals around the table, cozy nights by the fire. Dougie had started school, and Ruby worked as a seamstress, insisting on paying Ellen something for rent, nominal as it was.

Together they all made it work, and nearly three years after having moved to Glasgow, Ellen felt as if she could finally call it home. All that was left now was to receive her certificate, and then begin teaching in September.

She glanced at the crowds now filling the gallery, people murmuring excitedly about the works that were to be unveiled. She wished someone from her old life could have been here to share her success, but who?

Uncle Hamish was still in Seaton, but he'd closed the general store that he and Aunt Ruth had started when they'd emigrated to America and now worked behind the counter at the new, fancy department store in town. Ellen had written him to tell him of her plans, and Hamish's reply had been full of praise, but his handwriting had been spidery and, with a pang, she realized he was becoming quite frail.

She'd written the McCaffertys too, of course, and Aunt Rose, who had been a faithful weekly correspondent, had assured her she was thrilled for her, although sad that Ellen would not be returning to Amherst Island as she'd promised.

Ellen was sad, too; part of her longed to be back on the island, among family and friends, while another part recognized that she had changed, and perhaps her beloved island had, as well. It wasn't the home for her that it had once been, and at nearly twenty-three years old, she needed to make her own way.

Still, she wished she could have seen the McCaffertys. The children would be so grown up now; Peter about to start Queen's, and Caro at Glebe for high school. Sarah and Gracie were now in their teens and Andrew, whom she'd known since he was a baby, was a strapping ten years old. How strange that seemed! How quickly time had passed.

Ellen knew the McCaffertys would never be able to visit her in Glasgow; Rose had sailed once from these shores and possessed neither the means nor the desire to return.

Then, of course, there was Jed and Louisa, in their new farmhouse on the other side of the Lyman property.

Ellen had written Louisa several times over the last few years, but had had no reply, which had saddened her. She wondered if her friendship with Louisa was truly over, and suspected that it most likely was.

Still, Rose had kept her informed of the young Lymans; the summer after Henry's death, Ellen had learned that Louisa had had a baby boy, Thomas, who was now two years old, and, according to Aunt Rose, a lovely little lad. That, at least, brought Ellen no pang of sorrow; she was genuinely happy for them both. Her heart had healed in that regard, at least.

Six months ago, Lucas had written to Ellen; he'd been a faithful correspondent for her entire time in Glasgow, and he wrote then that he'd been accepted as partner at the law firm where he worked, and he'd hinted that there was a young lady of some interest to him.

Ellen had felt a strange welter of happiness and surprising jealousy, but happiness won out. She expected Rose would write imminently with the news of Lucas's engagement, and she imagined receiving letter after letter—engagement, marriage, birth, death, the whole cycle of life that she would gaze at from afar, and yet never truly participate in.

All of the island happenings and people seemed far away now, almost as if that life had belonged to someone else, someone she looked at the way you studied a stranger in a photograph. Of interest, but then you put it aside.

Her Glasgow life was real and satisfying, and yet even so, in occasional, solitary moments, Ellen missed the island quite desperately. She wondered if she would ever go back, and how she would feel when she did. She could not even imagine it.

"Ladies and gentlemen!" Norah's voice rang out among the crowd, and the murmurs ceased as everyone waited expectantly for the works of the certificate pupils to be revealed.

Ellen's stomach did a queasy little flip, for she had poured so much of herself into her painting, and revealing it felt like exposing her soul, far more than the *Sketches from Springburn* had. It was raw and real and spoke of sorrow and loss, grief and pain. Showing it to people was revealing something she'd chosen to keep hidden.

Moments later, the sheet was drawn away from her painting, and Ellen tensed as everyone drew a collective intake of breath and gazed at the massive canvas.

It was titled *Starlit Sea*, and it was a painting of the sea at night, stretching endlessly into the clouds of darkness, as it must have when the *Titanic* had sunk. The only sign of the presence of a ship, however, was a few ripples in the forefront of the canvas; the painting was mainly taken up with the expanse of water, and the reflection of stars on its surface, each one a pool of light that looked almost as if it were rising up from underneath the water, the souls of the dead offering both hope and their lament.

"Oh Ellen, it's magnificent," Ruby whispered. "It makes me want to cry, and I don't know why."

It made Ellen want to cry, but she blinked the tears back and simply squeezed her friend's hand.

Amy came up and threw her arms around her.

"You clever, clever thing," she exclaimed. Amy had stopped her lessons at the School of Art a year and a half ago, when she'd married Charlie Whittaker; she was now expecting her first child, although her tiny bump was barely noticeable.

"Thank you," Ellen answered as she hugged her friend. "For everything. You've been such a strength and support to me, Amy."

"Me, the dilettante?" Amy joked, even as she dabbed tears from her eyes. "Goodness, I do weep at everything these days. Charlie is heartily sick of me, I assure you."

"I doubt that very much indeed," Ellen returned. She knew Amy's husband adored her. She caught sight of a familiar face in the crowd and hurried forward. "Letitia!" she called and, with an ear-splitting grin, her old friend hurried towards her. "I didn't think you'd be able to get away," Ellen exclaimed after they'd hugged and kissed each other. Letitia had just started as a junior doctor at The Bruntsfield Hospital for Women in Edinburgh.

"I did, at the last minute," Letitia said breathlessly. "I was almost late for the great unveiling—oh, Ellen, it's magnificent!"

"It's nothing compared to what you do—"

"Nonsense, I do what I do so you can do what you do. They are both entirely worthwhile. And I'm so proud of you, being a lecturer already! Really, you are clever."

A short while later, Norah came towards Ellen and kissed her on both cheeks. "Ellen," she said, as if making a pronouncement. "Dear, dear Ellen. I miss you, you know."

"You'll still see me every day," Ellen protested. Although she was no longer living with Norah, they would both be teaching on Renfrew Street.

"Yes, but it's not the same. The student becomes the colleague… it is a different relationship." She smiled whimsically. "I shall miss instructing you, I confess, but I am glad to serve by your side."

Ellen could hardly believe she was the colleague of an indomitable woman like Norah Neilson Gray. Although she'd gained much experience and worldly wisdom in the last two years, she still felt a bit of the country bumpkin inside, and suspected she always would. But she didn't mind any longer; it was part of who she was, and she'd made peace with it.

Several hours later, Ellen, Ruby, and Dougie walked back to the little terraced house they all now called home. The air was sultry for mid-June, the evening still light despite the late hour, syrupy sunlight touching the rooftops with gold.

Ruby and Ellen walked with locked arms, humming tunelessly; despite all the tragedies of the past, in that moment Ellen felt almost perfectly content. There was so much to look forward to: teaching at the school, sharing her house with Ruby and Dougie;

participating in the Society of Lady Artists, and planning for the autumn exhibition. The summer stretched ahead of her, both pleasant and exciting.

She'd spoken with Ruby about renting a house in the country for a few weeks in August, near the English Lakes. Ruby had resisted, but Ellen had assured her the cost was minimal, as the place was so remote. She'd used up most of Henry's bequest buying her little house, but there was enough left to tide her over until she began teaching in September.

Those lazy days in Windermere in early August felt, in retrospect, like the last of Ellen's innocence, and the simple pleasures she would enjoy. The farmhouse was low and whitewashed and comfortably shabby; they ate in the kitchen and took long walks by the lake. Dougie's cough improved in the fresh air, and Ellen spent hours sketching the beautiful gray-green fells of the Lakeland countryside, the waters of Windermere sparkling beneath the steep hills. Then, on the fourth day of their holiday, church bells began to ring in the village, long, dour notes.

Ruby and Ellen exchanged uncertain looks. "Has something happened, do you think?" Ellen asked. "A wedding, perhaps?"

Ruby shook her head. "It's not merry enough for that."

Indeed it wasn't; the continuous tolling of the one, low bell was a lament, not a celebration. Ellen felt a wave of inexplicable dread. What could have happened?

"Should one of us go into the village, to see?" Ruby asked uncertainly.

"I'll go." Grabbing her hat and a shawl, Ellen hurried out into the late-afternoon sunshine, the air already becoming chilly up in the hills. She walked down the street towards the village church, noting how people were congregating in the streets, shaking their heads and whispering in tight clusters.

A young buck of eighteen or so let out a cheer, and someone else hushed him.

A little boy picked up a stick and began firing it as if it were a gun, shouting "Pop! Pop! Pop!" His childish voice echoed in the street, which otherwise, Ellen realized, was quite quiet.

She approached a middle-aged woman with a careworn face and tired eyes. "Pardon me, but what's going on? What's happened?"

The woman shook her head. "Ye're haven't heard, then?"

"No…"

"They've gone and declared war on Germany."

"What?" Ellen stared at her blankly. She'd been aware of the rumblings of political discontent that had been happening all year, and had culminated in the assassination of the Archduke Ferdinand by anarchists in Sarajevo at the end of June, but neither she nor any of her friends or colleagues had thought it would amount to much. Sarajevo was a world away, and had little to do with life in Scotland. "Why on earth?"

"The Huns have gone and attacked France, haven't they?" a young man said, pushing his way into the conversation. "Gone through Belgium two days ago, thought we wouldn't mind. They'll get a taste of their own medicine, they will. And I'll be the first to show 'em!"

"Oh, be quiet, Harry," the woman said tiredly. "You don't know what you're talking about."

"I'm going to enlist. I'm going to fight, Mam."

The woman just shook her head, looking even wearier.

Ellen headed back to the farmhouse a short while later, unable to discover any more information. Half the villagers seemed wary and afraid, the other half, mostly the young men, ebullient.

"What is it, Ellen?" Ruby asked as she came through the door of the farmhouse. "What's happened?"

Ellen shook her head slowly. "England has declared war on Germany." She felt as if she were playing some monstrous joke, especially when Ruby simply stared at her, as blankly disbelieving as she had been.

"What… what do you mean?"

"Germany attacked France through Belgium," Ellen said, repeating what the young man had told her. "Two days ago, it seems. We haven't been aware of any of it, tucked away as we are here. England told them to retreat, and they wouldn't, so war has been declared." She pressed one hand to her cheek. "I feel as if I don't even know what that *means*."

"War," Ruby repeated wonderingly. "But for Belgium's sake? Or France's? Why?"

"They have a treaty with England," Ellen explained. She'd read that in the newspaper a few weeks ago, although she hadn't thought all that much about it. "They have to."

"Surely they don't *have* to…"

"I don't know. Perhaps they've called Germany's bluff, and now they will retreat."

Ruby grabbed onto that like the lifeline it seemed. "Yes, that sounds likely, doesn't it? No one wants a war."

Ellen thought of the young man in the village, determined to enlist and "teach the Huns a lesson". "I'm not sure about that," she said slowly. "But I hope you're right."

Over the next few days, however, it became all too clear that Ruby wasn't right. Men were enlisting in their droves; recruiting centers had been set up in all the major cities, and a man came to the village where they were staying, putting up posters and speaking by the village green. England was being carried away on a wave of patriotism, and all Ellen could feel was dread.

When they returned to Glasgow several days later, it seemed a different city. Recruitment posters papered walls and windows, and in disbelief Ellen saw men already in uniform, ready to march. It was all happening so quickly, she could scarcely believe it. In the newspaper, she read that three thousand men were enlisting every day.

Ellen felt as if her life were a chessboard and a giant, invisible hand had suddenly upended all the pieces. Plans she'd counted on now were as nothing; young men and women alike were mobilizing for war, eager to join up as soldiers or volunteer as nurses.

Even Amy's husband, Charlie, enlisted, and Amy was determinedly proud. "It will be over by Christmas, anyway," she said, when she came to Ellen's house for tea. "That's what everyone is saying, and no one's better than the British."

"One hopes," Ellen murmured. She did not feel so sure. When she looked at all the men enlisting, and the fever of patriotism that seemed to be running high, she could not imagine everyone trooping dutifully home in a matter of months, and yet she hoped and prayed that was exactly what would happen.

"It will," Amy said stubbornly, her eyes glinting with challenge—and fear.

Wordlessly, Ellen reached over and clasped her friend's hand. The truth was, no one knew anything.

At the beginning of September, just a few days before Ellen was meant to start teaching, Norah paid a visit to her little house. She sat in the kitchen, her hands cradled around a cup of tea as she subjected Ellen to one of her intense gazes.

"This war won't be over before Christmas," she began in her stern, no-nonsense way. "Any fool can see that."

"I suppose," Ellen said slowly. She had never really believed it, but she still didn't like admitting it. It all felt so bewildering—the boys in khaki, barely older than Peter, marching to the train.

Norah was silent for a moment, her lips pursed in thought. "I know I've always proclaimed how art is important," she finally said. "And it is. It's one of the things that makes life worth living." She paused, her face drawn in sober lines. "But sometimes more is needed, and this is one of those times."

Ellen said nothing, for she had no idea what her former landlady and current friend was getting at.

"I intend to join the Scottish Women's Hospital at Royaumont," Norah concluded. "I've given in my notice at the school."

"You mean as a nurse?" Ellen said in surprise.

"Yes, although I have no formal training, so my duties will be minimal, and most likely menial. I still need to do my part."

"Royaumont… I've never even heard of it."

Briefly, Norah explained the origins of the hospital: it had been founded by the suffragette Elsie Maud Inglis only recently. Rejected by the British army despite having raised five thousand pounds, the Women's Hospitals had offered their services to the French, and, joined with the French Red Cross, they were planning to set up a hospital to treat the French wounded.

"They won't be able to take patients until January, but I intend to leave as soon as possible, to help in the organization," Norah said.

"That's very good of you," Ellen told her. "I shall miss you."

"One does what one must." Norah paused to take a sip of tea and then, putting her cup down, said, "You trained as a nurse, did you not?"

Ellen's mouth dried as her friend's implication became clear. "Only for a year…"

"Then why don't you join me, Ellen? There can be no greater cause than serving the wounded, and women with skills are so desperately needed. I will be doing nothing more than making beds and emptying bedpans, but you have training—"

"Very little training," Ellen protested. Her stomach seized with fear at the thought of leaving Glasgow, and Ruby and Dougie, as well as her dear little house and the teaching she hadn't even started. She'd arranged her life so pleasingly, and now Norah was asking her to give it all up?

"Still, it's something," Norah persisted. "And it will be needed. All those boys out there in khaki?" She nodded towards the window, and the sunny September day outside. "They have no idea what awaits them. They've never seen a war, and plenty of them have never even seen a *gun*. They think they're heading out for a lark, and they are so badly mistaken." She leaned forward. "They are going to need women to bind them up, and give them water when they are thirsty. They will need nurses to change their bandages and stitch their wounds, and hold their hands as they are dying. Think of your painting, Ellen, all those lost souls on the *Starlit Sea*. How many more lost souls will be on the battlefields of France?"

By the end of this impassioned speech, Ellen had tears in her eyes, even as she shook her head. "I don't know… what about Ruby and Dougie? They depend on me now…"

"They can still live here while you are away," Norah answered with a shrug.

Ellen knew that was true, but she wanted to cry out for all the other things she would miss—her own comfort and safety, the pleasure she had in painting and drawing, and the anticipation she felt for teaching. All of it gone in a single moment, if she agreed to go with Norah to France.

And yet how could she not? How could she put her comfort above those of the soldiers who might die on muddy battlefields, calling for their mothers? Boys who played at war and paid the greatest price. She swallowed hard.

"The school will be here when the war is over," Norah soothed her. "We shall all have to pick our lives back up, one way or another. But now, we are needed *now*. You see that, don't you?" Ellen didn't answer, but Norah saw her reply in her eyes. "You'll do it," she said, a statement, and slowly, feeling both a sense of dread and one of duty, Ellen nodded.

CHAPTER THIRTEEN

Royaumont Abbey, France, December 1914

The ghostly arches of Royaumont Abbey were illuminated only by a sliver of moonlight as the lorry, soon to be an ambulance, pulled up in front of the building. Every muscle Ellen possessed ached not just from the jarring journey across the rough countryside under the cover of darkness, the sound of the shells a constant, distant thunder, but the train journey from London to Viarmes, and the sea crossing before that. She felt as if she'd been traveling forever.

She, Norah, and her old friend Letitia Portman had crossed the Channel nearly a week ago, on a military convoy in the middle of a stormy night—by far the worst sea journey Ellen had ever endured. She, who had prided herself on never being seasick, had been as wrung out as an old dishrag.

The commanding officer at Folkestone had wanted them to wait for calmer waters, but the indomitable Frances Ivens, an obstetrician who was Royaumont's chief medical officer and surgeon, had insisted they travel as soon as possible.

Arriving in France had felt surreal, the city of Paris possessed by gaiety and sobriety in turns. Ellen, who had once dreamed of going to Paris to see the paintings of the Old Masters, now found herself wandering streets, trying to buy bread and coffee, waiting for a train that kept being canceled because the Germans had blown up the rail line.

The last few weeks had felt both fraught and surreal as Ellen had begun the process of dismantling her life in order to come to France. She'd registered as a nurse with Norah, and they'd arranged transportation to London directly. She had barely had time to write letters to Aunt Rose and Uncle Hamish, and have a tearful goodbye with Ruby and Dougie. Everything had felt precious and fragile and fleeting.

Frances Ivens had left them in Paris so she could go ahead, to arrange accommodation, for apparently "the fine house" the owner, Monsieur Gouin, had leased to them, "with ample accommodation, good drainage and water supply, and electric lighting," had nothing of the sort.

"It needs a bit of work," Miss Ivens had admitted, in a way that Ellen suspected meant it needed a lot.

They'd spent four days wandering around Paris, waiting for a train, and feeling guilty for sightseeing when a war was going on. But Paris was still Paris, with the Eiffel Tower and the Louvre, the Tuileries Gardens and the electric-lit Champs-Élysées. Ellen had seen it all, filled with both wonder and dread.

Now, as she and the others disembarked from the lorry, she wondered what awaited them at Royaumont. The abbey looked ghostly in the moonlight, a tower to rival that of Notre Dame pointing towards a starlit sky, the ground blanketed with crisp white snow. It was beautiful, in an ethereal sort of way, and it hardly seemed a likely place for a hospital, but Letitia had told her how she'd heard of all sorts of buildings being used as hospitals—town halls and schools, small and great houses. Why not an abbey?

Two heavy wooden doors guarded the entrance to the abbey, and when Norah knocked, the sound seemed to be absorbed by the stillness and the snow. Then, after what felt like an age standing out in the bitter cold, the air freezing painfully in Ellen's lung, the door creaked open and Frances Ivens stood there, tall and sturdy, her homely face split by a smile, an oil lamp in one hand, casting a yellow circle of light on the stone-flagged floor.

"Ah, the Scottish contingent!" she exclaimed, for Ellen had heard that the women recruited for the Scottish Women's Hospital came from all sorts of places, even Canada and Australia. They were some of the only Scots. "Come in, come in. I'm so glad you've arrived. And you'll be pleased to know you have something to sleep on—the mattresses arrived last night, thank heavens."

Ellen stepped into the vast entrance hall, the ceiling soaring up into darkness, the smell damp and musty. Royaumont was an imposing structure, but it was not the welcoming place Ellen had naively hoped it would be, despite all warnings to the contrary.

As Miss Ivens guided them through the rooms towards the back of the abbey, Ellen was struck by the improbability, and even the impossibility of the situation—how on earth could this moldering wreck be turned into a hospital? It would take months, if not years, and, as Miss Ivens cheerfully told her, they did not yet have any medical equipment or supplies, because they could not find someone willing to ship them.

"No one wants to do a favor for a woman," she said with a philosophical shrug. "Isn't it ever the way?"

The kitchen, at least, seemed welcoming, in a ragtag sort of way; a huge blackened range took up one side of the large room and threw off a reassuring amount of heat, and two long trestle tables occupied the main space, where around twenty women, of all shapes, sizes, and ages, sat eating their evening meal.

Miss Ivens made a quick-fire round of introductions that Ellen knew she'd forget, and then told her, Letitia, and Norah all to sit down and set to the simple but nourishing fare: a vegetable soup with brown bread.

As Ellen sat and ate, she was regaled with tales of spiders, rats, and worse occupying many of the rooms; one room was full of straw and horse manure from when the Uhlan—the Germany Cavalry—had bivouacked there during the Battle of the Marne.

"The only thing the abbey possesses," Miss Ivens announced with her unique combination of humor and asperity, "is space. Too much space, I fear."

That night, Ellen curled up on a thin straw mattress, wearing every single piece of clothing she'd brought in an attempt to keep warm, and wondered what on earth she'd got herself into.

The next morning, her muscles aching and her fingertips and toes numb with cold, she crept out of the dormitory back to the abbey's kitchen, the only place she knew she might find some warmth.

Dawn light stole across the stone flags of the floor, streaming in from the high, arched windows. In daylight, the room was even bigger than Ellen remembered, with no corners lost in shadows. It was also empty, save for Miss Ivens, who sat at one of the tables, a tin cup of coffee cradled between her hands.

"Ah, Ellen. You, like me, must be an early riser. Isn't the light beautiful? The way it glimmers on the snow… you could almost believe there isn't a war going on, or that the Germans are less than twenty miles away."

"Are they that close?" Ellen asked, her insides tightening. Last night, as she'd listened to the shells, she'd lulled herself into believing it was distant. The ancient abbey, with its medieval arches and towers, seemed untouchable, the war not quite as remote as it had been in Glasgow, but almost.

"Yes, and I'm afraid they will certainly come closer. But you can hardly have a hospital too far from the fighting, can you? Especially not with the state some of these poor chaps are in." She sighed and then nodded towards the pot on the stove. "Fresh coffee, weak but hot. We've got to make it last."

Ellen poured herself a cup, sipping the watery liquid with appreciation for its warmth. "Miss Ivens," she asked tentatively once she'd joined her at the table, "do you really think you can turn this place into a hospital?"

Miss Ivens subjected her to a frank look over the rim of her cup. "No, I don't," she said. "But we can."

Ellen had already heard from some of the other volunteers— orderlies and nurses and two game ambulance drivers—that Frances Ivens was something of a force of nature. Always cheerful, invincibly determined, she radiated capability and confidence. After talking to her for just a few minutes, Ellen started to believe that Royaumont could indeed become a hospital, and even in time for the inspection by the Croix-Rouge—the French Red Cross—on Christmas Eve in just a few weeks' time, which it needed to pass before they could officially open.

The next few weeks almost felt like some strange sort of holiday, sleeping on straw mattresses in the big, empty rooms, and making do for meals with a handful of dishes and cutlery borrowed from the local ironmonger, as well as a single knife they passed around, as the clerk administrator, Cicely Hamilton, said, "so everyone can have a chop with it."

There was, Ellen found, something surprisingly invigorating about scrubbing stone floors by candlelight, and singing as they washed the dishes with buckets of icy water brought in from the spring, knowing in just a month's time, God willing, the hospital's one hundred beds would be filled with men needing their care.

When the medical equipment arrived, and the water and electricity came on, it started to seem as if it was all really going to happen.

One sunny morning just before Christmas, when the sun on snow made everything crystalline-bright, Ellen made up twenty beds in one of the wards, gazing around at the neat beds with their tight hospital corners, with both pride and hope. She imagined them filled with soldiers, men who had fought bravely and were now receiving the care they so desperately needed.

She knew it was a hazy image, pleasant in its vagueness; she had not yet seen the realities of war, had not experienced it other than in the canceled trains and the distant thunder of the guns. A sudden ripple of apprehension chilled her; what was it really going to be like, when the beds were filled and the hospital was up and running?

First, however, the hospital had to be inspected by the Service de Santé of the Croix-Rouge, and Miss Ivens and her team received yet another setback when the hospital failed to pass its inspection on Christmas Eve.

The wards they'd worked so hard on had been dismissed by the inspectors as "cowsheds", too large and ill-equipped to be of any use to potential patients. Some of the orderlies were in furious tears as the officious inspectors left; Miss Ivens, however, was far more pragmatic, and within mere hours of the inspectors' departure, she was calling to Ellen and the others to help her shift beds and sweep floors.

Despite the bad news from the Service de Santé, the twenty-five women who comprised the first contingent of doctors, nurses, orderlies, and drivers had a merry Christmas. The cooks, under the leadership of Dorothy Littlejohn, rose magnificently to the occasion, and provided a traditional Christmas dinner, although no one knew from where.

Cicely Hamilton, who had been both an actress and a playwright as well as a suffragette back in England, designed a pageant of the abbey through the ages, which some of the women gamely took part in, while Ellen watched and laughed at the women's determined theatrics, celebrating in the face of hardship and tragedy.

A local woman had given them mistletoe decorated with flags and ribbons, and everyone's spirits were raised by the festivities so that they returned to their work with renewed vigor. To everyone's relief, including Ellen's, the second inspection on the sixth of January passed without a hitch.

By the thirteenth of January 1915, The Scottish Women's Hospital at Royaumont was open for patients, with all of its staff full of fresh optimism for what was ahead, eager for beds to be filled and men to be treated.

"You see, Ellen?" Miss Ivens said cheerfully as she clapped her on the shoulder. "Anything is possible when you turn your mind and, more importantly, your hand to it." She nodded towards the arched windows that provided a perfect view of snow, sun, and sky, the fields outside the abbey blanketed in pristine white. "Soon the men will come, the wounded both in mind and body, in desperate need of care. I've been to the front lines and seen what happens. It's tragic, the men dying for lack of care." She shook her head. "This is our last moment of peace before the storm." Her normally cheerful face fell into serious lines, her friendly eyes becoming shadowed. "This is the last, before the war truly comes to Royaumont."

CHAPTER FOURTEEN

May 1915

"Nurse Copley, you are needed in theater."

Quickly, Ellen nodded, sparing only a minute to tidy her hair and wash her hands. For the first few months of 1915, both Germany and the Allies had been enduring a stalemate on the Western Front, with trenches running all the way from Verdun to the coast south of Ostend. Then, in February, the fighting had been renewed and the French had lost fifty thousand men by the end of March.

Ellen could not remember ever having worked so hard, or feeling so tired. Often she felt as if she were stumbling through a fog, binding wounds, checking fevers, and changing bandages without even realizing what she was doing. She fell onto her straw mattress every night to catch a few hours of sleep, before the porter's horn sounded again, signaling an ambulance had been sighted coming up the abbey's sweeping drive.

When the hospital had first opened in mid-January, they had only been sent French soldiers who were ill from fevers or the flu, men who were tired and hungry and dirty. Miss Ivens had remarked, rather tartly, that the men needed a bath and a hot meal more than they needed medical care, but those things were provided as well.

Ellen was moved by the gaunt-faced men who clutched her arm and told her, in broken English, that she was an angel, and that Royaumont felt better than heaven. She didn't like to think what horrors they must have endured to be so grateful for a warm blanket, a bowl of soup, and a female touch.

The men had also needed new uniforms, as the French army did not replace ones that had become rent or worn. Miss Ivens arranged for a woman nearby to take in the uniforms for repair so that the French soldiers left the hospital well-fed and properly vested.

"It seems a shame that we're just sending them back to the misery of the Front," Letitia had said when they had seen off a convoy of soldiers back to Ypres. "You patch them up and get them well, just so they can have a chance to be blown up again—and for what?"

It was a refrain they all felt sorely, for as the months slogged on, and men died by the thousands, nothing seemed to be gained. The Front moved a few feet this way or that, a town was lost, and then retaken, but there was no end in sight at all. Ellen recalled Amy's assurance that the war would be over by Christmas and knew now what naïve, wishful thinking that had been.

After the first wave of soldiers, the doctors and surgeons at the Front were satisfied that the women of Royaumont could treat men properly, and in February they began to send the wounded.

The first convoy of wounded soldiers had been a shock; Ellen didn't think anything could have accustomed her to the sight of men with their heads half-open or their stomachs strewn out, far more gruesome than any of the amputations she'd seen in her nurse's training. Far too many of the wounded came to Royaumont only to be comfortable while they died.

"It's worse at the clearing stations on the Front," Letitia told her grimly. "There are so many, and so few skilled medics and surgeons, not to mention morphine or proper equipment. They do what they can…" But it never seemed like enough.

By the end of February, the one hundred beds were filled with French soldiers, most of them privates—or *poilus*, as they were known. Norah was an orderly while Ellen, thanks to her training back in Kingston, had been made an auxiliary nurse. She spent her days assisting Miss Ivens and the other surgeons in operations, changing bandages and bedpans when an orderly could not be found, and administering what medicines they had. She fell into bed each night exhausted and frozen to the bone, and woke with the gray light of dawn to drink a quick cup of coffee and hurry back to the wards. Sometimes she didn't even sleep; the woman on duty would sound the porter's horn if she sighted an ambulance, and everyone would tumble out of bed, hurrying into aprons and caps, to greet whatever horrors awaited them, and do their best to mend and heal.

Letters had, somewhat to her amazement, found her at Royaumont by early spring. She learned that both Jed and Lucas had joined Canada's First Expeditionary Force as soon as it had formed; Jed was a private and Lucas an officer, thanks to their differences in education, which seemed hard to Ellen, but she knew that's simply how it was, and she suspected Lucas would feel worse about it than Jed. It was strange to think of them here in France with her, perhaps not even that far away. They felt as if they were from a different time, a different life.

She'd also heard from Aunt Rose, who had said that Peter was planning to enlist in the summer, and Caro was training to be a Canadian VAD nurse. She was hoping to go to a British military hospital on the Front, but Rose wrote that she thought it was more likely Caro would be assigned to a convalescent hospital in Kingston. Ellen knew Rose would be relieved by that; she did not want to send more than one of her children to the Front, with all of its dangers. In her letters Ellen had tried to be vague, but she knew her aunt would still read between the lines—and suspect the worse.

Now Ellen entered the theater, steeling herself for the sight of a man with shrapnel littered through his intestines. Miss Ivens' face was grimly focused above her surgical mask. Ellen's job was to take the recovered pieces of bloody shrapnel and put them in a pan. Hardly glamorous work, and yet essential.

Her eyes felt gritty with fatigue, her body aching as she stood next to Miss Ivens. Every so often, the room shuddered from the force of the shells exploding only a few miles away; the Front had been, as Miss Ivens had predicted, drawing ever closer, inch by bloody inch. Now and then, the lights would blink or go out completely, and Miss Ivens would demand someone fetch an oil lamp, or even a candle. She'd performed more than one life-saving surgery practically squinting in the dark, but such were the times they lived in.

And yet, Ellen thought in her darker moments, it all felt so *pointless*. No matter how many soldiers they operated on, bound up, and sent on their way, yet more came. The stream of wounded felt never-ending; even if there was a brief lull in the fighting, when it started again, the soldiers came in a flood, each one seeming more broken and hopeless than the last.

In April, the Germans had begun to use the awful new chlorine gas against French and Algerian soldiers at Ypres, causing mass death by asphyxiation and sending the Allied forces into a shocked tailspin. The only saving grace, Norah told Ellen, was that the Germans had been so shocked by the success of the trial, they had failed to take full advantage and push forward. Despite the devastation, the Allies had kept most of their positions.

But now, in May, when the weather was warm and the air sweet with cherry blossom, the Germans had pushed forward again and the Allied forces had fallen back to Ypres.

It was early evening by the time they finished in theater; Miss Ivens had removed all the shrapnel from the poor man, but his prognosis, as with many stomach wounds, was not good.

"If he lasts the night, he has a fighting chance," she said grimly as she washed the blood from her hands. "More than some others, at any rate."

As Ellen left the theater, the Nursing Sister, Helen Watts, told her to check the patients in the Ecosse Ward before going off duty. "The patient in Bed Five needs his dressing changed. Please see to that first."

"Yes, Sister." Ellen hurried back to the ward; the *poilu* in Bed Five blinked up at her as she approached.

"*Bonjour, monsieur,*" Ellen said with a smile, and checked the bandages on his arm where he'd been hit by some flying shrapnel. The bandages were soaked with blood, and the sutures, she saw, had come undone.

She shook her head at him, for she knew he had probably fussed with the bandages, as many of these poor men did. They were sad cases, and not just because of their injuries. When the first *poilus* had arrived back in February, Ellen had been appalled by their state. Their officers, some of whom also came to Royaumont, had little use for them away from the battlefield. Letitia, who was one of the few women at Royaumont who spoke fluent French, had overheard an officer say in disdain, "At the Front, the soldier may be a hero; in the rear, he is merely tiresome." Another officer whose men were being treated in a separate ward had not even inquired about their health, but had merely complained about his own lack of hot food and fresh water.

"You must leave the bandages alone," Ellen now told the *poilu*, and he smiled at her blankly. "*Ne touchez pas!*" she said severely and he grinned and nodded.

Despite their rough looks and ways, the *poilus* loved the abbey, which they called The Palace, for both its comforts and the kindness of its staff. One *poilu* had called the nursing staff "the happiness of Royaumont."

Smiling, Ellen patted the soldier on his good arm and moved to the next bed.

By the time night had settled like a soft, dark blanket over the abbey, Ellen had checked all the soldiers in the ward, settled the restless ones, and administered what medicines she could.

She was just going off duty when she heard the sound of footsteps on the gravel outside, and she peered out of one of the abbey's ancient, arched windows to see several drivers hurrying to the row of trucks that served as makeshift ambulances, and then the sounds of cranks turning and engines sputtering to life in the still, spring air.

She turned to Edith, the nurse who had come to take over her shift. "The wounded are arriving at Creil again?"

Edith nodded. "We just received word. The hospital will be full again. So much for sleep," she said, her lips twisting ruefully, and Ellen nodded in sympathy.

Life at Royaumont was conducted in frenzied, staggered bursts; they might have days or even weeks of peace, when the fighting had stopped and the operating theater remained thankfully empty. In those times, Royaumont could be a jolly place; once, two orderlies had dressed up in the French *horizon bleu* uniform and pretended to be patients, much to the delight of the soldiers who called them "the naughty Misses". There might be card games and singing, and jokes and laughter and celebrations, but when the porter's horn sounded, any merriment was forgotten and the staff might be working for days at a stretch with little or no sleep.

Ellen had got used to the stop-and-start pace, and it had forced her, along with everyone else, to find their happiness and pleasure while they could, in the simple things—a cup of tea, a game of cards, the roses that still bloomed in the garden, tightly furled pink buds, nearly ready to unleash their heady scent.

"I have enough time for a cup of tea, then," Ellen said with a smile. Creil was nearly ten miles away, and although they moved fast, it would take some time for the drivers to get the wounded on board.

The monks' refectory where the staff ate their meals felt like a welcoming haven after the intensity and pervasive despair of the operating theater, and a big brown pot of tea was always at the ready for whoever could sit for a moment and have a cup.

As Ellen entered the room, she saw Norah sitting at one end of the long table, her chin in her hand, her expression as weary as Ellen suspected hers was.

"Hello, Norah." She poured herself a cup and sat opposite her old friend and colleague. Now that Norah was an orderly and Ellen a nurse, their positions were essentially reversed. It had been strange at first to see Norah, so elegant and sophisticated, emptying bedpans and sweeping floors, given the lowliest of chores because of her lack of medical training. Norah, to her credit, had not complained; Ellen thought it took a special sort of courage to admit your own failings and accept your limitations. "It's quiet now," she said as she sipped her tea. "But I just heard the drivers starting up the ambulances. We have an hour, perhaps."

"And I can still hear the guns," Norah replied. They had been booming ceaselessly for nearly a month, as the second battle of Ypres raged on, just a little over one hundred miles away. "It never seems to stop."

"How are you holding up?" Ellen asked gently. Norah's face looked particularly careworn tonight, in the dancing shadows of the oil lamp.

"I'm all right." Norah hesitated, her gaze focused on her cup of tea. "I heard word today that my cousin fell at Ypres. Three weeks ago now, right at the beginning. All this time, I didn't know."

"Oh, Norah, I'm so sorry."

She shook her head, the movement quick, as if denying the truth of her loss. "He was only eighteen, poor lad. Eighteen! His whole life ahead of him, and now we'll never know what he might have achieved or dreamed."

Ellen just shook her head, knowing no words were adequate. Grief was all too common these days, but it still hurt. It always did. And she feared for those she loved—Peter, of course, and Lucas and Jed. Would she feel it if they'd died? How long would it take before she found out if they were wounded?

"Sometimes I feel as if we are losing two or three boys instead of just one," Norah said slowly. "Because we're losing the potential of him. These young boys… I saw a *poilu* who couldn't have been more than sixteen, although he would have denied it. He died from that wretched chlorine gas, and who knows what he might have done? He could have been a doctor or an artist, an architect or a lawyer, or even just a simple farmer. But he'll never know, and neither shall we. A whole generation is losing its potential, Ellen, and I shudder to think of what will happen after this bloody war, and what it will mean for us."

Ellen could not imagine the war ending. She'd been at Royaumont only for six months, but it felt like a lifetime, and there was no end in sight. No end at all.

"They say there have been over fifty thousand deaths of British soldiers in the last month," Norah continued. "And thirty-five thousand French. Six thousand Canadian."

"Six thousand?" Ellen could not keep a tremor from her voice. There were only thirty thousand in the Canadian Expeditionary Force, in which Jed and Lucas, and soon Peter, all served.

"Yes." Norah's voice softened. "Have you had any news from home?"

"Not recently." Her last letter from Aunt Rose had been three weeks ago, right at the start of the latest push. How long would it take Rose to find out, and then to write to her?

She'd written to Lucas herself, back in February, but she had no idea if he'd received her letter; getting mail to soldiers was a dicey business. In any case, he hadn't written back.

Now, as her tea grew cold, Ellen mouthed a soundless prayer for the safety of both Jed and Lucas, and all the island boys who had crossed the Atlantic to give the Germans what for.

After finishing her tea, Ellen hurried upstairs to her sleeping quarters, a drafty room on the top floor of the abbey that she shared with three other nurses. Her bed was nothing more than a straw mattress on the floor, her chest of drawers a few wooden crates, and her dressing table an old door propped on top of some blocks. Still, the view was unparalleled, with the meadows, now filled with wildflowers, glinting under the moonlight.

Ellen didn't bother changing out of her uniform as she lay on her mattress for a brief rest before the ambulances came back with the wounded.

She managed to doze for an hour before she was wakened by Rosemary, another nurse, and she hurried to tidy herself and slip her nurse's veil back on.

"It's bad," Rosemary said, her face pinched and gray.

Ellen stilled for a moment, glancing at the other woman. "It's always bad."

"Yes, but…" Rosemary shook her head, swallowing hard. "How can men do such things to one another?"

Tense with awful anticipation, Ellen hurried downstairs. The wounded were coming through the front doors of the abbey, which had been flung open to the night. Those who could walk did, some staggering, and others were carried in on stretchers, heads and bodies swathed in bloody bandages, many of them moaning piteously.

For a second, Ellen simply stood there, watching this flood of wounded humanity, and thinking how it never ceased. Tomorrow or the next day, there would be yet more coming. The war, it seemed, would continue until there were no men left to fight.

"Nurse Copley!" Sister Watts' sharp voice startled Ellen from her melancholy thoughts and quickly she hurried forward.

"Yes, Sister," she called, and she placed a hand on a soldier's elbow to help him into the ward. Perhaps the fighting would cease one day, but for now it continued, and there was work to be done, and men to be tended to and hopefully healed.

CHAPTER FIFTEEN

June 1915

As summer blossomed around the abbey, the staff and soldiers of Royaumont experienced a brief respite as there was a lull in the fighting. The aftermath of the battle at Ypres had been both bloody and deadly, and far too many men had died in their wards and theaters.

Now, however, with the roses in bloom and the sun shining high above, the only men left at Royaumont were the ones who had survived and were convalescing. Although most of the patients were French, some others were British, Canadian, and some from the French Colonies in Africa. One of the Scottish orderlies had been shocked, having never seen a black man before several privates in the Algerian division came to the abbey.

Ellen had asked one of the Canadian soldiers if he knew of Jed or Lucas Lyman, but the man had shaken his head sorrowfully. Ellen longed for news; she still hadn't heard from anyone on the island, and although she'd written him again, there had been nothing from Lucas.

Still, it was hard to keep oneself in a constant state of anxiety, and Ellen did her best to be cheerful, for the patients' sake. She was continually amazed and humbled at the forbearance the patients showed again and again, and how they were able to laugh and joke in even the most tragic of circumstances; she would never forget the tight-lipped, uncomplaining faces of the soldiers with mangled limbs who had to be adjusted on the hard metal table for an X-ray, or the one-armed *poilus* playing draughts, or the soldiers blinded by the dreadful gas who painted watercolors of the wildflowers from memory.

Their fortitude was a lesson she took to heart, considering the tragedies in her own life, and she had vowed that whatever happened after the war, she would face it with the courage and cheer that the *poilus* had shown her so many times.

One afternoon in mid-June, Ellen came into the ward to find an Algerian soldier protesting at the top of his lungs and Letitia standing at the foot of the bed, her hands planted on her hips as she looked at him in exasperation.

"*Monsieur, s'il vous plaît,*" she said for what Ellen suspected was not the first time. She continued in French that Ellen could only just understand, "I must see to your wound's dressings. If you will only permit me…"

The man held the bed sheets to his chest, his face red with both fury and humiliation. "*Non, mademoiselle,*" he returned. "*Non, non, non!*"

Ellen suppressed a laugh at the absurdity of the interaction; a few of the patients in nearby beds, those who were well enough to sit up, were watching the scene unfold as if it were a great drama on the London stage for them to enjoy.

Ellen touched Letitia's arm. "What is the matter here?" she asked quietly. "Can I help?"

"Only if you can hold this man down long enough so I can check his dressings," Letitia answered shortly. "He is being ridiculous."

"Where is his injury?"

Letitia's face, already flushed nearly as red as her patient's, turned a shade rosier. "On his buttocks. He was hit with flying shrapnel. I sewed him up myself a week ago while he was unconscious, but he is now insisting that he cannot show himself to a woman, and—*oh!*" She shook her head impatiently. "He is at a hospital with all women staff. There is no one else, as you very well know."

"Does he know that?" Ellen asked.

"I have explained it to him several times." She tried again. "*Monsieur, s'il vous plaît—*"

The man shrank back against his pillow, wincing as his wound pressed against the mattress. "*Non!*"

"Oh dear," Ellen murmured. She was trying not to smile, but there was something ludicrous about the situation, and as they all learned, you had to find your humor where you could. "Are you sure they need to be checked right at this moment?"

"It has been a week," Letitia huffed. "And it is clear the wound is paining him. If they're not checked, he could develop an infection in the blood which may very well prove to be fatal."

"That is indeed no laughing matter," Ellen continued soberly. "I'm sorry, Letitia." She touched her friend's arm lightly. "How can I help?"

"You cannot, unless you can turn me into a man," Letitia retorted in exasperation. She turned to the patient, who looked as obdurate as ever. "You will reopen your wound!" she warned the man, shaking a fist. "And then what? You shall die of sepsis, sir, if you are not careful!"

"Perhaps I can help, *mademoiselle*?" A man appeared in the doorway of the ward, speaking in English. He was a patient, but well enough to walk, and clearly an officer, judging by the dressing gown and slippers he wore. The *poilus* had nothing but the tattered uniforms they came in.

"Perhaps you may, sir," Letitia answered as she drew herself up with dignity. "Do you know this man?"

The officer's gaze flicked to the man in the bed and he smiled. "I do. He is in my regiment. Private Henri Sahnoun." He spoke to the man in French, rapidly and in a low voice so neither Letitia nor Ellen could make out what he had said.

Amazingly, the man in the bed grunted his acceptance and rolled onto his stomach so Letitia could inspect his wound; as she had feared, the dressing was soaked with blood and looked to be infected.

Ellen stepped back to give the man some much-needed privacy. She glanced at the officer, who was leaning on a cane, his face now pale and haggard.

"*Monsieur*, your help is greatly appreciated," she said quietly, "but I think perhaps you should return to your bed."

He nodded wryly and Ellen took his arm as she helped him out of the ward to one of the other wards reserved for officers.

Ellen was just settling the man into his bed when Letitia came into the ward. She looked more composed, her face its normal color, her coat of gray-blue with its *caducées* of surgeon-major in silver now straightened. "I must thank you, sir, for your kind intervention. What did you say to the man?"

The officer leaned back against his pillows and smiled. "I simply told him he was fortunate indeed to have a lovely young woman such as yourself inspecting his backside."

Letitia's flush returned and her eyes sparkled with anger. "I'd thank you, sir, to remember I am a doctor."

The man inclined his head in acknowledgment, his blue eyes flashing in amusement. "And a woman, *mademoiselle*," he returned. "A beautiful one, at that. But let me introduce myself." He extended one hand, which Letitia did not take. "Lieutenant Lucien Allard."

Letitia stared at him a moment and then nodded stiffly. "Thank you again for your assistance, Lieutenant Allard," she said and, turning on her heel, she left the room.

Lucien Allard met Ellen's gaze with a humorous one of his own. "I fear I have insulted the good doctor."

"She is merely tired," Ellen demurred. Letitia was the youngest and most newly qualified doctor at Royaumont, and had thus been given the status of medical dresser rather than fully fledged doctor. As a result, she was, Ellen suspected, always trying to prove herself, to the staff as well as to the patients.

News of the dashing Lieutenant Allard and his rescue traveled around the abbey quickly enough, for any interesting news was always greeted with both humor and excitement. By dinnertime as they gathered in the kitchen to eat the meat and fruit that comprised their evening meal, a few orderlies dared to tease Letitia.

"It seems you have an admirer, Dr. Portman!"

"He is in the French Foreign Legion," another sighed. "So romantic."

Letitia did not answer, choosing instead to saw the single piece of stringy pork that their new chef Michelet had dressed up with stewed apples. He had served at one of the country's great houses before the war; after convalescing as a patient, Miss Ivens had worked her considerable charm to have the chef seconded to the hospital for the duration of the war. "He has a way with meat and potatoes," she told the staff frankly, "that is quite unparalleled. And good food increases morale, I am sure."

"Don't you think he is handsome?" Charlotte, another orderly with a penchant for story papers, pressed. "Such dark hair…"

"I did not notice his hair," Letitia returned shortly. "I notice men's wounds, not their looks."

"Still, wouldn't it be wonderful to have a romance at Royaumont? All these women doctors and nurses…" Charlotte's eyes sparkled. "And all these male patients!"

"That is quite enough, Miss Evans," Miss Ivens intervened, although her tone was friendly. "We have enough to do as it is, without filling our heads with such nonsense."

Lucien Allard, however, did not seem to agree, for as June waned into July, he became determined to win Letitia's favor, if not her heart.

Despite a wound to his knee, he was well enough to walk, with the help of his cane, and one sunny afternoon he went outside to the abbey's gardens to pick a posy of flowers that he offered to Letitia as she was doing her rounds.

Her face red, Letitia took them with a suffocated whisper of thanks and stuffed them in the pocket of her uniform coat. Ellen watched on in bemusement; Lucien Allard, with his dark hair and tanned skin and sparkling blue eyes, cut a dashing figure indeed. There had been, over the course of her time at Royaumont, a few flirtations between the staff and soldiers; one of the orderlies wrote letters regularly to a French private who had returned to the Front. Letitia, however, hardly seemed susceptible to the lieutenant's charms.

"Don't speak to me of that dreadful man," she warned Ellen one afternoon when, during a lull, they were sitting out in the cloisters, enjoying the warm weather and the beautiful countryside.

At a moment like this, Royaumont felt as if it were untouched by the war; how could there be muddy trenches, bombed-out villages, and hollow-eyed men just a few miles away?

Of course, one only had to catch the eye of one of the soldiers sitting in the cloisters to be reminded. Miss Ivens had decided that fresh air and sunlight worked wonders on convalescents, and so she insisted that as many men as possible take the air when they could. It was pleasant to see the men playing draughts or cards, tilting their faces to the sun. In these moments, they seemed like men, rather than soldiers.

"Surely that's a bit unfair, Letitia," Ellen argued with a smile. "He's far from dreadful." Lieutenant Allard, in fact, had won over many of the staff's hearts, save Letitia's. He was charming and seemed to know it, not that anyone minded. Last night, he had serenaded the nurses in his ward in a lovely tenor voice, with the wartime song "*Noël des Enfants*." Even the staff who didn't know enough French to understand its touching story of the lost children of France had been visibly moved. Letitia, however, would not be moved by any of it.

"He is dreadful," she insisted, her face reddening as she gazed out at the gardens of the abbey, full of roses and birdsong. "He is making a fool of me."

"Is that how you feel? He doesn't mean to, Letitia. He just admires you."

"Admires?" she scoffed. "Or fancies?"

"Both, I suppose. Is that so bad?" A surprising little flicker of envy rippled through Ellen before she quickly suppressed it. It had been a long time since she'd had anyone interested in her… or felt that spark herself. She had no designs on the lieutenant, but for a moment she imagined what it would feel like to love someone again, or even just like them a little.

"He jeopardizes my reputation," Letitia continued in a low voice, "and makes a mockery of my calling." She set her jaw. "I am a doctor, not some flighty, fluttery miss to fall in love."

"Even doctors fall in love," Ellen reminded her, although in truth none of the staff at Royaumont were married. Some of them certainly wanted to be, however, at least one day.

"Not this doctor," Letitia said firmly. "Lieutenant Allard can pick as many wilted posies as he likes. I will not be moved. Besides, his wound is healing nicely and he'll be packed up to the Front again in no time at all. He's sure to forget about me then."

Ellen regarded her friend with quiet curiosity, for something in Letitia's tone made her wonder if she actually wanted to be forgotten.

A week into July, when Lucien Allard had been given his marching orders and the sun baked the earth so even the cool, shadowy rooms of the abbey were stifling, Ellen and Letitia packed a picnic of cold cheese, meat, and fruit and headed off for an afternoon's much-needed leisure.

As they waded through the waist-high grass, the only sound the babbling of the nearby brook and the occasional twitter of birdsong, it seemed incredible to think they were not all that far from the barbed-wire and barren fields of the trenches, the burned-out villages, houses and barns reduced to rubble, as war cut its bloody swathe through France and Belgium.

Ellen spread a blanket by the brook while Letitia set out their meager feast.

"I think I have been hungry since this war began," she said as she portioned the scraps of meat onto two plates. "But not as hungry as the men we treat, I suppose."

Ellen tucked her feet under her skirt and picked an apple from the basket. "When do you think it will be over?" she asked quietly.

Letitia smiled wryly and plucked a grape from the bunch. "Do you remember how at the beginning they said they'd be home by Christmas?"

"Miss Ivens never thought that," Ellen countered. "She set up the hospital in December!"

"I think women can see sense more than men can," Letitia answered with asperity and Ellen smiled.

"I suppose you are thinking of Lucien Allard."

Letitia pressed her lips together. "I don't ever think of him."

"He's leaving soon, anyway, isn't he?" Ellen said.

"Yes, he'll be gone in no more than a few weeks, if his knee continues to heal without infection." Letitia popped the grape in her mouth. "Good riddance, I say."

"Do you, really?" Over the last week, Lieutenant Allard had continued his charm offensive, but just as the war was fought in battles of tiny increments, his push to win Letitia's affections did not seem to gain an inch.

"Yes, I do," Letitia insisted, perhaps a bit too much.

"He's very solicitous towards his men. Some of the French officers are horrible. They treat their men like cattle, or even worse, fodder for the cattle. Completely expendable."

"And some of the Colonial troops have it even worse," Letitia agreed soberly. "Many of the Senegalese have been forced to fight by the chiefs of their village, so others aren't taken by force."

"It's terrible." Ellen had heard about the tribal politics that had led men to war, men who could have had absolutely no idea what they were signing up for… yet Ellen didn't think any boy could have had an idea. Surely the boys she knew from the island couldn't have conceived of the muddy trenches, the booming guns, the clouds of chlorine gas. It was like something out of a nightmare.

"Still," Ellen couldn't keep from saying, "that makes Lieutenant Allard's conduct all the more admirable."

Letitia sniffed. "Perhaps."

"He is handsome," Ellen pressed mischievously, and for a moment she thought Letitia would admit to some small affection.

"He is handsome enough, I suppose," she answered after a moment. "But honestly, Ellen, you are worse than some of the orderlies! I am not here to have a grand romance."

"Of course not. But if one *happened*…"

"With Lieutenant Allard? I grant he is certainly charming, but then what Frenchman isn't? And he lives in Algeria, of all places, after all." For a second, Letitia's face looked bleak. "What future could we possibly have?"

"You have thought of all that already?" Ellen asked in surprise. "Then you must like him more than you've let on, even to think of it like that."

"I don't," Letitia answered quickly, but she blushed and Ellen laughed, daring to tease her friend a little more.

"You do! Oh Letitia, I am glad for you. I think you could use a little levity, and even a little romance, in your life."

Letitia didn't answer; her face looked frozen and then, to Ellen's shock, it crumpled and she held up her hands to hide her expression.

"Oh, I'm sorry," Ellen exclaimed, full of contrition. Her teasing suddenly took on a meaner cast. "I didn't realize…" she began, for she now could see Letitia's feeling ran deeper than anyone might have expected, even Lieutenant Allard himself. "I've been so thoughtless, teasing you the way I have. Letitia, I am sorry."

"No." Letitia shook her head and dabbed at her eyes. "I'm being so foolish. It's only… hope is such a dangerous thing, isn't it? I see that now more than ever. We bandage these poor boys up and push them out the door, most likely to their deaths, and they most likely know it. How can they not? They've already looked it in the eye more than once." She took a gulping sort of breath. "And so much of the suffering is needless, so terribly pointless…" She shook her head, her tears drying on her cheeks. "We are perhaps a few feet ahead of where we were last summer, after Ypres. A whole year of fighting, and who knows how many thousands dead, and for what? A few paltry feet of ground?" She sank back onto the blanket, her expression turning grim. "I hate this war," she said flatly. "I truly hate this bloody, bloody war."

Ellen remained silent, for what could she say? She hated the war too; they all did by now, though few spoke of it. Miss Ivens was adamant that her staff keep their spirits up, and yet as the months had slid by and so little had changed; as each battle had become bloodier and the casualties had mounted up and the soldiers who had once been cheerful and chipper become more gaunt and hollow-eyed, who could keep from questioning the point of it all?

"I can't care," Letitia said quietly. "I can't care about any of them, Ellen, and certainly not Lieutenant Allard. It's simply too dangerous. He'll be going back to the Front in a few weeks, once his knee heals. That's all that matters."

Ellen continued to reflect on her friend's words as they packed up their picnic and headed back to the abbey, the mood more somber than it had been when they'd set out. She understood Letitia's sentiment all too well; she'd felt it herself. Losing Jed to Louisa and then, far worse, losing Henry when the *Titanic* had sunk had certainly made her wary of caring about anyone ever again.

But to keep your heart safe, wrapped up and tucked away, was a lonely way of living. As they brought their picnic basket back to the kitchen with thanks to Michelet, Ellen hoped Letitia would dare to risk her heart one day. Perhaps she would too, if this war ever ended.

CHAPTER SIXTEEN

July 1915

As the wounded continued to flow into Royaumont, Miss Ivens took the decision to open several new wards, and they spent a few days sweeping out rooms full of rubble and rubbish and then setting up beds and arranging for electric light. Workmen tramped through the hospital, and in addition to her nursing duties, Ellen found herself on her knees, scrubbing the stone-flagged floor, along with orderlies and doctors alike. Everyone had always chipped in at Royaumont, no matter how menial the work, thanks to Miss Ivens' example.

"What needs to be done, must be done," she would announce, taking a broom herself. Thankfully, there had been another lull in the fighting, which gave them the opportunity not just to prepare new wards but to spend time enjoying the lovely French summer.

One afternoon in late July, Ellen came downstairs to find a letter waiting for her from Ontario. It was from Aunt Rose, and Ellen prayed it had good news of Jed and Lucas.

She took it outside to read, sitting on a stone bench by a fountain whose water made a merry tinkling sound as it splashed and sprayed.

Dear Ellen,

I'm sorry it has been so long since I've written. Life has become very busy on the island, as we man the home front, doing our best to continue with the war effort. Even Captain Jonah has done his bit—he offered his little tug as a hospital ship, but I'm afraid he was politely refused, which has put him rather out of sorts.

I am the proud mother of an enlisted soldier now, although my heart trembles to write that. Peter has joined the Expeditionary Force, and he sailed for France last week. Caro has been, as I had expected and certainly hoped, posted to the convalescent hospital in Kingston. The rest of us continue on, managing the farm and knitting more socks than we know what to do with… but hopefully they will keep our poor boys' feet warm. I have read about the terrible cases of trench foot, and I'm sure you've seen them where you are.

We had news of both the Lyman boys; Jed has been fighting at Ypres and, a few months ago, Lucas was appointed to do something in London, so at least he is safely out of the fighting, although he cannot say what he is up to, and of course everyone wonders.

Lucas in London! A wave of relief pulsed through Ellen. But Jed in Ypres… at least he hadn't been wounded, or Aunt Rose would have said. She tried to imagine Jed crouched in one of the trenches like the soldiers who came through the hospital, tired and dirty and scared, the shells flying over his head, their white flares lighting up the sky. She could not imagine it; in her mind's eye, she still saw him in the kitchen of the Lyman farmhouse, his gray eyes laughing at her, but that, of course, had been years ago now, before the war, before Louisa. Ellen turned back to Aunt Rose's letter.

Louisa and Thomas are doing well, all things considered. He is not a hearty boy, but Louisa dotes on him. He is coming up to three years old now, and he is a very sweet little thing, with Jed's gray eyes and Louisa's curls.

She would not let that hurt her, Ellen told herself. It was too long ago, and too much had happened since then.

It is so strange to think of how the world has been turned upside down. I'm sure none of us could have imagined it, with most of the island boys in France, and the ones who can't go wishing they could. It all feels so very far away, and yet so horribly close. Yesterday an island family—the Boyles, I don't think you knew them—learned their son Henry was missing in action. No one knows if that's better or worse than knowing he's been killed. It's frightful, what you hear the Germans are capable of. I can scarce believe some of the stories they print in the papers.

I hope you keep well and safe, dear Ellen. Write soon.

With all my love, Aunt Rose.

Ellen put the letter down, closing her eyes briefly as she pictured Amherst Island in the heady throes of summer, with the raspberries dripping like fat, red jewels from the bushes, the blue-green waters glinting in the sun, the smell of haymaking in the air.

"*Mademoiselle!*"

She opened her eyes to see a patient smiling and pointing to her feet, where a ball had rolled. The men who were well enough were all taking in the summer sunshine, and several soldiers were playing a game of football, which Ellen knew must be good for their spirits. This sunny garden was a universe away from where they were headed all too soon.

With a little smile, Ellen kicked the ball back to the men, and then laughed as they all cheered.

"*Merci, mademoiselle, merci!*"

She watched, smiling, as they continued their impromptu match, some of them hobbling a bit, and she hoped none of them had stitches that would be pulled out by their antics. She suspected a bit of football was as beneficial to the convalescing soldiers as a dose of sodium salicylate.

She observed that Lucien Allard was one of the men playing, although he limped quite a bit. Letitia would not approve, Ellen thought with a smile. Over the last few weeks, Letitia had thawed slightly towards the charming lieutenant, which was all the more meaningful now that Ellen knew of her deeper, hidden feelings.

As she watched the game, smiling at the men's enthusiasm, Lieutenant Allard suddenly stumbled and then sprawled across the grass. A cry went up from the men as they clustered around him. Before Ellen could rise from her seat on the bench, Letitia was striding across the lawn, her face a mask of anxiety.

"*Prenez un peu de recul,*" she cried, and obediently the men shuffled back. Letitia crouched by Lieutenant Allard as Ellen hurried forward, blanching at the sight of his graying face and fluttering eyes. He was half-unconscious already.

"He was smiling and laughing but a moment ago…"

"Because he's an idiot, and always puts a brave face on things," Letitia answered bitterly. "He's reopened his wound, the fool, and now it looks infected. He should have known better. *We* should have known better. He was always saying he felt perfectly fine…" Her voice caught and Ellen put a hand on her arm that Letitia shook off, her face drawn in lines of tension and anxiety. "Call some orderlies. He'll need to be carried back to his bed."

A few minutes later, Lucien was settled in his bed, his wound cleaned and his bandages changed. A fresh convoy of wounded had come into the abbey, and so Ellen wasn't able to check on the lieutenant or Letitia until late that night, after the most serious cases had been dealt with.

As ever after a rush, she felt tired and dirty and dispirited, having seen so much hopeless, pointless suffering and pain. A boy no more than fifteen years old had come in with his head practically in pieces; he hadn't even made it up the steps.

Ellen had sat with him by the door of the abbey, one arm around him as he muttered incoherently in French. She knew he most likely only had minutes to live. At one point, his eyes, a vivid blue, had opened wide and he'd looked around in a panic.

"Marie?" he'd called desperately. "Marie, *es-tu ici?*"

"*Oui, je suis ici,*" Ellen had answered gently, smoothing his hair back from his fevered brow. "*C'est moi. C'est Marie.*"

He'd relaxed then, his eyes fluttering closed as he slumped back against her. A few seconds later, he'd died.

Ellen's heart had been heavy as she'd arranged for him to be taken to the mortuary. Over the last few months, as men had breathed their last, she'd been Marie, Elise, Suzanne, daughter, sister, friend, fiancée, wife, and mother. *Maman.* Men always seemed to ask for a woman when they died, usually their mother.

Although she was weary and aching, dawn only an hour or two away, Ellen knew she needed to find Letitia and check on Lieutenant Allard before she grabbed a few hours' sleep. When she spoke with the nurse on duty on his ward, her manner was grave.

"He's been tossing and turning all night, but he's gone quiet now. His fever is still high."

"Has nothing been able to lower it?"

"We've done what we can," the nurse, who had a higher rank and more experience than Ellen, said a bit repressively. "I fear the wound might go septic." Which was almost always fatal.

"After all this time…" Ellen shook her head, filled with sorrow for both Lieutenant Allard and Letitia, who knew her heart even if she hid it from everyone else, and especially from the lieutenant.

"He was out and about when he should have been resting in bed," the nurse said with a sigh. "It's no wonder it became infected."

"He was due to return to the Front in just over a week."

"He won't be, now."

Thanking her, Ellen left the ward and went in search of Letitia. She was off duty and not in her room, which meant she could be anywhere. Ellen was tempted to wait till morning, but some instinct told her to keep looking.

She finally found her in the most unlikely of places, a room full of rubble that hadn't yet been cleared for a new purpose. Letitia was sitting in a deep stone windowsill that overlooked the moonlit meadows, as bucolic a sight as anyone could wish for, although the distant thunder of the guns was audible, and Ellen could see the strangely beautiful white arcs of light the artillery made against the night sky.

"How are you?" Ellen asked quietly.

Letitia let out a shuddery sigh as she leaned her head against the window's stone archway. "I'm not sure I know."

"Have you seen Lieutenant Allard?"

"Yes, a while ago. His fever hasn't broken. It looks as if his wound might go septic." She sighed. "Stupid man."

"I'm sorry, Letitia."

"Miss Ivens said she would amputate in the morning if his leg isn't looking better. Better the loss of a leg than the loss of a life."

"Perhaps it won't come to that…" Ellen said, although even to her own ears the words sounded feeble.

"Perhaps it will," Letitia countered grimly. "If there's one thing I've learned in this war, it's that happy endings are never guaranteed. They usually don't happen."

Ellen thought of the boy calling for Marie, spending his last moment in a strange place, in a stranger's arms. And for what? *For what?*

"It's been a difficult night," she said at last.

"It's been a difficult month. A difficult year. A difficult, bloody war." Letitia let out a hard, bitter laugh. "I wouldn't mind, you know, any of it, if I felt it was for a noble cause. A higher good. If we were actually accomplishing something, fighting something worth fighting."

"Surely we are—"

"The Germans aren't evil, Ellen. I know we try to act as if they are, because that makes it worthwhile, somehow. We can justify all the loss and even the stupidity if we're the ones on the right. But they aren't evil. Maybe the Kaiser is, who knows? Or perhaps he's been caught up in the futility of it all, just as we have. But the German soldiers are just boys, too, the same as ours. They're terrified, they suffer from the terrible shock, they call for their mothers. I can't blame them. I'm not sure I can blame anyone, and that's what makes it so unbearable. *Why are we here?*" Her voice rang out, her eyes like dark pits of grief and despair.

"To help the wounded," Ellen said as steadily as she could. She was shaken by Letitia's words, and the bitter conviction with which she'd said them. "I agree with you, the longer this war goes on, the less sense it seems to make. But there's nothing we can do about that, Letitia, not a single thing. So in the meantime we do what we can—we bind up the wounded, we hold their hands, we act as their mothers. We show them care and kindness." She sighed heavily. "I don't have any other answers. I don't know what else to do."

"Nor do I." Letitia shook her head. "And still it goes on, and on and *on.* The men coming in tonight have been fighting for control of a few pathetic yards up in the Vosges. Thousands have died, and neither side has gained any advantage at all. It's so *pointless.*"

It had been the same in Ypres—positions barely held, a few feet gained or lost after weeks or months of pitched battle and endless shelling. Trenches abandoned, trenches dug, the whole world turning into a muddy, murky no man's land. Ellen knew she had no wisdom, no solace, to offer anyone. The only thing she knew to do was to keep going, keep trying to help whomever she could.

"Why don't you get some rest?" she suggested.

Letitia shook her head. "I can't sleep."

"You need to, Letitia. We are no good to anyone if we don't get some rest while we can."

Letitia's gaze rested on the pink dawn streaking the sky, the rumble of the guns stilled for a blessed moment of quiet. "I love him, Ellen," she said softly, so softly Ellen almost didn't hear her. "Isn't that the most foolish thing you've ever heard?"

"I think it's the most wonderful," Ellen replied, a lump forming in her throat. She would like to see both Letitia and Lieutenant Allard happy. "Heaven knows we all need some good news now, something to remind us why life is worth living, what joy it can bring."

"He might not live," Letitia said, the words ending on a shudder she cut off, pressing her lips together to keep the tears at bay. "He might lose his leg, or his life. And even if he doesn't…" She trailed off, shaking her head, biting her lips.

"Even if?" Ellen prompted gently.

"I told you before, there's no life for us. He's French Algerian and I'm American. We live in completely separate worlds, and absolutely everyone we know will remind us of it."

"I won't," Ellen returned with a bracing smile. "It's challenging, I admit, but not impossible. Nothing is impossible, Letitia, when it comes to love, and love is the one thing I know is worth sacrificing for. Fighting for."

Letitia gave her a fleeting smile. "You sound so wise."

"Perhaps more hopeful than wise, but I truly believe it."

Letitia sighed. "I wish I could." She glanced again at Ellen. "What about you, Ellen? In all the years I've known you, there hasn't ever been anyone, has there?"

"No, I suppose there hasn't." Ellen thought of Henry, whom she hadn't told Letitia about, and then she thought of Jed, both of them more wished-for than real relationships. In the years since Henry's death, she'd come to realize how little time or experience they'd shared. Yes, her grief had been real, and she had been planning to marry and spend her life with him, but the truth was they'd hardly spent any time together. She grieved their lost future more than their shared past. "I'm still looking, I guess," she said. "Still hoping."

"None of the officers have caught your eye?" Letitia teased with a wan smile.

"No, I'm afraid not."

"And no one from back in Canada?"

"No," Ellen said after a second's hesitation when, for some reason, she thought of Lucas, who had always been a friend and nothing more, no matter that he'd told her loved her. "No," she said again, more firmly, letting the word reverberate through her. "There's no one."

After a few hours of sleep, Ellen returned to duty to discover that the angry red streaks on Lieutenant Allard's leg had not gone down; in fact they'd become worse.

"I'm afraid it doesn't look at all well, Dr. Portman," Miss Ivens said to Letitia while Ellen stood by the door, her heart feeling as if it were suspended in her chest. "Look at the angry redness all along his leg," she continued. Lucien was alarmingly still from the fever, his face pale and gray, his forehead beaded with sweat. "The infection has entered his blood. I'm afraid we are looking at am amputation." Her eyes were gentle as she glanced at Letitia, clearly guessing something of her feelings. All of Royaumont knew about Lieutenant Allard's affections for Dr. Portman, certainly.

Now Letitia just nodded, her eyes grim, her jaw set. She said nothing as two orderlies moved Lieutenant Allard, who had fallen unconscious, onto a stretcher.

Miss Ivens nodded towards Ellen. "You may assist, Sister," she said, and with her heart seeming to beat its way up her throat, Ellen followed them into the operating theater.

Just a few minutes later, the thing was done, and Lucien's leg was amputated above the knee, the blood staunched, the wound bandaged.

"Poor man," Miss Ivens said as she washed her arms up to the elbow in a big stone sink. "Pray that the infection went no farther, and he survives." She glanced at Ellen. "For both their sakes."

Ellen spent the rest of the day on duty, dealing with the men in her care who still needed wounds dressed, foreheads mopped, and sheets changed. She didn't see Letitia, and she wondered how her friend was coping with the news of the lieutenant's amputation. He was still unconscious, and did not know of it himself, and Ellen hated to think of his usually cheerful demeanor changing. Most men struggled with an amputation, especially of a leg, and some bitterly wished they'd died instead.

Ellen knew life was hard for a man maimed in such a way, and she shuddered to think of the grim future after the war, when so many men of her generation would be crippled, blinded, shell-shocked, or worse. How did anyone go on from here? All she wanted was for the war to be over, and yet she could not imagine what life would be like for anyone when it was.

Finally, in the early evening, she found Letitia out in the cloisters, sitting a little bit away from the soldiers and staff who were enjoying the cooler part of the day. Even the interior of the abbey, behind its thick, stone walls, had been stifling in the heat of summer.

Now Ellen paused a few steps away from her friend. "Letitia…"

"It's so peaceful here, isn't it? So lovely. I've been watching the sun set. Without the noise of the guns, it feels like it could be a summer back home. We used to spend the summers on Cape Cod, have I told you that?"

Ellen shook her head. "No, you haven't."

"So, so peaceful." Letitia lapsed into thought and Ellen waited. "If he survives," she said after a moment, as if they had been in the middle of another conversation, "what sort of life can he have? An amputation above the *knee*, Ellen. It doesn't bear thinking about."

Ellen came to sit next to Letitia. "We've seen plenty of men with similar amputations," she said quietly. "They will all have to find a way forward, after this war is over." Even if neither of them could imagine it.

"After this war is over," Letitia repeated, and rested her forehead against the cool stone wall. "Sometimes I wonder if that is ever going to happen."

"The tide will turn soon, surely," Ellen answered with more conviction than she felt. "If America enters the war…"

"They seem remarkably reluctant to do so," Letitia answered. "To my own shame. But in any case, the players may shift, but the terror will never end. And when it does…" She lifted her head to gaze bleakly out at the abbey gardens; a couple of soldiers were laughing and playing boules. "What will happen to men like Lucien? Do you think his country will provide for him? There will be so many wounded, blinded, maimed… and I fear by that time everyone will just want to forget. The wounded will be a reminder no one wants to see. What will they do, all these poor boys of ours?"

Ellen thought of Jed and Lucas, safe as far as she knew, but who really knew anything? She had not seen them in all the time she'd been in France, and what news she had gleaned came from Aunt Rose far away on Amherst Island.

Amherst Island… it felt a more distant memory than it ever had, with its maple trees and the blue-green water of Lake Ontario, the happiness and the simplicity of the place that now seemed like no more than a children's story Ellen had once read and then grown out of.

"I don't know," she admitted to Letitia. "I don't know what will happen when the war ends, Letitia, as much as I long for it." She laid a hand on her friend's arm. "But if you love Lieutenant Allard…" She trailed off, unsure how much to press. Would Letitia still love a man who had lost his leg? The improbability of a future together loomed even greater now.

Letitia didn't speak for a long moment; her face remained bleak, her expression shuttered. "Does it matter?" she finally asked, and rose from where she'd been sitting.

After a pause, Ellen followed. She went to her room and tried to sleep, but her troubled dozing was plagued by dreams of blood and gore and the cries of the wounded, even though the hospital was now all peace and quiet.

By dawn it had already become too hot to sleep, and she rose and washed and dressed in her plain skirt and blouse; today was her day off, and she thought perhaps she would travel into the nearby village of Asnières-sur-Oise, simply for a change of scene. She felt heavy in both spirit and body, weighed down by fatigue and the endless grief of the war, and the parade of wounded men who had come through the abbey with their missing limbs, their pain-filled eyes, their hopelessness and even more heartrendingly, their determined cheer.

It was mid-morning as she was just tidying her hair when Edith came up to see her, breathless, her face red from both exertion and heat.

"Ellen! There's a soldier here to see you!"

"A soldier…?" Ellen repeated blankly, and Edith nodded.

"Yes, he cuts quite a dashing figure in his uniform. He speaks English too, like a Yank."

"What…" Ellen's breath came out in a rush as she hurried down the abbey's twisting stairs. Hope was a dangerous thing, she reminded herself, and yet she could not keep it from ballooning inside her as she rushed to the abbey's magnificent entrance hall, where a soldier in the uniform of the Canadian Expeditionary Force waited, his cap in his hand, his smile wry as his warm gaze met Ellen's startled one.

Her mouth dried as she came to a halt in front of him, shaking her head slowly. "Lucas," she said wonderingly, and then she rushed into his arms.

CHAPTER SEVENTEEN

Lucas's arms closed around Ellen and she pressed her cheek against his chest, the buttons of his coat digging into her skin. She didn't care. She was so glad to see him, she could barely speak. Joy and hope rose like bubbles inside her, buoying her soul.

Finally, with a self-conscious laugh, she eased away from him. "I'm sorry… I haven't seen anyone from home for so long! I can't tell you how good it is to see you. How long has it been?"

Lucas smiled wryly. "Four years."

Four years. She shook her head slowly, the events of the last four years—her time in Glasgow, and this hard year of war—tumbling through her mind. "It's so very good to see you, Lucas. Truly."

"And you, Ellen. I wasn't even sure I'd find you here. Your Aunt Rose had told me you were planning to serve at Royaumont Abbey the last time I was on the island, but that was back in December."

"Do you have news?" Ellen asked. "You must tell me everything. Letters from Aunt Rose only get through rarely."

"I'll tell you all I know," Lucas said, and glanced around as if looking for chairs.

"I was just going out," Ellen told him. "To the nearby village, Asnières-sur-Oise. Why don't you come with me? If you have time…"

"I'm not due back to London until the day after tomorrow."

"There's a little café in the village. It's nothing much, just a few tables and chairs in someone's front room. But Madame Loisel makes some lovely cakes, and there's usually coffee." Even if it was made with old grounds or even acorns.

"All right," Lucas said, and Ellen fetched her hat and cloak before they set off into a warm summer's afternoon.

It felt so strange and yet also bizarrely right to walk with Lucas along the dirt road that led to the small village a few miles from the abbey. Bumblebees flew lazily through the air, landing on the poppies and wildflowers that grew by the side of the road, and the only sound was their drone and the rustling of the wind through the trees.

"If I close my eyes," Ellen said, "I can almost believe we're back on the island, walking by the pond between our houses."

"I don't even have to close my eyes," Lucas answered as he smiled and looked down at her. "You haven't changed a bit, Ellen."

"Oh, I have," Ellen protested. She lifted a hand to her cheek, conscious of how tired and worn out she must look. She'd lost weight since she'd begun nursing; although the food at the Abbey was more plentiful than in other places, the hours and exertion and the hasty meals she managed had left her a little gaunt. "I'm not a young girl anymore, Lucas." She would be twenty-four in October. Most women her age, back on Amherst Island at least, were married with several children already.

"And I'm not a young man," Lucas agreed. "But you still don't look any different to me." His smile lingered on her, like the warmth of the sun.

They waited until they were settled in the front room of Madame Loisel's house, with cups of weak coffee and pastries, before they spoke properly.

"So tell me all the news from the island," Ellen said as she took a sip of coffee. She studied Lucas over the rim of her cup; he looked dashing in his uniform, but older too. There were new lines around his eyes and mouth, and his light brown hair had a few faint streaks of gray by the temples, even though he was only twenty-four.

"I don't know how up to date my news is," Lucas answered. "Many of the island boys joined up with the First Expeditionary Force in 1915—me and Jed, of course, and the Tyler twins, Andrew Parton…"

"But you're not with them now, are you?" Ellen asked. "Aunt Rose told me you'd been doing something in London."

"I was commandeered to join a specialist operation in the spring," Lucas told her. "And I'm afraid, at this point, I can't tell you more than that."

Ellen eyed him mischievously. "It sounds quite intriguing."

"I like the work," Lucas admitted. "As for the island boys… Jed's made it through all right so far, thank God. He took a bullet in the shoulder at Ypres, but it was only a flesh wound and he was back on the Front in a couple of weeks. Some of the other boys didn't do so well."

"They didn't?" Ellen's heart sank as she thought of the young boys she'd gone to school with, so many years ago. Six thousand had died at Ypres, she remembered Norah telling her.

"Andrew Parton died at Ypres, from that wretched gas. One of the Tyler twins was wounded at Artois. I don't know about the others." He paused and said, "Have you heard from Rose about Peter?"

"Yes, he's enlisted." She shook her head. Tousle-haired, impish Peter, now a soldier. It was terrible to imagine. "I hate to think of little Peter out in the trenches," she admitted, "even though I know he's not little anymore. I've frozen the island and everyone there in my mind, but they've all moved on, of course. It's just been so long."

"It has," Lucas agreed. "We've missed you, Ellen." A faint blush touched his cheeks and he took another sip of coffee as he avoided her gaze.

"Have you been back often, Lucas? Before the war? I don't even know what your news is." She paused uncertainly and then plunged ahead, resolute. "You wrote me back in 1914, before the war started, that you'd met someone…"

Lucas stared at her in surprise. "Met someone?"

"A girl, I mean," Ellen said, and now she was blushing. "In Toronto. I remember you said she was someone special…"

Lucas shook her head, his mouth tightening. "There never was anyone in Toronto, Ellen."

"But I remember," Ellen insisted. "You said there was a young lady of interest, I'm sure of it…"

Lucas gazed at her, frowning for a moment before his expression cleared and he laughed, the sound a bit hollow. "Oh, Ellen, that was a joke. I was talking about the dog my landlady had. She'd been delivered of puppies, and I took one."

Dimly Ellen remembered some reference to a dog in the letter, and she laughed in embarrassment. "I must have misread it completely. I just wanted you to be happy, I suppose."

"Buttons was a good dog," Lucas said. "I brought her back to the island when I enlisted. Dad still has her."

"And Jed?" Ellen asked after a moment that felt thick with memories. She'd tried to keep her voice light, casual, but she had a feeling Lucas was not fooled. "How is he? And Louisa? And their little boy?"

"I haven't seen much of him since the war started, to be honest. After I left the battalion we met up in London once when he was on leave. And you know Jed. He's not much of one for letters."

"And Louisa? Have you heard anything about her?"

"Dad wrote to tell me she went back to Seaton in the spring, with Thomas. She wanted to be with her parents, I suppose."

"Oh, I see. Aunt Rose must have written me before that happened." Although she could understand it, Ellen thought it a bit disloyal of Louisa to the island, to leave it as soon as Jed had gone.

"Truth be told," Lucas said, "I don't know if Louisa will ever come back from Seaton. She never settled there, as much as she tried, although I don't know how much that was."

"Rose seemed to think she was—"

"Rose has always seen the best in everyone. Louisa wasn't made for island life. She'd always find it a trial."

"And if she stays in Seaton…?"

"There is a job for Jed at her father's bank, apparently. I think he might be willing to take it, for her sake, as well as Thomas'. He's not a particularly strong child, and there is better medical care in Seaton than on the island."

Ellen nodded slowly. In which case, who knew when she'd ever see either of them again? It all felt so strangely and sadly distant.

"And what about you, Ellen?" Lucas asked. "You've been nursing here in France since the war started, I know, and your Aunt Rose told me you were set to take a teaching post at the School of Art back in Glasgow. Will you do that when the war is finished?"

"I don't know," Ellen admitted. Glasgow seemed almost as far away as Amherst Island; it was too far to travel on her few leaves. She'd had a few letters from Ruby, who was busy with the war effort, and knew that she and Dougie were managing all right, but other than that… "I can't imagine what life is going to be like after the war. What any of us are going to do."

"Celebrate, I hope, as best as we can."

Ellen shook her head, her smile turning sad. "I suppose we will have to try. If there's anything left to celebrate."

Lucas leaned forward and covered her hand with his own, his hazel eyes glinting with determination. "There will be, Ellen. I'm sure of it. It might take some time to find our happiness again, *ourselves* again, but we will. You certainly will. Look at how much you've experienced already. You're a survivor, Ellen." He squeezed her hand and Ellen smiled.

"I suppose I am a survivor," she said slowly. She thought of the days nursing her Mam in Springburn, and then the trip to America when she'd been so full of hope, and the deep disappointment of her father's abandonment and Aunt Ruth's chilly welcome. And then losing Jed… and dear Henry… yes, she'd survived it all, and perhaps she was even stronger for it. "I think I want to hope for more than survival," she said at last. "Everyone has been just subsisting for so long, ploughing through the days to get to the end of this wretched war. I hope happiness might be in our grasp again, one day. I hope it is for you as well, Lucas."

"Well." Lucas smiled wryly and removed his hand from hers; Ellen found she missed its comforting warmth. "I hope so, too." He looked away, not seeming to want to meet her eye, and with a lurch, Ellen wondered if he still felt something for her. Surely not, after all these years, and yet the realization gave her a foolish little flicker of disappointment that she knew she had no right to feel.

"Will you go back to Toronto when the war is over?" Ellen asked. "To your law practice?"

"I suppose so," Lucas answered. "It depends what Jed and Louisa do. Dad will need help on the farm, if they end up in Vermont."

"I can't see Jed as a banker," Ellen admitted. "And I can't see you as a farmer, to tell the truth. You've always liked your books."

"And you your pencils." He leaned forward, his expression turning intent. "I do hope you go back to Glasgow, Ellen. You've done so much there, and I think you'd make a wonderful drawing instructor. Don't give up on your dreams. This war will be over one day, and we'll be able to go back—not to the way things were, but perhaps even something better, because we know what tragedy looks like. It will enable us to enjoy what we might once have taken for granted."

"That's a nice thought." Ellen sipped her coffee, mulling over Lucas' words. *Had* she given up on her dreams? The trouble was, perhaps, she didn't know what her dreams were anymore. To live as a Lady Artist in Glasgow, giving lectures and attending gallery openings? Ruby and Dougie would be waiting for her there, and a scattering of friends from school. But even after three years in Glasgow, it still didn't feel like home, now that she was so far away from it, and the drive to paint or draw had left her entirely. "I don't know what I'll do," she said. "Do you know, I haven't drawn a thing since I arrived in Royaumont? I haven't so much as picked up a pencil." Even though she'd packed several sketchbooks and pencils. Norah had found inspiration at Royaumont; during their quieter moments, she'd sketched and painted, and was hoping to exhibit several after the war.

Why, Ellen wondered, had she not been able to access that same wellspring of creativity? There were so many things she could have sketched… a wounded soldier reading a letter in bed, a faint smile on his face… a nurse holding a man's hand, only to realize he'd already died… the way the sun streamed through the tall windows, gilding everything and making even the buckets of dirty, blood-soaked bandages look strangely beautiful. The fields of poppies, their blowsy red heads dancing in the wind. She'd drawn none of it.

"You haven't had time," Lucas suggested. "That's entirely understandable…"

"Oh, I've had time," Ellen assured him. "Life at Royaumont has always been in fits and starts. We'll have a mad rush and no one will sleep for a week, and then it's days, or even weeks, of peace afterwards, almost like a holiday." She frowned as she mulled it over in her mind. "It's not even that I can't, although that's part of it, I suppose. It's that I don't want to."

Lucas frowned. "But why not?"

"Because some things are too painful to draw." She thought of *Starlit Sea,* and how that had plumbed the depths of her grief over Henry and transferred it to the canvas. Yet that grief seemed so personal and even petty compared to what she'd seen and experienced now. How could she reduce so many men's unbearable suffering into a picture people might admire? How could she cheapen their sacrifice by turning it into some silly little scene? "Some things can't be drawn," she finished, and after a moment Lucas nodded slowly.

"Yes," he said, his voice quiet and thoughtful. "I do think you're right."

Lucas paid for their coffees and pastries and they walked back to the abbey, the day still drowsy and warm.

When they arrived back at Royaumont, they found things in surprising and delightful uproar.

"The *poilus* have revolted!" Elsie, one of the orderlies, exclaimed. "They're taking over the hospital and are insisting on a garden party."

"What?" Ellen exclaimed, laughing.

Elsie pointed at Lucas, her eyes sparkling with both merriment and determination. "Every able-bodied man is commandeered to stay and help! We're bringing the tables outside."

"What on earth?" Lucas looked mystified.

"It's not all sorrow and suffering here at Royaumont," Ellen told him with a smile. "We have fun sometimes, too."

"At a hospital?" Lucas sounded doubtful.

"Yes, even at a hospital. Like I said, it's fits and starts—a mad rush when we have wounded coming in, but now it's just convalescents and the men want to have fun." Feeling suddenly light-hearted, Ellen reached for his hand. "Why don't you join us? After all, we do need every able-bodied man."

Laughing a little, Lucas shrugged. "All right, then. I suppose I'd like to see what you sisters get up to!"

It was a perfect afternoon for a garden party, with the air just starting to cool and the sun gilding everything. Laughingly, Lucas helped a few orderlies lug the two long trestle tables from the refectory out into the abbey garden.

"Our chef, Michelet, has made a cake," Elsie told Ellen. "Isn't he a marvel?"

"A cake? Where on earth did he find the sugar?" Ellen exclaimed.

"Who knows? We don't ask."

Soon enough, they had all assembled outside, Michelet's impressive cake the centerpiece on the table, complete with chocolate layers and fondant icing. There was tea and platters of biscuits, plates of cold sausage, as well as bread and cheese, and the daintiest little *tarte Tatins* that Michelet had conjured from old, dried apples. Even though Ellen had already had cake and coffee at Madame Loisel's, she couldn't resist all the offerings, and neither could Lucas.

After the food, they cleared the tables away for dancing, with several soldiers seeming to produce instruments out of thin air. They had a harmonica and a little flute and a violin, and it was enough to get everyone who could up on their feet.

Ellen couldn't remember laughing so much, as she whirled from smiling soldier to smiling soldier, finally finding herself partnering Lucas.

"This is quite the most fun I've had all war," he exclaimed as they danced up and down the aisle made by clapping couples.

"For me, as well," Ellen agreed as he spun her around.

Finally, as the stars came out in sparkling pinpoints against the velvety night sky, some of the nurses chivvied the men back to their beds, and Lucas helped to lug the tables back inside, while Ellen and others took all the tea things back to the kitchen. Her muscles ached from dancing and laughing, so different from the way her neck and shoulders usually tensed, standing next to Miss Ivens in theater, or carrying pails of water or piles of blankets.

This was a pleasant ache, an ache that made her remember how much fun life could be.

"It's too late for me to catch the train back to Paris," Lucas said wryly when he found her in the kitchen. "Your CMO has said I can stay here."

"Oh, Miss Ivens? That was kind of her." Ellen smiled at him. "It won't put a dent in your plans?"

"No, I'm not due back at HQ until the day after tomorrow. As long as the trains keep running, I should be all right."

"As long as the Germans don't blow up the lines," Ellen said, only half-joking. "We're farther away from the fighting now, but when I first arrived in France, we were stuck in Paris for days because the track had been blown up."

"Yes, it can be quite a challenge to move around France. Once it felt as if we'd traversed half the country to get from Paris to Senlis." He smiled down at her. "I'm glad I stayed."

Later, when Lucas had been settled in one of the spare rooms and Ellen had retired to the small room she shared with two other nurses, the questions came.

"So who is that dashing Yankee?" one of the nurses, Charlotte, teased. "They make them right across the pond, don't they?"

"He's Canadian, not a Yankee," Ellen said as she unpinned her hair. "And he's just a friend."

"Are you quite certain about that?" Rosemary, the other nurse, asked. "It looked to me as if he couldn't take his eyes off you."

"Nonsense," Elle murmured, but she felt herself start to blush. Lucas hadn't been that attentive, she was quite sure of it, but now that both Charlotte and Rosemary were asking questions, she found herself starting to wonder. "We're old family friends," she said, as much to herself as to the other women. "And we hadn't seen each other in several years. That's all it was."

"And is that all you want it to be?" Charlotte asked shrewdly.

"Yes," Ellen answered automatically, because that had always been her answer when it came to Lucas, because of Jed…

But Jed was married now, with a wife and son. And Lucas…

No, she couldn't possibly be thinking that way about Lucas. She was just starting to doubt herself because she'd been alone for so long, and it had been so wonderful to see a familiar face again. She was confusing affection with something deeper, something she'd never felt for Lucas, and it wasn't fair to either of them to entertain such thoughts, even for a moment.

"Yes, it really is," she said firmly, and both Charlotte and Rosemary both laughed.

"You keep telling yourself that, Ellen," Rosemary said as she stripped down to her shift and settled on her thin straw mattress. "Perhaps eventually you will believe it."

Ellen lay on her mattress, her hair sticking to her pillow, the air stifling and still. Outside, a full, clear moon shone down on the gardens and meadows and for once the guns didn't boom in the distance; everything was peaceful and quiet.

Even so, it took a long time for Ellen to get to sleep.

The next morning, as she came down for duty, she found Lucas finishing a cup of coffee in the refectory, clearly making to leave.

"I'm glad I saw you before I had to leave," he said as he stood up to greet her. "One of your ambulance drivers is taking me to the station at Viarmes."

"So soon?" Ellen blurted before she could think of it.

"I need to get back," Lucas said apologetically.

"Of course, of course, I'm sorry, I didn't mean…" She shook her head. "It's just been so lovely to see you."

"And you." He arched an eyebrow, smiling in that affectionate old way of his. "Will you walk me out?"

"Yes, of course." Ellen ignored the speculative and even knowing looks of the other nurses and orderlies in the refectory as she accompanied Lucas outside.

Their steps slowed as they came to the front door of the abbey; Ellen had an urge to postpone the moment of farewell, fearing she might cry.

She turned to Lucas, smiling even as she blinked back the sting of tears. "I can't tell you how good it has been to see you, Lucas. You've been such a balm. I've missed the island so much, and it's been so long…"

"It's been too long." Lucas smiled back at her. "I'll write you, Ellen, now that I know for certain where you are. And I hope you'll write me. I'll give you my address in London where letters can reach me. I'm not always there, but I should get them eventually." He took out a stub of pencil and a scrap of paper and scribbled for a moment before handing it to her. Ellen tucked it into the pocket of her apron.

"I will write," she promised, and Lucas took hold of her hands, clasping them loosely.

"Don't forget me, Ellen," he said softly and he leaned forward and kissed her cheek. His lips were surprisingly soft even as the faint whiskers on his jaw scratched her cheek. He smelled of soap and coffee. She closed her eyes, savoring the moment, trying not to cry. She didn't want to say goodbye; she didn't want to see him go.

With one last squeeze, Lucas released her hands and stepped back. She gazed at him, wanting to memorize his features and hold in her heart how dashing he looked in his uniform—and yet still so wonderfully familiar and dear. The terrible thought that she might never see him again seized her by the throat and for a moment she couldn't speak.

"Goodbye, Ellen," Lucas said and Ellen managed to choke out,

"Goodbye, Lucas."

She stayed outside by the door and watched him as he walked all the way down the lane, sunlight touching his hair with bronze, and then he disappeared around the corner as sunshine bathed the meadows and hills around the abbey in golden light.

CHAPTER EIGHTEEN

July 1916

The shrill bleat of the porter's horn startled Ellen awake from an uneasy sleep as, around her, Rosemary and Charlotte started to pull on their uniforms.

The guns had been blasting non-stop for nearly a week, the arcs of light of the artillery turning the night sky to fire. Even the windowpanes had rattled, and it seemed as if it would never end, the constant sound putting everyone on edge.

Then, finally, there was silence, blessed and awful, because now that the shelling had stopped, the assault would begin. It seemed almost as if a hush had stolen over the world, expectant and dreadful. The Battle of the Somme, as it would later be known, had begun.

There had not been a great offensive since the Battle of Verdun in March, and the hospital had been lulled into a false sense of peace, as snow had blanketed the meadows around the abbey and the convalescing soldiers had amused themselves with games and cards. Lucien Allard had left Royaumont in September 1915, and Letitia refused to speak about it. Ellen chose not to press. Whatever had or had not happened between the two of them, it had clearly been very painful.

Christmas that year had been a surprisingly jolly affair; the army bakery in Boran donated a large tree that they decorated with what ribbons and candles they could find and set up in the refectory. Christmas dinner was a feast prepared by the wondrous Michelet, and someone had rustled up a box of Christmas crackers from who knew where.

That jollity seemed far away now, as the porter's horn sounded not once or twice but four times—every ambulance the hospital possessed had gone to Creil and come back full of wounded.

"Quickly, now," someone called from the corridor, and Ellen and her roommates hurried to pin hair and put on caps before going downstairs to greet whatever awaited them.

The night was sultry and sticky, the air thick with both humidity and fear as the ambulances pulled up in front of the abbey, one after the other. Ellen started forward to help; as usual, the men who could, walked; the men who couldn't were either helped or carried on stretchers, and Ellen and the other nurses performed triage, to see who needed care most urgently.

After two and a half years at Royaumont, Ellen had thought she was accustomed to the sight of wounded, the many grievous injuries, the men wheezing and choking from the awful chlorine gas, the mangled arms and legs, the missing fingers and toes. But nothing had prepared her for the unending stream of wounded humanity that came through the abbey's doors that night, man after man, moaning, mangled, faces filled with shock and horror and pain. They came from everywhere—French, British, Canadian, a desperate flood as all the auxiliary hospitals in France were filled to overflowing.

Soon, stretchers lined the halls as beds were filled and more moved into the refectory to create another emergency ward. Miss Ivens and the other surgeons worked through the night, as the lights flickered on and off, trying to save as many men as they could. No one slept.

Ellen found herself retreating into an emotional and physical numbness that felt like the only way to survive as she tended as many men as she could, knowing they were only likely to die.

"The new steel helmets are meant to keep them from head injuries, aren't they?" Charlotte said bitterly as another man with his head half-blown away moaned in a bed, destined to live only hours, if that.

Ellen did not reply; all her energy and focus had to be on the wounded, and more than ever she was aware of how little they could do. Even Miss Ivens, with her surgical skill, was limited by her equipment and medical supplies, and the fact that many men had been lying in a battlefield for hours before they'd been taken to the clearing station, and then on to the train to Creil, before finally arriving at Royaumont. For far too many of them, it was just too late.

Twenty-four hours passed without anyone going off duty or having a wink of sleep, and still the men kept coming. It seemed as if the ambulance returned the moment they left, disgorging more and more wounded.

"There's no room," Norah cried, as she carried another stretcher in with the help of another orderly. The halls were stacked with men on stretchers or even just lying on the floor. "Where do we put them?"

"The less injured ones can share beds," the matron said shortly. "That's all we can do."

The soldiers were beautifully acquiescent, insisting on giving their blankets to those who needed them more, gladly sharing the already narrow beds, even making jokes, when everything in Ellen ached and screamed that this was wrong, it was evil, it was *senseless*.

Still it went on. Day after day, the ambulances left and brought back more wounded, wounded they could accommodate only because enough had died that the beds were now free. Eight days passed in this manner, with the staff only getting an hour or two of sleep at a time, if that.

By the time the last rush stopped, Ellen was so tired, she felt as if she were existing in some strange bubble, everything distant and wavering, as if viewed through a glass. The reports had started to come in, along with the men—sixty thousand British casualties on the first day alone, twenty thousand Canadians. The French casualties had been less, thanks to their heavy artillery that captured more ground.

With the reports of all the losses came the senseless stories that Ellen couldn't bear—the gas canisters that exploded in the trenches before they could be fired, maiming many horribly. The artillery that had bombarded the enemy for days but tragically fallen too short of their deeper trenches. The tanks, used for the first time in the war, that had broken down before they could be any use. Together it all seemed like a litany of failure and disaster, but the soldiers she spoke to remained firm.

"We did the best we could, and we'll always best the Germans."

"Yes, of course we will," Ellen said, because she could not imagine anything else. Yet in the privacy of her own bleak thoughts, she wondered how long the war would go on. It had been nearly three years, and they were no closer than they'd been at the beginning, as far as she could tell. France was still a muddy no man's land of barbed wire and trenches; a few yards taken or lost, depending on the day. And millions of men dead or wounded; by the end of November, when the Somme offensive had finally ended, it was said that over a million men had died in it since July.

Thankfully, Lucas and Jed were not among that terrible number. Ellen received a letter from Lucas just before Christmas 1916, assuring her that he was well and that Jed had fought in the Somme but survived. Aunt Rose wrote as well, telling her that Peter was well, the last she'd heard, at the end of November. Ellen was thankful that the men closest to her had been spared, even as she wondered if they actually had.

More and more, it was becoming clear to the staff at Royaumont that the men whose bodies were not badly wounded had minds that were.

"War neurosis, they call it," Letitia explained flatly while she and Ellen were having a tea break. Outside, the ground was iron hard, the trees stark and bare, and despite the coal stove emitting a cheering warmth, the abbey refectory was freezing. "No one knows what causes it, really. At first they said it was being near the exploding shells—but men who aren't on the Front line have experienced it, as well."

Ellen shook her head slowly. "It's so terrible to see." She'd found men moaning in their beds, in the grip of a nightmare that seemed all too real. Other men were deaf or blind or mute, sometimes all three, lost in a paralyzed world of their own.

"The thousand-yard stare, they call it," Letitia said when Ellen had described a soldier who, although physically fit, could not eat or drink, speak or listen. "Poor souls. They won't get the sympathy the man with a mangled leg will get, but in their own way they're just as wounded."

All too often, such men were deemed physically fit and forced to return to the Front, although some shook and wept and begged not to be. Ellen's heart twisted with pity at the sight of the poor wretches, whose minds had been wrecked by this terrible war, even if their bodies hadn't.

Those who were not considered well enough in mind as well as body were sent to convalescent homes back in Britain, with the faint whiff of shame about them, as if they hadn't been strong enough to stand what other men could.

"I don't think anyone is strong enough," Norah said savagely after a young boy, only nineteen years old, had been forced back to the Front. "No one should be. No one should be asked to endure what these men must, day after bloody day."

And yet they did, and the war continued on, the Front moving farther and farther from Royaumont, so by the spring of 1917 the rushes of the Somme seemed almost—but not quite—like a distant memory, as Royaumont became more of a convalescent home than a casualty clearing station.

One day in June, Miss Ivens called all the staff together in the massive refectory; Ellen sat on a hard wooden bench, fanning herself, for although it was early in the summer, it was already hot, the grass outside bleached yellow, the air inside stifling and still. Miss Ivens stood in front of the forty women gathered there, looking at each in turn.

"As you know," she began, "we have been investigating the possibility of organizing an advance casualty clearing station that is closer to the Front."

Ellen knew that Royaumont's status as a convalescent home rather than a military hospital frustrated Miss Ivens no end; they had the capability to deal with the most serious of cases, and had also pioneered some new innovations with X-ray treatment of those affected by the dreadful new mustard gas, or "Hun Stuff" as it was known. None of it was useful, however, when the soldier would have to travel so far to obtain it.

Miss Ivens had already explained how having access to early operative treatment was shown to greatly improve the soldiers' mortality rates, and reduce the cases of gas gangrene that they'd seen at Royaumont so depressingly often, and so she was determined to be able to provide it.

"I have looked at various sites over the course of the spring," Miss Ivens continued, "and we have finally found one that is deemed suitable. Therefore, in a few weeks' time, I will be sending a team to Villers-Cotterêts to begin to prepare an advance casualty clearing station. Anyone who wishes to be part of this new endeavor may speak to me regarding the opportunity."

Everyone was buzzing with the news as Miss Ivens dismissed them. Ellen glanced at Norah, whose face was alight with interest. Norah was always someone who liked to be leading a charge;

Ellen had no doubt her former landlady and mentor would be keen to do so at Villers-Cotterêts.

Ellen saw Letitia walking quickly away and went to catch up with her. Although Lucien Allard had left eighteen months ago, Ellen knew her friend felt his absence sorely. She still had not got to the bottom of why things had never happened between the two; she was hesitant to ask Letitia about it.

"Do you think many people will want to go to this new place?" she asked now. "I've been at Royaumont so long, it almost feels like home. I can't imagine going elsewhere."

"I suspect some people will relish the new challenge. And it *will* be a challenge," Letitia answered with a shrug. "I heard from Mrs. Berry that the place they've chosen is little better than a few sheds. It used to be an evacuation center, and it is right beside a railway station. They've got oil-papered windows and composition roofs."

Ellen thought of the abbey with its lovely cloisters and gracious rooms. Filled with rubble and dust at the start admittedly, but even when it had been a mess, the abbey had always been a beautiful place, a refuge from the horror of war.

"At least it will be convenient, so close to the station," Ellen offered.

"Yes, there is a covered walkway between the station and the buildings. Very convenient," Letitia's mouth twisted. "Perhaps I shall put my name forward. Miss Ivens is looking for several doctors, along with nursing sisters and orderlies."

"You're thinking of going?" Ellen said in surprise. For some reason, she had thought Letitia would stay in Royaumont, as she had been planning to do.

Letitia gave her a swift, sharp look. "Why shouldn't I?"

"I don't know… I thought perhaps you'd want to be where you could hear news…"

"News of whom?"

Ellen decided to go ahead and say it. "Of Lieutenant Allard. I've seen from the envelopes in the hall that he writes you on occasion."

Letitia's lips twisted. "You think I should stay back just for a few letters?"

"Someone has to stay. Royaumont still needs to be staffed."

"True enough, but I think I'd like a distraction."

"What happened, Letitia?" Ellen asked gently. "It's been so long since Lieutenant Allard left, and it seemed… for a little while… as if you both cared for each other."

"We did," Letitia answered after a moment, not looking at Ellen. "But it wasn't enough."

"But why not?" Ellen cried. "I know his amputation was a hard thing, but surely—"

"Oh Ellen, you have no idea." Letitia passed a hand over her face as she shook her head wearily. "Lucien has been in the army since he was twenty-one. He has only had an active life."

"He can adjust—"

"His father was in the army as well. And life in Algiers is hard—"

"You aren't one ever to shrink from a challenge—"

"Perhaps it isn't up to me," she said rather sharply.

"What do you mean?"

Letitia was silent for a long moment, her hand still covering her eyes. "He refused me," she finally bit out, and dropped her hand. She let out a broken laugh at Ellen's look of shock. "No, I don't shrink from a challenge, do I?" she said, her voice ragged and a little wild. "I asked him to marry me, Ellen. Can you imagine that? The scandal of it? I asked, and he said no. He said he wouldn't tie me to a cripple." She looked away, setting her jaw even as she blinked back tears.

"Oh Letitia," Ellen whispered. "I am so sorry."

"So am I," Letitia said in a hard voice. "So am I. He still writes, but only as a brother or a friend, and in truth those letters tear me up inside, because I don't see him that way, and never will. So now perhaps you can understand why I might put my name forward to go to Villers-Cotterêts."

Letitia and Norah, along with several other doctors, nurses, and orderlies, left for Villers-Cotterêts in late July. Ellen hugged Letitia goodbye, knowing she would miss her but also accepting that a change would be good for her friend.

As the hot, muggy summer started to give way to a crisp, clear autumn, and as the abbey was still far from the fighting, over the next few weeks Ellen had some leisurely days walking through the meadows surrounding the abbey, enjoying the strange interlude of peace amidst so much war and devastation, and yet still feeling as if the whole world was waiting, longing for the end of this war… and yet what then?

"For we know that the whole creation groaneth and travaileth in pain together until now," Miss Ivens quoted scripture with one of her wry, whimsical smiles, while she and Ellen were sitting in the refectory, having a cup of tea. "It does feel as if even the earth is groaning, does it not?" she asked as her smiled turned sad. "As if it is the end of the world."

It wasn't like her indomitable leader to wax so philosophical. Ellen raised her eyebrows. "Perhaps not the end of the world, Miss Ivens, but hopefully the end of the war."

"I fear they are one and the same. Oh, yes, we want an end to this dreadful fighting, of course we do. No more senseless killing, no more clouds of that dreadful gas, no more men with that terrible, terrible stare." She paused, her face drawn into stark lines. "But what then, Ellen? What then? I cannot imagine how the world will cope and recover, with an entire generation maimed, mangled, destroyed." She shook her head. "I'm old enough that

I feel I've had my time. It will be your generation that must learn to soldier on, when there is no longer any war."

Her words reverberated through Ellen as the weeks slipped by and the war lumbered on; what would she do when it finally finished? She could not imagine going back to Glasgow; she could not imagine going anywhere else. It was as if life would cease when the guns did, but she knew, or at least she hoped, it would be a beginning. Heaven knew everyone needed one.

Letitia wrote her long letters about life at Villers-Cotterêts:

> We are only five miles from Soissons, which is under fire. The noise of the guns seems like it shall bring the walls right down, and you can see the searchlights at night even though we are not all that far from Paris. We have talked of planting a garden if we're still here in the spring, which it seems we will be. Before the war, Mrs. Berry was a farmer's wife, and her expertise is standing us in good stead.

In October, Letitia wrote that a Canadian camp was near the hospital, and the officers had come over to visit. Ellen's heart lurched to think of Letitia perhaps meeting Jed, but she did not ask her friend the names of the officers who came to Villers-Cotterêts. She did not even know if Jed *was* an officer; perhaps he had been promoted to an NCO, but as he was obviously not looking for her, she hardly felt she could go looking for him, something that saddened her.

She hadn't seen Lucas since that charmed afternoon when they'd had the garden party more than two years ago, although he'd written many times. She longed to see a familiar island face, but Lucas was in London, Jed hadn't been in touch, and Peter was fighting too far away, at Passchendaele.

A few months later, a glorious, golden autumn gave way to a hard, cold winter. January 1918 was the coldest month Ellen had ever known; at night, the nurses' hair froze to their pillows, and their rubber boots to the floor. When the cook spilled hot water on the floor of the kitchen, it had frozen within minutes. Ellen couldn't remember ever being so bone-numbingly cold, and she knew it had to be much worse for the men in the trenches, with only frozen ground to sleep on. At least it saved them from the mud.

And then the German offensive began again, and life as Ellen had come to know it changed completely. Royaumont, a peaceful oasis for months now, became the center of action again as it was once more at the front of the fighting.

Bombs fell on Paris and some landed so close to the abbey that the windows blew in, scattering broken glass across the wards, so Ellen had to carefully pick up dangerous shards from the patients' bedclothes.

The fields and meadows that surrounded the abbey, once so pleasant and pastoral, a refuge from the horror of war, were now cut through with trenches, the green grass flattened, with jagged gashes crisscrossing the earth. When accompanying a driver to Creil, Ellen saw the craters made by bombs only a few hundred yards from the abbey, and even more unsettling, the endless stream of war refugees, women and children who carried all their worldly belongings in ragged, cloth-wrapped bundles, tragedy and grief etched in hard lines on their faces. This was the terrible reality of war, the ugly, scarred face of it, and it made her tremble.

How long? she wondered silently. *How long would this horror last?*

Troops and guns streamed along the dirt road too, so the refugees had to step aside or scatter, as the military rumbled towards the ever-shifting front line. Royaumont, which had been a backwater only weeks ago, had become part of the war's Front.

The quiet life Ellen had become pleasantly accustomed to was now a thing of the past, as was sleep. The Germans made one push after another, desperate attempts to keep themselves going, especially now that America had entered the war.

As wounded came continually into Royaumont, which had been officially recognized as a casualty clearing station, Ellen worked eighteen- or twenty-hour days, sometimes snatching no sleep at all before she was making her rounds again. When she did manage to crawl up to her bed, she was often woken by the screaming of the sirens or the distant crash and thunder of the bombs falling on Paris, although after a while, some desperate and exhausted part of her brain was able to drown it all out; it simply became the backdrop of everyday life, as common a sound as birdsong or the breeze in the trees.

Every bed in the hospital was occupied, with fifty wounded or more coming in every day. Convalescents were shipped out as quickly as they safely could be, to make room for the more seriously injured, and men with the "thousand-yard stare" were given less consideration and compassion than they had been before, much to Ellen's regret. There simply was no space.

The eighth of April was Royaumont's busiest day yet, with over eighty operations performed, and nearly two hundred wounded admitted. Even Miss Ivens looked ready to drop, her face haggard, although her eyes remained bright, her gait as brisk and determined as ever, as if she would take on the entire German army if she could. "It won't be much longer," she kept insisting. "Surely it won't be much longer."

Ellen tried to match her supervisor's stride and smile, for the patients' sake if nothing else. The men who came to Royaumont were, she saw, broken in both body and spirit in a way they hadn't been before. The war had simply gone on too long; the bonhomie, the camaraderie, the fighting spirit… all of it was flagging, and it was no wonder. God willing, it wouldn't be much longer, but sometimes another day felt like too long.

"I forget what I was like, before the war," one soldier told her as she changed the dressing on the stump of arm he had left. "So I don't suppose it matters that I've lost a hand, since I don't remember who I was."

"I'm not sure I remember who I was," Ellen told him with a sympathetic smile. "And even if I did, I couldn't go back to being that person."

"That's it exactly, Sister," the man said, looking relieved that she'd been able to put his feelings into words. "You can't go back, even if you wanted to." His eyes clouded as he looked at his bandaged arm. "The trouble is, will everyone else want us to?"

Ellen patted his shoulder, knowing she had no real words of wisdom to offer. Like Miss Ivens, like everyone, as the end of the war hovered ahead like a mirage, he was wondering what the future could possibly hold for the likes of him, or for anyone.

In the middle of May, the Germans' offensive relented and the stream of patients thankfully lessened to a trickle. Miss Ivens suggested Ellen and a few others go up to Villers-Cotterêts for a rest, as the field hospital had not experienced nearly the rush that Royaumont had, and was now more of an oasis of calm, as the abbey had once been.

"It seems strange to be going to what was meant to be the forward station for a rest," Ellen told Charlotte wryly as she packed her one small bag. "But there you are. The map of war is being continually redrawn, like a child scribbling over his picture."

"I wish everyone would just leave it alone," Charlotte answered with a sigh. "Four years on and you'd think one side would have made more progress than the other, but I fear we're no closer to anything than we were at the beginning."

Ellen grimaced. "It's terrible to think about, especially when you think of all the men who have lost their lives." She sighed tiredly, not wanting to give in to the discouragement that always loomed.

Charlotte clapped a hand on her shoulder. "You'll feel better with a rest," she said bracingly.

"Yes—although it's not that much of a rest. Villers-Cotterêts is still an operating hospital!" Ellen smiled wryly. "Letitia has written to tell me of all the cases they are receiving."

"Not like here, though."

"No," Ellen agreed with a sigh as she thought of the crowded wards, the blown-in windows, the endless sound of the guns. "Not like here."

One of the ambulance drivers, Iris, drove her to Creil, along with a truckload of convalescents, where she caught the train to Villers-Cotterêts.

"Say hello to everyone for us!" Iris called gaily, determined to keep her spirits up. "Don't have too much fun, darling."

Ellen laughed and rolled her eyes. "Cocktails and dancing every night," she teased. "Just as if we were in Paris!"

CHAPTER NINETEEN

"I can't tell you how good it is to see you!"

Letitia embraced Ellen warmly as soon as she'd stepped off the train. As she hugged her friend, Ellen could feel how thin and gaunt Letitia had become. But then she supposed she was just as thin; the recent rush of patients had left little time for eating or sleeping, and food was scarce anyway, and had been for over a year.

"It's not as gracious as the abbey," Letitia told her, linking arms as they walked along the covered walkway from the station to the hospital just a short stroll away. "But it is very convenient, as you'd said! So close to the station… no porter's horns necessary. We're right here."

"Yes, indeed," Ellen murmured.

After the ancient elegance of Royaumont, the sight of the basic sheds that comprised the hospital was a bit jarring. The exposed elevation meant the buildings were constantly swept by the wind and the roofs and windows rattled like coins in a tin. It was as different from the huge, soaring space of the abbey, the quiet and peace found in its ancient walls, as could be possible.

Still, Ellen felt a certain relief as she settled into work at Villers-Cotterêts; the trickle of patients was nothing like the rush she'd experienced at Royaumont, when her mind and body had both been pushed to the brink of exhaustion. She and Letitia were able to take an afternoon off and walk up to the forest that skirted the village and have a picnic of bread and cheese among the pasqueflowers that grew there in abundance.

"You could almost believe there was no war here," Letitia said as she tilted her face to the sunlight. "Like back in the old days, before Royaumont was on the Front. Has it been terrible, Ellen?"

"The worst yet," Ellen admitted. "Worse even than the Somme rushes."

Letitia shook her head. "It's so hard, isn't it?"

"We must do our part. It's much harder on the soldiers."

"Still."

Ellen reclined against the sun-warmed grass, enjoying the sense of peace; the only sound was the lazy drone of a bumblebee. "It's so quiet here," she remarked. "I haven't heard a bomb falling since we arrived."

"Long may it last," Letitia said with a grim twist of her lips, her glance skittering away.

Impulsively, Ellen reached over and grabbed her friend's hand. "And how are you, Letitia? Are things… better for you at Villers-Cotterêts?"

Letitia shrugged and picked a flower, shredding its purple petals absently. "As good as they can be, I suppose," she said. "I like being busy and it's better… not to think about Lucien."

"Has he written recently?"

"No, and I have not written him for nearly a year now. It's better that way. Otherwise I'll get my hopes up, and what is the point of that?"

"Hope is what keeps everyone going, these days," Ellen objected with a small smile.

"Hope, or sheer bloody stamina? I'm not sure I know." Letitia tossed the ruined flower aside. "We should get back. A train is due to arrive this evening, and who knows how many wounded will be on it. Peace never lasts forever."

Letitia's words were true enough, for a train pulled in just a few hours later, and Ellen and the other staff were kept busy all through the night. By the next morning, the pressure had lessened a little, and Ellen was able to catch a few hours' sleep and have a wash, necessities which had started to feel like guilty pleasures.

Then, on the twenty-seventh of May, the Germans began a massive bombardment and the little hospital's few weeks of near-tranquility were shattered. Ellen had experienced nothing like it, not even during Royaumont's worst days, when the windows had blown in and it had felt as if the ground beneath them were shaking, the world ending.

This was a never-ending onslaught, the wounded and desperate refugees pouring into the hospital, the patients spilling out of the wards, too many to deal with beyond a cursory fashion. Desperately, Ellen moved from bed to bed, trying to staunch bleeding and bandage wounds as fast as she could, her fingers fumbling in her haste. At one point, one of the doctors, Dorothy Hayes, told her not to bother with the men who were sure to die in the next few hours; they didn't even get a bed, just lay on blankets or stretchers in the corridors, moaning piteously, if they could make any sound at all.

"We simply can't afford the time or the equipment on the dying," Dr. Hayes said in a low voice. "It's terrible, I know, for them to die alone and untended, especially in a hospital, but what else can we do? We're here for the living. We have to be."

Ellen knew she was right, but she could not keep from flinching and cringing with guilt when she passed by, some of them reaching out their hands and catching her skirt, pleading with her for something—a drop of water, a loving touch, an end to their pain. She could give them none of it.

"It feels like a circle of hell," Norah said, her lips pinched tight, as she stepped around a man in his death throes, his breath a rattle in his throat as his hands reached out in clawed desperation. "How can we live with ourselves? How will we ever forget this enough to go on?"

The questions remained unanswered even as they circled through Ellen's numbed mind. The continuous bombing had cut the electricity, and the doctors had to operate in the dark; Ellen held a candle over Dr. Logan's head, her arm trembling with the continuous effort, as she amputated a man's leg at the thigh and the sirens wailed, a never-ending shrieking in their ears, the shells crashing close enough to make the whole building shake.

"Miss Ivens sent me here for a *rest*," Ellen told Letitia in a gasp, during a few minutes' break, and then suddenly she was laughing as if she couldn't stop, her sides aching as she wrapped one hand around her middle.

The slap Letitia gave her was sudden and sharp. "You're hysterical," she stated calmly. "It's understandable, but we can't indulge in such histrionics now, Ellen. Take a few minutes to compose yourself and then return to the ward."

Every trace of laughter was gone as Ellen spent a few minutes outside in the warm spring air, her cheek stinging. She felt ashamed of herself for reacting in such a way, and yet so exhausted she couldn't even summon the strength to care.

Then, all of a sudden, a sob erupted from her that she didn't even understand. How could she be laughing one minute, and crying the next? And yet she was; the sobs tore from her body, physical, guttural sounds that escaped even as she clapped her hand over her mouth to suppress them, her shoulders shaking with their force.

She fell to her knees, her nurse's veil dragging on the ground, as the tears she hadn't realized she'd been holding back flowed down her cheeks.

Then, suddenly, someone's arms were around her, rocking her like a child.

"There, there. There, there. It's all right, Ellen, it's all right to cry."

But it wasn't, Ellen thought even as the sobs continued to wrack her whole frame. It wasn't, because Letitia was right, there was no time for histrionics, they had to keep going. Men were dying every second, simply for want of care. She struggled to stand, but the woman held her fast.

"It's all right," she said again, and Ellen realized it was Norah holding her, and she relaxed a little, resting her head on Norah's shoulder.

"I'm sorry," she whispered. "I'm ashamed of myself."

"Don't be. It's a wonder that any of us can still walk and talk and breathe."

"*They* can't," Ellen burst out. "I watched a man die from across the room—I was bandaging another man's leg, but he was dying all alone, no one to help him or hold his hand as he called out." She struggled to draw a breath. "It's so awful, Norah. I can't bear it."

"None of us can, and that's what makes us human. What gives us souls."

"But we have to," Ellen protested in a trembling voice.

"Yes," Norah said steadily. "We have to."

After an endless moment, Ellen stood up on shaky legs. "I'm all right now," she said, as she wiped her cheeks and tucked her hair under her veil. "Thank you."

Norah patted her on the shoulder before moving away.

Ellen took a deep breath, letting it fill her lungs and buoy her battered soul. Then she turned and walked back into the ward.

Miss Ivens arrived later that night to help with the wounded, but Ellen had barely spoken to her in the rush. She hoped Miss Ivens hadn't heard of her near-breakdown, although she knew there were few secrets in the close quarters. Still, she hated the thought of the admirable and indomitable Miss Ivens knowing her weakness.

Then, only a few days later, the Medecin-Principal told Miss Ivens that everyone at Villers-Cotterêts, patients and staff, would be required to evacuate, taking as many patients as they could back to Royaumont.

"And how are we to get there?" Miss Ivens had demanded. "Every car and ambulance has already been commandeered, and our telephone line has been cut. There is no way to go anywhere. We are stuck."

Ellen, who had been in the operating theater with Miss Ivens and heard her talking of it, felt a strange new shiver of apprehension. They were on the Front, and they were cut off from the rest of the world. She'd seen the streams of cars and people fleeing down the muddy road, searching for salvation. She'd noticed the hollow-eyed looks of refugees who carried all their worldly possessions in a single string bag, the children who looked like wizened old men from hunger and seeing too much war, the flood of refugees staunched by the occasional troop of soldiers or weary cavalry, sometimes a lumbering tank.

It was odd that in her nearly four years of service, she had never truly been afraid for her own life. She'd been concerned for others, and for her work, but not for her very self. But now, with the bombs falling all around them, with the windowpanes and roof rattling and far too many wounded to move, she felt a sudden, terrible surge of fear, raw and primal, for her own life.

I haven't lived enough, she thought frantically. *I haven't loved enough. It's too soon for me.* She thought of the boy back in Royaumont who had died in her arms; the soldier who had cried out across the ward, alone and aching. It was too soon for everyone.

"There is a train," the Medecin-Principal told Miss Ivens. "For the wounded. Your staff may go in cars as you can find them. Pack all your valuables and be ready to move tonight."

Ellen felt as if she were living in a dream, a terrible, waking nightmare, as she packed her few possessions and then set about helping the patients to be ready and as fit for travel as they could be, although some struggled even to be moved from a bed, unable to put a brave smile on, as they once might have done.

"This is absurd, a farce," Letitia said in a low, furious voice as she supervised the removal of patients from a ward, the men looking too dazed and ill to protest. "These men can't be moved."

"Then they'll be killed," Marjorie Dunmore, one of the doctors, said bluntly. "Do you think the Germans will spare them? Any of us? It's move or die, Doctor. Move or die."

Somehow they managed to get all the patients out of the hospital, stumbling or on stretchers, onto the train platform. Spring sunshine bathed everything in warmth, even as desperation pulsed through the air like a live current. The Germans were said to be less than eight miles away, and moving fast.

Ellen could not imagine what would happen if the enemy army came upon dozens of soldiers and staff, everyone unarmed, simply *waiting*. Miss Ivens had said no staff should leave until the wounded were safely on board the train, and yet evening came and the train did not arrive.

An awful sense of impending, unimaginable disaster came upon the patients and staff like a dark mist. How could they just stay there, when everyone else was fleeing as fast as they could?

Ellen met the terrified gaze of a little boy with a scrawny chicken under one arm, trying to keep up with his mother, who was holding a little girl of no more than two in her arms. They could not move very fast, and Ellen's heart ached for them and all the other refugees whose lives had been completely destroyed.

She'd heard horrid tales of what the Germans did—put babies on spits and roasted them alive; shot down mere children as if for sport. She didn't know whether to believe them or not; surely the German soldiers were just men, like the British and Canadians, the French and Senegalese? All just dirty, tired men who were so weary of war.

But this was the Front, and the tide was turning against the Germans, or so people hoped. Who knew what they would do in this situation? Anything could happen. Anything might.

Ellen realized that she had, in all her time in France, never actually seen a German soldier. She was half-expecting a monster, even though she knew him to be a man. She wondered if she would see one—or many—tonight.

At eight o'clock, the train finally pulled into the station, and everyone on the platform exhaled in tremendous relief. Then Miss Ivens discovered, to her immense ire, that there was only room for half of the hospital's patients.

"And what shall we do with the other fifty?" she demanded as the train pulled away, her hands bunched into futile fists at her sides. No one had any answer.

"What now?" one of the orderlies asked uncertainly. The hospital had no cars or lorries; they'd all been commandeered by the military, or broken down.

Then, like a miracle of heaven, several cars from the nearby American base pulled up to the station, and a ragged cheer went up from the motley crew still on the platform.

Miss Ivens managed to find places in cars or lorries for the rest of the patients; the Americans promised they would come back for the staff. Ellen exchanged an uneasy look with Letitia, wondering how long it would be that they would have to wait in this ever-increasing hell.

As the sky lit up like a massive firework, streaks of white light arcing against the stars, several of the staff started to walk.

"They won't come back," Letitia said matter-of-factly. "They won't be able to turn around. I've heard say the Boche are only three miles away now, and coming on even faster."

With her heart feeling as if it were thudding up her throat, Ellen fell into step with Letitia. "Where are we going?" she asked and Letitia shrugged.

"Miss Ivens says to make for Royaumont. There might be a train at Crépy."

"But that's miles away," Ellen exclaimed. "A whole night's walking, at least."

Letitia shrugged, too despondent to be moved. "What else are we to do?"

Ellen glanced back at the remaining staff milling about on the platform, looking lost and uncertain. "What about the others?"

"They can come if they want to."

Ellen hurried back to see what the others were doing; while most chose to wait, in desperate and perhaps pointless hope, Norah and a few others set off with her and Letitia, joining the now-trickle of humanity still trying to flee the Germans.

They walked in silence, the sky lit up all around them, the air filled with the scream of sirens and the boom and thud of bombs falling in the distance. It felt like a nightmare that would never end, and yet with each step, Ellen found her fear receding. No one, she supposed, could stay afraid for that long.

Perhaps that was what the soldiers at the Front felt; after that first surge of pure terror, some part of them accepted the risk and danger, and simply got on with things. Then she remembered the dazed stare of so many who had seen so much, and wondered if that was just wishful thinking on her part.

They were not alone on the road; along with a handful of the staff of Villers-Cotterêts, refugees from the surrounding villages continued to trudge towards whatever safety they could find.

At one point, a bomb fell so close they ran for shelter in a falling-down barn on the side of the road, putting their arms over their heads as the dust and dirt rained upon them, and the noise rang in their ears, leaving them all stunned for a second.

Several hours later, Ellen was hungry, filthy, and too tired to feel anything, never mind fear, any longer. She could barely put one foot in front of the other, and they were still miles from the train station at Crépy. The stream of those fleeing had reduced to a trickle, as some sought shelter for the night, and others simply sat by the side of the road, too tired to go on.

Ellen's ears rang from the noise of the bombs and every muscle ached and screamed in protest, yet they still had to go on… and on and on. Some of the other nursing staff had fallen behind, while others had marched ahead. Only Letitia stood next to her, trudging alongside, her head bowed. Ellen heard the sound of a motor behind her, and then Letitia grabbed her arm hard.

"Someone's coming," she hissed, and pulled Ellen off the side of the road, so they both fell headlong into a ditch, bruised and muddy. There could be no telling if the lorry that was hurtling down the dirt road was friend or foe, and Ellen's heart started to thud in heavy, hectic beats. She could still feel fear, after all.

The vehicle, whatever it was, stopped nearby, its motor still running. Letitia and Ellen exchanged a wide-eyed look of uncertain terror. Then Ellen poked her head up, enough to see the markings on the lorry.

"It's Canadian," she said, her body sagging with relief. "Perhaps they can help us."

They scrambled up from the ditch, and one of the soldiers at the side of the lorry stared at them in surprise, two mud-splattered women barely recognizable in their disarray and dirty clothes.

"We're nurses evacuating from Villers-Cotterêts," Letitia called out. "British. We're trying to get to Royaumont, or at least Crépy, for the train."

The soldier shook his head. "There are no more trains. The line has been bombed."

Ellen thought of the wounded on the train with a lurch of grief. What had happened to those poor men?

"We'll go anywhere," Letitia said. "Anywhere away from here. Can you take us?"

The soldier consulted with the driver, and then shrugged as he opened the back of the lorry. "I don't know if there's room, ladies, but you're welcome to cram in and find a space if you can."

Ellen and Letitia hurried to the back of the lorry and saw that it was fit to bursting with evacuating soldiers, shoulder by jowl, faces and uniforms covered in mud. As Ellen hauled herself up into the lorry, she fell flat on her face, bruising her cheekbone, before she scrambled up to a seated position. She blinked around in the gloom; she was surrounded by soldiers who were too weary and dazed to offer her a smile or even a hand.

Then, suddenly, someone was gripping her shoulder, peering into her face.

"*Ellen?*"

Ellen blinked at the stranger's face, helmet and mud splatters making it impossible to make out who it was… but the voice. Oh, the voice.

"*Jed…*"

Jed grabbed her arm, hauling her up next to him, and a few soldiers obligingly and silently shuffled over to give her a tiny amount of space. On the other side of the lorry, Letitia had managed to find a bit of bench.

Ellen blinked in wonder at Jed, scarcely able to believe he was there—his gray eyes glinting, even in the darkness. His face was streaked with mud and the set of his mouth was both familiar and grim. It had been seven long years since she'd last seen him. "*Jed.*" She shook her head, unable to believe it still, and tears started in her eyes.

Clumsily, Jed pulled her into a one-armed hug. "I can't believe it's you. Lucas told me you were nursing in France…"

"At the Scottish Women's Hospital at Royaumont. Not far from here. We tended mostly French soldiers."

"All this time…"

"And you've been on the Front…"

"In the artillery." He gazed down at her face as if trying to memorize her features. "I haven't seen anyone I've known for months."

"What about Lucas?"

"I don't even know what he's been doing. No one does. Our leaves have only allowed us to meet up once."

"That's terrible," Ellen exclaimed. "All this time… and what about Peter?"

"He was in a different division, since he joined up later. I haven't seen him in months. I haven't heard anything bad, though, but it's complete chaos out there. No one knows anything."

Ellen nodded soberly. "It feels like the end of the world."

"I think it is." Jed shook his head grimly. "We'll never go back to the way we were, after this. I don't think we'd even know how."

"What about the other island boys?" Ellen asked, both eager for and afraid of news.

Jed shook his head again, and Ellen listened with a leaden feeling of dread as he listed all the boys, far too many of them, who had been wounded or killed.

"Little Tommy Boyle…" Ellen exclaimed with a soft sound of dismay.

"Not so little anymore. He was nineteen."

"*Nineteen.*" Ellen looked away, biting her lips to keep from crying out. Why the death of a boy she'd barely known should affect her so much then, she didn't know. She'd certainly seen enough death already. And yet… Tommy Boyle. He'd had gap teeth and freckles, and she remembered when he'd been about six. "And what about Louisa?" Ellen asked after a moment, knowing she needed to mention her old friend. "How is she? And your little boy…"

"I don't know how they are." Jed looked away from her, hunching his shoulders. "Louisa hasn't written me since she left for Seaton, back in 1915."

"What!" Ellen stared at him in shock. "Not even once?" Jed shook his head. "But why…"

He shrugged, his gaze still averted from hers. "It's been hard on her," he said in a tone that suggested he wasn't going to say anything more about it, and she'd better not ask.

Ellen wondered what he meant—what had been hard on Louisa? The war? Her marriage or motherhood? Island life? All of it?

"I'm sorry, Jed," she said quietly, and he shrugged.

"The war has changed everybody, not just those at the Front."

"Perhaps you just haven't received her letters…"

"That's not how it is, Ellen." Jed's tone was final, and Ellen bit her lip, determined not to say anything more.

They rode in silence for a few minutes, the lorry bumping and juddering over the deep potholes and muddy ruts in the road, no one speaking or even looking at each other, everyone desperately tired, and also desperate to escape the shelling.

Then, a sudden whistling rent the air and an explosion threw everything in bright relief as for a second the entire world seemed suspended as if in a terrible spotlight, and then the lorry turned over and over, down into the ditch, the world exploding into fragments around them.

Ellen felt herself flying through the air, too stunned to scream, everything a bright blur, and then she landed hard on the ground, pain ricocheting through her head. She stared up at the lit sky, thinking distantly how bright the stars were, and how very beautiful, before darkness claimed her.

CHAPTER TWENTY

Ellen blinked up at the vaulted stone ceiling high above her as someone raised a glass towards her lips. She choked on the single sip, the water dribbling down her chin.

"There, now. You're all right. Nothing broken, thank goodness."

Ellen tried to raise her head, but she felt utterly exhausted, as if her body was weighed down by heavy stones. She couldn't move at all, not even a flutter of her fingers against the sheet. Memories came trickling in: the madness of the last days at Villers-Cotterêts, the hurried evacuation from the hospital as the bombs fell over Paris, the sky lit up like a giant firework, *Jed…*

At the memory of Jed, she struggled to sit up again but fell back against the pillow with a groan without having moved more than an inch.

"Where…" Her voice came out hoarse and scratchy. "Where am I?"

"At Royaumont, of course." The woman who was speaking to her leaned closer, and Ellen saw it was her roommate and fellow auxiliary nurse, Rosemary. "You did get struck on the head, Ellen, but surely not that badly?"

"I don't know." Ellen lifted one trembling hand to her head; she could feel a large lump by her ear, painful to the touch. Of course she was at Royaumont. She should have known simply by her view of the arched stonework above her. But everything was so muddled in her mind, and she didn't know how long she'd been in bed. The last thing she remembered was being in

the lorry with Jed, he'd been telling her about the island boys…
and Louisa…

She took a few even breaths and tried to order her thoughts.

"How did they find us, Rosemary?" she asked at last. Her voice came out in a scratchy whisper. "What happened? The Germans…"

"Thank goodness you remember me at least," Rosemary answered with a little laugh. "The cars with the staff were traveling in convoy behind you. The Americans had come back, after all. They stopped when they saw the lorry had been hit." Rosemary fell silent and Ellen closed her eyes, everything in her straining in denial even as the memories trickled through her—the thud of the shell, the debris raining down as she'd been hurled from the truck as if by a giant hand, the world fading to black.

"And… the soldiers?" she asked. "The Canadians? Are they all right?"

"Some of them," Rosemary allowed soberly. "Some were badly injured, and a few… a few died. The shell hit the front of the lorry, Ellen. The driver and the man next to him didn't have a chance."

Ellen thought of the driver who had stopped for her and Letitia, the soldier in the passenger's seat who had opened the back of the lorry for them. She couldn't recall their faces, but she knew they'd been kind. They had given their lives for her and Letitia, even if they hadn't realized it. If they hadn't stopped, perhaps that shell would have missed them. They would all be away safely somewhere. The thought was unbearable.

"Letitia," she said with a sudden gasp. "Is she…"

"She's in the bed next to you," Rosemary said, and Ellen turned her head and thankfully caught a glimpse of her friend. "She's sleeping," Rosemary continued. "She broke her arm. Miss Ivens set it herself, and said it should mend nicely."

"What about the soldiers?" Ellen asked. "The Canadians? Did you bring them to Royaumont as well? Are they here?" She thought of Jed with a sudden, frightened urgency. What had happened to him? Was he injured, as well?

"Yes, I think so." Rosemary frowned in puzzlement. "Why are you so concerned about them, Ellen? Surely you hadn't known any of them?"

"Yes, I did. *Do.* One." It seemed a terribly cruel twist of fate for her to be reunited with Jed only to have it all blasted apart seconds later. What if he'd died?

But then, Ellen reminded herself, she hadn't *really* been reunited with Jed, not in the way it had felt for one surprising second when he'd put his arm around her and she'd pressed her cheek against the rough wool of his jacket. He was a married man still, and always would be. That wouldn't change. But it had been so very wonderful to see him again.

"Rosemary, please… could you discover if one of the Canadians, Jed Lyman, is here at Royaumont, and how he fares? He's in the artillery. He was a friend of mine, from back home. I'd… I'd like to know how he is."

"I'll try," Rosemary said. "But it's not as it once was, Ellen… the abbey is filled to the rafters, not just with patients, although we've hundreds of those, but with refugees of all sorts. The entire nursing staff from another hospital has come here, and they weren't even fully dressed when they came! Ran out in their pajamas and dressing gowns. They won't lift a finger to help," she added with a sniff. "The cook is quite put out, and he makes sure their porridge is cold, although I don't blame them, not really. They've had a dreadful time. Everyone has. It feels like the end of the world."

Just as she'd said to Jed. "How long have I been here?" Ellen asked, and Rosemary grimaced.

"You've been in and out for sleep for three days. I would have thought the shelling would have woken you, but you didn't do much more than moan, even when the window—the last one with glass that we have, I think—blew in just over there." She nodded towards the windows at the end of the ward, now empty of glass, a bright blue sky visible framed by its stone arch.

"Goodness." Ellen closed her eyes, overwhelmed by how much had happened and changed. Her head pounded.

"You should rest," Rosemary said. "I'll look out for this Canadian of yours. Jed Lyman, you said? Someone might know if he's here." She gave Ellen's arm a squeeze before rising from the chair by her bed.

Ellen lay there for a few minutes, gazing up at the ceiling, her mind spinning both from the bump on her head as well as the realization that Jed could be close at hand—or he could be lost to her forever.

"Please God," she whispered. "Please have him be safe."

It was another two days before Ellen felt well enough to rise from her bed, and even then Miss Ivens insisted that she rest and recuperate rather than report for duty. She felt as weak as a kitten as she went back to her old room, although she longed to search the wards for Jed. Rosemary, at least, was still looking.

"Heaven knows we need all the willing hands we can muster," Miss Ivens had told her severely, "but you won't do me or anyone else any good at all, Sister, if you fall into a faint when I need you to hold the candle steady. It's straight to bed for you, at least for another few days."

Royaumont was indeed, as Rosemary had said, filled to its very rafters. Beds and stretchers lined every room, even those that had not been put into use before, because of their draftiness or inconvenience. Shells rained steadily down all around them, and refugees camped in the meadows outside the abbey, a field of makeshift tents and shelters made of boughs or brush. It looked like a cross between a circus and a battlefield.

As Ellen returned to her old room on the top floor of the abbey, it seemed strange to think a few days ago she'd been unsure whether she would live or die; it had felt like the end of the very world, and yet here she was, back in her old bedroom, putting her chemises away in an old milk crate. She touched the thin cotton, mended thrice over, and wondered yet again how long the war would go on. Surely, for better or worse, the end would come soon?

She'd just finished putting her things away and was more than ready for a rest when Rosemary came into the room, breathless from the climb up the steep stone stairs.

"I've found your Jed Lyman," she said.

Ellen blushed at that, even as her heart turned over at her friend's news. "He's not mine, Rosemary," she protested. "I told you, he's a friend from my childhood, nothing more."

"Well, he's not mine," Rosemary answered with a small smile.

"You've found him? How is he?" Anxiety tightened her insides. "He's hurt…" He must have been, to be at Royaumont at all.

"He's in the Blanche de Castille ward. He was insensible for a while, which was why I couldn't find him. But he's sitting up and talking now."

"Is he well?" Ellen asked, anxiety sharpening her voice. "He wasn't… he wasn't too badly hurt?"

Rosemary hesitated and terror surged through Ellen. She didn't like the hesitant look on her friend's face. It spoke of something she dreaded to think about.

"But of course he's hurt," she murmured. "If he was insensible…"

"It's not that," Rosemary said. "He was hit on the head, but it wasn't too serious."

"But something," Ellen clarified. "I can tell by the way you're looking at me—oh, Rosemary, just say it, please. I can't stand not knowing."

"What is he to you?" Rosemary asked bluntly and the flush Ellen had been battling returned in full force.

"A friend, nothing more," she insisted. "He's married to one of my old school friends—Rosemary, you don't mean to tell me that he's… that his life is in danger?"

"No, nothing like that," Rosemary answered. "But when he was thrown clear of the lorry, he shattered his elbow. It might have been all right, I think, if it had been dealt with right away, although I suppose he would have always had a sore arm. But that's the trouble with a time like this—it wasn't dealt with. Nothing was. So many soldiers had to wait. We had them lining the hallways, bleeding to death, while Miss Ivens operated as quickly as she could…"

Ellen blanched at the image, one she was all too familiar with. "I wish this wretched war would just end," she burst out.

"I'm so sorry, Ellen." Rosemary's face was drawn in weary sadness.

"So he'll lose his arm?" Ellen stated flatly, for she knew Rosemary could mean nothing else, and her friend nodded.

"Miss Ivens said she is going to amputate this afternoon. She's afraid of blood poisoning otherwise. It has started to look infected. It won't heal."

Ellen nodded mutely. She'd heard such a story a hundred—a thousand—times before. It was the same as Lucien with his leg; it was the same as dozens and dozens of other soldiers who had come through Royaumont too late to save their arms or legs. The fact that it was Jed made no difference… except to her, and of course to him. And to Louisa, as well, perhaps, even though she hadn't written.

She sank onto the bed, her head pounding worse than ever. "Poor Jed," she murmured. "An amputation above the *elbow*… he's a farmer," she explained, as she looked up at Rosemary and blinked back tears. "A dear little farm on the prettiest island in Ontario you'd ever hope to see…" The tears thickened in her throat and she dropped her face into her hands, not wanting Rosemary to see her cry. She'd thought she had no tears left, but still they threatened to come. She'd cried for so much already, for wounded soldiers and dead boys and men stretching their hands out, longing only for a human touch as they breathed their last. But she hadn't cried yet for Jed, who would lose an arm and perhaps his livelihood, and maybe even his wife, as well, if he hadn't already lost her. *Jed, poor Jed…*

"Oh Ellen, I'm sorry," Rosemary said, and came to sit next to her on the narrow bed. She put her arms around her and Ellen leaned against her friend's shoulder, willing the tears back.

"It's the same everywhere, I know," she said. "So many men… so many shattered limbs and broken dreams, so many lost lives… and for what?"

"Don't think on it," Rosemary implored. "You'll lose your soul if you do, and most certainly your mind. The only way to keep going is to put your head down and work. You can't think about all of it. Any of it. You just can't."

"I know," Ellen answered with a shuddery sigh. "But it's so hard sometimes, Rosemary. I feel like screaming at how pointless it all is."

"I know. I do, as well. Scream into your pillow, if you must. Sometimes you have to." Ellen managed a wan smile at that, and Rosemary was silent for a moment. "They say the end might be in sight, you know."

"You think we'll manage to push the Germans back, when the bombs are falling all around us?"

"One hopes," Rosemary answered wearily. They exchanged sad smiles, needing no more words.

*

The next day, despite her still-aching head, Ellen reported to duty, and was amazed at the orderly chaos that life at Royaumont had become. Staff were sleeping in barns and on chairs; night and day staff shared the same beds, one falling into it as soon as another had risen. Patients were everywhere… every bench or board or blanket had been used to create makeshift beds for the more able patients, and stretchers lined the hallways as men, groaning and bleeding, waited for surgery they should have had hours, if not days ago.

Ellen worked for eighteen hours straight, assisting Miss Ivens in the operating theater, before she finally stumbled off duty, filthy and exhausted. It was past midnight, and she could hear the shelling; sometimes the impact shook the rafters, sending down a shower of dust and even rubble, and once that evening as many as could fit went down to the abbey cellars to wait out the bombing. When they emerged again, a huge crater had appeared in the field behind the abbey, bathed in moonlight, looking strangely beautiful and otherworldly.

After tidying herself as best as she could and bolting down a cup of tea and a piece of bread and butter, Ellen went in search of Jed. She hadn't had a moment to spare to find him and talk to him, and in truth she felt anxious about what she might say when she did. Jed could be surly at the best of times… how would he be with the prospect of an amputation?

She found him, as Rosemary had said, in the Blanche de Castille ward, lying in bed with a bulky bandage covering his right shoulder and what little was left of his arm, which had been amputated about three inches above the elbow. Miss Ivens had done the amputation that morning, before Ellen had come on duty, and the nurse on the ward assured her it was healing well.

Jed was sleeping, and Ellen watched him for a moment, noting the gray streaks in his dark hair, the shadows on his face, the new lines from nose to mouth. The war had changed him, as it had changed everyone, and yet he was still Jed, still the same boy who had picked her up from the ferry station and driven her through the dusk to Jasper Lane. She felt near tears again and she willed them back. Then Jed opened his eyes. His mouth twitched in a tiny, wry smile before remembrance flickered across his features and he closed his eyes again, shutting out the world.

"Hello, Jed," Ellen whispered. "It's so good to see you. How are you feeling?"

"I don't know." His voice was scratchy and he cleared his throat. "They've given me something for the pain."

"That's good."

He opened his eyes and glanced down at his shoulder, his expression shuttering. "I suppose."

"At least you're alive."

"There's that," Jed agreed. "Although what use I'll be to anyone, I don't know. You can't pitch hay with one arm."

"Oh, Jed." Quickly, Ellen dashed the tears from her eyes before he could see them. She sat on the chair by his bed. "You might be surprised by what you find you're able to do. We've had quite a few amputees through here, and they soon get the hang of things. A man with no arms at all can actually hold a pen between his toes!"

A blaze of anger lit up Jed's eyes and he glared at her. "Do you think I want that? To be some sort of circus freak? To be nothing more than an… an *amputee?*" His mouth twisted as he spat out the word.

Ellen berated herself for her thoughtlessness. It was far too soon to be offering that kind of encouragement. She knew that well, from her past experience with other men who had had amputations. "I'm sorry, I didn't mean anything like that. It takes some getting used to, I know."

"I'll never get used to it." Jed spoke heavily, his voice filled with grim despair. He closed his eyes again. "I'm sorry, Ellen. I shouldn't have spoken like that. I'm sure that man is admirable indeed." He took a deep breath that shuddered through him. "But I don't want to talk about me or what you think I'll be able to do with one arm. Not yet. I just… can't."

"I understand," she whispered.

He opened his eyes and studied her for a few quiet moments. "It's been a long time, Ellen."

"Seven years."

"A lot has happened to both of us, I reckon." His mouth twisted in acknowledgement, and Ellen nodded slowly.

"Yes."

"Rose told me a bit about Glasgow. You had an exhibition…?"

Ellen thought of *Starlit Sea*. It felt like a thousand years ago. "Yes, at the end of my course."

"You'll go back to Glasgow when all this is finished?"

"I… don't know. I suppose." She wondered if she still would have her position, if the School of Art would go on the same as ever. It seemed hard to imagine, and yet what else would happen? Life would go on. One day, life would go on, perhaps not as it always had, but in some form. It had to. "And what about you? I saw Lucas a long time ago now, but he said you and Louisa might move back to Seaton? You could work in a bank, he thought."

"With one arm?" he said, his voice caught between bitterness and wryness. "I can't ever see myself working in a bank, and I'm not sure Louisa even wants me to."

Because she hadn't written? "Surely she'd like that, Jed…" Ellen said uncertainly. She didn't know what Louisa wanted any longer.

Jed shook his head, and Ellen fell silent. "When I was in the trenches," Jed said after a long silence, "I used to picture the island. I'd walk down the lanes in my mind, and I'd be able to imagine every tree, every leaf. I could see how the sun fell on the fields, turning them to gold, and how the frost tipped the grass, turning them silver. I could hear the waves lapping the shore, see how blue-green they looked in the summer sunshine. I saw it all, Ellen." His voice choked and he turned his face away.

Ellen reached for his hand. "It's still there, Jed. It's still there just as it was. You can go back. We can all go back."

"And what would I go back for?" Jed looked at her, his face full of misery and despair. "For my own father, my own wife to take care of me, an invalid and as good as a cripple? She could just about tolerate me when I had two good arms."

"Oh, Jed…"

"Am I to be nothing but a burden to the community I'm meant to serve?"

"You have served," Ellen protested. "At home, and for all of this wretched war. You'll find a way, Jed. This doesn't have to be the end of everything. What about your little boy?"

"He doesn't even know me. He was barely more than a bairn when I left. And Louisa hasn't written to me about him." He shook his head. "I'm a stranger to my own family, and that's without this." He gestured to his bandaged shoulder.

Ellen decided not to press the matter. Jed's injury was still new, and she knew that a man had to grieve the loss of the limb, the loss of the life he'd expected to have, before he was able to think of any kind of future.

"What about you, Ellen?" Jed asked eventually. "Do you think you'll ever come back to the island?"

His words caused her an ache of bittersweet longing. "I… I don't know," she admitted. "I don't know if there's anything for me there anymore." She looked away, afraid he'd take her meaning to be about him. And maybe it was… at least a bit. Seeing Jed again had stirred up those feelings a little, like the ashes in a long-dead fire.

"Rose would welcome you," Jed insisted. "You've been like a daughter to her. And times are hard for her, you know. I'm sure she could use some help."

"Are they?" Ellen felt a lurch of alarm. "Why? I mean, I know it's hard, with Peter fighting…" Ellen trailed off at the look on Jed's face. "You know something," she stated numbly. "Don't you? Lucas hasn't written me for months, and I haven't heard anything from Rose since before Christmas. What's happened?"

"Dyle died in January," Jed told her quietly. "My father wrote me about it. He had a heart attack. But he died in his own bed, in his sleep, as any man would want to."

"Oh, no." Ellen pressed a hand to her cheek, reeling from this shocking news. "Dyle…" She thought of how she'd hugged him goodbye all those years ago, his scratchy coat against her cheek, how he'd made her promise to return. "*Dyle.*" She shook her head as if to deny it, although it was just one more casualty of the war. There had been far, far too many.

If Dyle had had Peter home to help him with the farm, perhaps he would still be alive today. Andrew was fourteen, and Ellen knew he had to be of some help, but there had still been so much to do. If Peter hadn't had to go to war… It was, she knew, an unhappy, pointless thought. "Poor, poor Rose. She'll have to manage the farm with only Andrew, until Peter comes back." *If* he came back. If she'd learned one thing in these last four years, it was that *nothing* was certain. Although Ellen couldn't bear to think about losing Peter as well.

"Yes," Jed agreed, meeting her eyes with that same old steadiness she'd always found so reassuring. Even now, in his own bleak state, he possessed the strength to offer her some comfort. "When he comes back."

The next few months blurred by in an endless round of snatched sleep and long hours in the operating theater or on the wards, which grew stifling in the summer heat.

Miss Ivens had requested more staff, and Ellen and the other nurses were subjected to a parade of new orderlies and auxiliary nurses, some of whom left after only a few weeks, or even days, complaining of the crowded conditions, the lack of private beds or baths, and the endless, backbreaking work.

"Did they think they were coming on holiday?" Rosemary asked grimly when an orderly, Doris Stevenson, left in high dudgeon, complaining that she could not work in such dreary circumstances. "There's a *war* on. What did she think it would be like? A tea party?"

"Apparently the place isn't fit for a gentlewoman," Ellen answered with a small smile. "Imagine that! We're actually getting our hands dirty." Absolutely filthy was more like it. Ellen couldn't remember the last time she'd had a proper wash; water was scarce, as was time.

By the beginning of July, the steady stream of wounded into Royaumont had finally begun to lessen, although the air raids continued nightly. Miss Ivens relayed the orders that the hospital was to be emptied as far as was possible, to make ready for the next wave of wounded when the French launched their counter-attack.

Ellen said goodbye to Jed on one stiflingly hot morning, a month after he'd arrived. As busy as she was, she'd had very little time to spend with him, although she'd stopped by his bed whenever she could, and encouraged him to write Louisa. Jed had experienced moments of both light and dark; often falling into despair before Ellen did her best to rouse him out of it. Before he'd left, he'd finally penned Louisa a brief letter, and Ellen had made sure it went in the post. She hoped and prayed Louisa would find it in herself to reconcile with Jed, and be the support he so clearly needed.

For now he was returning to England to convalesce, and then back to Canada. For him, the war was over, and she was thankful that at least he would be safe, out of the fighting… whatever the future held for him and his wife.

"Shall I see you again, do you think?" he asked as he embraced her lightly with his one good arm. His empty sleeve was pinned neatly back, and he stood tall and straight, as fine as any soldier could be, determined to conduct himself with dignity.

"Yes, of course you will," Ellen cried. In that moment, she could not imagine not seeing Jed or Lucas or Aunt Rose or the island ever again. "I shall come back," she promised. "When the war is over, I will. I'll need to."

Jed nodded, accepting her word.

"Until then," he said, and kissed her on the cheek.

Ellen stayed outside the abbey doors, watching the dust settle on the road long after the lorry that was taking him to the station at Creil had gone. She would see him again, she vowed. She would return to the island, if only for a visit. She had to, for her own sake as well as Rose's. She needed to see her home again, to remember her roots. They felt like the only thing anchoring her to this strange, shifting world.

A few weeks ago, when she'd sent Jed's letter, Ellen had written her aunt, but she had not yet had a reply. Post was incredibly difficult to get through with the German U-boats, so Ellen was not holding out for a response. But, God willing, the war would be over soon and she'd be able to go back to the island herself. *Go home.*

In August, the overworked staff began to feel the strain of their twenty-hour days and the constant shelling at night. Several doctors were sent home due to nervous collapse, and Miss Ivens wrote frantic letters for more staff to replace the ones that had gone.

Through it all, Ellen trudged on—working, sleeping, too weary even to dream of the day when it would finally all be over. It felt as if it never would; she certainly couldn't imagine it. She heard from Aunt Rose at last, who was worn down by grief and yet still ever pragmatic and even cheerful.

I long for the day when this is all behind us, and we can get on with life as best as we can. I know it won't be the same, nothing will be the same, but at least it will be ours. And I do hope and pray, Ellen, that you might find it in your heart to come back to your island, if only for a visit. I miss you so, and the island misses you as well. For it is yours—surely you know that? You feel it in your very bones.

Yes, she did.

Ellen lowered the letter to gaze out at the abbey's once-peaceful gardens, now cratered with shell holes and muddy tracks, a shadow of its once glorious self, just as all of Belgium and France was. But one day the flowers would grow again; the trenches would be filled in, perhaps even forgotten, although Ellen resisted that notion. They must all remember, so they could be grateful for what they had afterward. So it would never happen again, because surely no one could survive that.

Then, in September, just when things had reached an equilibrium of sorts, both staff and patients began to come down with *la grippe*—the dreaded influenza that had been striking the battle fields, as dangerous as any German artillery. Ellen was soon nursing her own compatriots along with the wounded who continued to fill the wards. Rosemary and Norah both succumbed to the 'flu but were back at their posts by October, while Ellen, perhaps because she'd endured a similar illness during her days at Kingston General Hospital, remained thankfully immune.

The days and nights blurred together and she sometimes fell asleep standing up, a cup of tea still in her hand. She had learned to sleep through the screaming of the air-raid siren or the thudding booms of the bombs, through the shuddering of the whole abbey, as if the ancient cloisters might collapse on top of them, and the endless groaning of the poor soldiers who suffered from such grievous wounds.

She'd jolt awake after a few minutes, or perhaps an hour, and hurry back to her duties. And so the months both slid by and stretched on, as everyone waited for word that there would be an end to all the madness and misery. Surely it would happen soon. Surely it had to. And yet the days crept by, each one bringing fresh injury and agony, and nothing happened.

Then, when it finally did, Ellen could hardly believe it was true. General Descoings came to the hospital at eight o'clock one November morning, his face solemn. "*La guerre est finie.*"

A stunned silence followed his pronouncement, one that went on too long, as if the news simply couldn't penetrate anyone's numbed minds.

Ellen stared at him dumbly, utterly unable to take it in. *La guerre est finie.*

Then, finally, a few raggedy cheers went up as the nurses and orderlies went through the wards, announcing the long-awaited news. The stunned silence and seeming inability to understand what had happened gave way to incredulous joy and tremulous hope. Tears pricked Ellen's eyes as the cries started up in every ward: "*Vive la France! Vive l'Angleterre! Vive les Alliés!*"

She found Rosemary and Norah and Letitia in another ward, and they hugged each other silently, tears of relief and incredulity streaming down their faces. It was over. It was starting to feel real; it was actually *over.*

A spirit of almost manic jollity swept through the hospital on a tide of emotion; someone found the old bell rope and pulled and pulled so the bell high above the abbey rang for at least five minutes. Impromptu concerts were had all over the wards as patients and staff alike sought to celebrate, finding instruments or even just pots or pans, making a joyful noise because they simply had to. It felt necessary, essential. Now, finally, it was time to celebrate. At last.

"I hardly know what to feel," Letitia admitted that night, as she and Ellen stared out at the frost-covered fields under a starry sky. All was blissfully, blessedly silent, a world at peace. "I don't know what I shall do now."

"Will you go back to Edinburgh?" Ellen asked. "And work in the hospital there?"

"I suppose." Letitia shrugged, her expression turning contemplative and a bit sad, and Ellen knew she was thinking of Lieutenant Allard, who had returned to Algiers, his heart still closed to her. "And what about you? Back to Glasgow?"

"Yes, I think so." Ellen thought of the island, and her promise to Jed. She did want to return to Amherst Island, to see everyone, but she could not afford a trip to Ontario and back, just for a lark. She sighed wearily. Perhaps next year, after she'd been teaching and earning money for a while. It felt like a long way away.

"We most likely won't leave France for months yet," Letitia said pragmatically. "Miss Ivens said soldiers wouldn't be able to return home till after Christmas, at the earliest."

Ellen supposed she shouldn't be surprised; war wasn't a game of cricket, where you simply picked up your bat and went home as soon as the match had finished. Still… Christmas, or even later. That felt far away, too, duty stretching on with no end in sight.

As it happened, the next few weeks slipped by, the same as any others, except without any more wounded coming in, thankfully. But men still needed their bandages changed, their medicine given, their bedpans emptied. Sadly, men still died, of wounds and infection and the terrible influenza that was raging through half the world, another war to be waged.

"It seems even more tragic, to have them die now," Letitia said sadly, one afternoon a few weeks after the war had ended. They were in the Canada ward, with Ellen checking on dressings and Letitia looking over some of her patients. Everything felt peaceful, the fields outside glittering with frost under a sky of hard, bright blue, the men in good spirits.

"Yes, but God willing, there should be no more." Already troops were being demobbed, and the word was that at least some of the soldiers would be home before Christmas.

One of the orderlies bustled into the ward, excitement sparkling in her eyes. "Dr. Portman, there is someone calling for you downstairs."

"Calling for me?" Letitia looked mystified. "Who on earth? I'm in the middle of my duties—"

"But nothing urgent," Ellen protested, curious as to who might be calling on her friend. "Surely you could spare a few minutes…?"

"I suppose." Letitia looked reluctant as she left the ward to tidy her hair and straighten her uniform. Ellen caught the orderly's eyes and something about the sparkle in them made her follow Letitia out of the ward and down the stairs.

At first, neither of them recognized the man standing ramrod straight despite the need of a crutch under one arm in the hall of the abbey. Although he was dressed in civilian clothes, his bearing was that of the soldier.

Then he turned around and Letitia let out a soft gasp. "Lu— Lieutenant Allard."

"Dr. Portman." He nodded, looking more serious than Ellen had ever seen the merry lieutenant, even after he'd lost his leg. His gaze was trained on Letitia, and Ellen stepped back quickly.

"I'll go back upstairs…"

"Letitia," Lucien said, stepping forward, his crutch scraping across the stone floor. He didn't even seem aware of Ellen or the orderly.

"Lucien," Letitia whispered. "Why…"

"The war is over."

"I know."

"We've lost so much. Everyone has… and it has made me realize I cannot waste another day. Not another moment."

Ellen's heart seemed to catch in her throat as she stood transfixed, awaiting Letitia's response, her heart buoyed with hope.

Letitia stared at him for a long, tense moment before she drew
herself up. "Does this mean you'll marry me?" she said rather
tartly, and Lucien drew back, startled.

"No," he answered. "It means *you* will marry *me*."

Ellen nearly jumped at the roar of approval that emerged
from behind her. She whirled around to see soldiers crowding
the hall and stairs—it seemed as if anyone who could walk had
done so, many using crutches or canes or holding onto nurses
and orderlies. They all wanted to see the spectacle for themselves.

Lucien grinned up at them and Letitia laughed, and then, to
the cheers of everyone, he took her in his arms and kissed her.

Celebration took hold of the wards again that night; an
impromptu party was held in Lucien and Letitia's honor, and
Ellen sat in the corner of the room, laughing as she watched as
three soldiers well enough to leave their beds did the cancan,
accompanied by cheers, jests, and lively music.

Norah came to sit next to her with a sigh. "I wasn't sure we
could experience such happiness again."

"Nor was I," Ellen agreed. "I hope it lasts."

"I hope you haven't become cynical."

Ellen raised her eyebrows. "Haven't we all?"

"Perhaps," Norah allowed. "How could we not, with all this?" She
sighed. "But at least it is over. Will you return to Glasgow, Ellen? To
the art school? Your position will still be there for you, I am sure."

"Yes, I suspect I will. I can't imagine what else I would do."
Ellen leaned her head back against a stone pillar. "In truth, I'd
like to go back to Canada, but I'm afraid there's nothing to go
back to anymore."

"Perhaps you need to see if that is true," Norah responded
with a wry smile. "But I hope wherever your travels take you,
you will return to Glasgow one day."

Ellen nodded slowly, still unsure as to what she would do. Was this deep-seated desire to return to Amherst Island a passing fancy, or nothing more than a sentimental desire to return to the past, now that the war was over? The sensible thing to do would be to return to Glasgow, settle in her little house with Ruby and Dougie, and make a life for herself. Take up her teaching, find her old friends. There really wasn't anything on Amherst Island for her—and yet…

Amherst Island was her home. It was where her family was, and her friends, and her very heart. Yet when—or if—she returned, would she find all three waiting for her there?

CHAPTER TWENTY-ONE

March 1919

Ellen stepped off the train into Glasgow Central Station, breathing in the old, familiar scent of soot and smoke, salt and sea. The smells of the city where she'd been born, and where she was finally returning, after four long years.

She'd been one of the last ones to leave Royaumont, choosing to stay behind with a handful of other doctors, nurses, and orderlies, to care for the hundred or so patients who could not yet be moved.

At Christmas, they'd opened the abbey doors to all the locals for a tremendous pantomime; two of the orderlies had trained as opera singers and Ellen had been enthralled by the production of *Cinderella* they'd put on; for once, everyone was able to celebrate without restraint, without the pall of war hanging over them like a shroud. It had been a joyous occasion indeed, full of laughter and cheer.

Over the course of those quiet, winter months, Ellen had heard from friends—Letitia and Lucien had married quietly and were living in Paris; Norah had returned to Glasgow to take up her position as painting mistress. Peter and Lucas had both thankfully returned to the island by January, and Jed several months before that, thanks to his injury. To Ellen's deep regret, Rose wrote with sad news of Jed and Louisa; she had returned a year ago, when Jed had, and they'd briefly tried to make a go of their marriage. But then their little boy Thomas had died of the influenza in October, and after the funeral Louisa had returned to Seaton, seemingly to stay.

> *Louisa is refusing to return to the island, and there is even talk of divorce, which would be quite a scandal, I'm sure I don't have to tell you. But I've come to realize that the war has left everyone with scars—even those who were not in France, and grief can be as destructive as death itself. I do feel sorry for them both—two hurting people who can't seem to find their way back to one another.*

Ellen ached with sadness to think of Jed living with his father at the Lyman farm, having lost both his wife and son. After having fought for four long years, it seemed unbearably unfair, and yet there were so many stories like it. The war had taken more than men's lives.

Rose wrote also of Lucas, which Ellen was glad to read.

> *Lucas has returned to Toronto, although he visits often as he can. He seems to enjoy his work there, and he's certainly well-suited to it! I do hope he'll come back to the island, one day. It's hard-going for everyone—I don't know whether the Lymans will be able to hold onto their farm, or whether anyone will. These are trying times.*

Ellen could guess what Rose was deliberately not saying; that she was struggling to hold onto Jasper Lane, without Dyle. Andrew and Peter would help, certainly, and perhaps the McCaffertys could make a go of it, but in these uncertain times, it would be hard.

> *Do let us know when you finally leave nursing; I imagine you will return to Glasgow but as ever you are welcome here,*

Ellen. The door is always open, and your little bedroom awaits! We all miss you terribly.

By March, there had been nothing left to do in Royaumont, and yet Ellen was still strangely reluctant to leave what had been her home for over four years. She'd seen so much in these soaring, vaulted rooms—so much sadness, of course, and yet also so much surprising joy.

She'd laughed and wept, sang and danced, served and been served. She heard the whispers of a thousand ghosts as she moved through the near-empty rooms—the soldiers she'd watched die, the ones she'd helped save, the friends she'd made and loved and lost. The war had been a terrible thing, and yet it had brought people together. It had united them in a cause. She'd realized, to her own surprise, that she was not ready to leave it all behind, and yet she had to, because the hospital was officially closing.

"It has done good duty," Miss Ivens, the last to leave, had said philosophically. "I shall miss it, which I know is strange."

"So shall I," Ellen had said. The chill March wind was bitterly cold, and she'd shivered as she reached for her case. "I didn't expect to, really."

"No." Miss Ivens nodded sagely. "Strange, isn't it? For four years we wanted nothing but for the war to be over, and now it is…" She shook her head. "Of course, I don't miss the fighting, or the senseless injuries, or the lack of medicine or beds or even light. But… it was something, wasn't it? What we did?"

Ellen smiled and nodded in acknowledgement. "It certainly was."

Together the last of the staff had traveled to Boulogne and then across the Channel, and Ellen had said her goodbyes before taking the train up to Glasgow by herself.

She stepped off the train with a sense of unreality; she had not been back since August 1914. She still wore her nursing uniform, and several passersby gave her warm smiles of gratitude for her service.

With just one kit bag to carry, she decided to walk the short distance from the station to the little house she'd shared with Ruby and Dougie, which she'd bought with the bequest from Henry McAvoy. Ruby had written regularly over the last five years, and Ellen knew from their letters that they had kept safe during the war, although Dougie had been further weakened by a bout of influenza that he'd thankfully survived.

Now she stood in front of the little house where she'd spent so many pleasant days, and shook her head, still amazed and almost disbelieving that she was actually there. It felt like a dream or as if she was living someone else's life. She realized she didn't have a key to her own home, and so she stepped up to the door and knocked.

Ruby answered the door, looking as cheerful and pretty as ever, if a little more careworn. Her mouth dropped open as she took in the sight of Ellen and then she threw her arms around her. "Oh, Ellen! You never even said you were coming back! We've wondered and waited… I knew you were staying at that hospital in France for such a long while, but…"

"I'm sorry," Ellen said as her arms closed around Ruby. "I should have sent a telegram. I didn't even think."

"Oh it doesn't matter, of course it doesn't!" Ruby exclaimed. "Come in, come in. You look ready to drop."

"I'm all right," Ellen said, and she followed Ruby into the little kitchen where they'd shared so many companionable cups of tea.

Ruby made a pot of tea and she and Dougie regaled Ellen with all the news they'd stored up over the last few years—how Ruby had started her own business, making up serviceable gowns, that had supplemented her seamstress work.

"People want things that are useful now. Everything's so different. There's opportunity for someone like me when there wasn't before."

"I'm glad to hear it," Ellen said. "At least something good has come from this war."

"It is a changed world," Ruby proclaimed with a new excitement firing her features. "Women can do so much more, Ellen. There's so much more opportunity now. Everything feels different, not always in a good way, I confess, but some changes *are* good."

"Yes, I can see that they are," Ellen answered with a smile.

The city certainly felt different than what she remembered from 1914; it seemed both more subdued and heartfelt. There could be no denying its population had changed, with far fewer men about, and many of them wounded in both mind and body. Ellen saw more than one man in a painted tin mask to hide his scarred face; she stepped aside as a group of blind men, one hand on the shoulder of the man in front of him, walked past in a crocodile on their way to the park, led by a matron as if they were little schoolchildren. It both heartened her and made her achingly sad. So much had changed. Everyone was adjusting because they had to; what other choice was there? And yet she felt as if she were drifting through her days, being blown by the winds of change without knowing where she would land, the sense of purpose nursing had given her gone and not yet replaced by something else.

She visited her old friend Amy, who now had two young children; she had, in Ellen's absence, become a cheerful matron who had grown just a little stout.

"Charlie had a good war," she said as Ellen sat in the sitting room of her comfortable house in Dowanhill. "As good as could be. He came out of it alive, at any rate." She shook her head sorrowfully. "Yet so many others lost... We must be thankful."

"Yes," Ellen agreed. "I am thankful."

"Will you take up your position at the School of Art?" Amy asked. "I expect they'll have kept it for you, even after all this time."

"Yes, they have," Ellen replied, because she'd had a letter from Fra Newbery offering her the position for a second time. She had not yet responded.

"It seems strange, to simply take up where one left off," Amy mused thoughtfully. "But what else is there to do? We can't go back. We must go on."

"Yes, I suppose we must," Ellen said, but she knew she didn't sound convinced. She didn't feel convinced; she felt, strangely, as if she were waiting, but she did not know yet what for.

She spent several days walking the streets of Glasgow, from Dowanhill to Springburn, recalling the strange and varied stages of her life. She stopped by Henry's house, remembering how she'd mounted the steps in Amy's emerald gown, full of nerves and hope. She walked by the offices of *The Glasgow Herald*, where she'd heard the terrible news of his death. And she remembered his funeral, when she'd stood apart from his family, having been loved by him in secret, and so not accepted by those he loved.

In Springburn, she walked down the crowded, narrow street where she'd spent her childhood, and past the same vegetable barrow she'd drawn seven years ago, now manned by a young girl with bright eyes and a cheeky smile. She felt like a ghost visiting a past life, or a spectator watching a play; none of it seemed to matter anymore, or at least not nearly as much as it once did. She couldn't settle, and she didn't know how to try. She was afraid she'd lost the knack completely. Just like the veterans who struggled to find a place for themselves in this new world, Ellen felt adrift.

"You're not happy here," Ruby stated a month after Ellen had returned to Glasgow. Spring had arrived and the city was ablaze with blooms, the fog of war and grief finally starting to lift, as if the world itself were determined to move on—trees budding just as they always had, skies washed the pale blue of spring, of rebirth.

"It's not a question of happiness," Ellen answered slowly. "Truly it isn't. I just don't know where I belong anymore, Ruby.

Maybe I've never known." She'd felt this sense of otherness before, although not as strongly as she did now. Where was her home, her heart? Where, truly, did she belong?

"We want you here," Ruby insisted and Ellen smiled and sighed.

"I know. You and Dougie have both been so understanding, so dear. And there's no reason why I shouldn't stay here—everything is already here for me." A job, a house, a life. She'd written Fra Newbery accepting the position as drawing instructor, yet she still couldn't even imagine it. Why, oh why, couldn't she settle? What was wrong with her? Everywhere she went, she seemed to feel adrift and alone; surely the problem lay in her, and not the place, wherever it was.

"It's as if something isn't finished," Ruby said slowly. "As if you're waiting for something more to happen. But do you know what it is?"

"No, and perhaps that's the trouble." Ellen sighed. "This is about me, not about Glasgow or teaching drawing, or anything like that." She hesitated and then said slowly, "The truth is... I have been thinking about returning to Canada. I don't know what would be there for me, certainly not a job. But it feels like something I should do. To see the people there. The people I love." She thought of Rose and all the McCaffertys, and of Lucas... and Jed. What was she hoping to find there? Surely nothing, even with Louisa in Seaton. Jed was still married. And yet... she was afraid to consider the matter too closely.

"Canada?" Ruby looked alarmed. "But that's so far!"

"I always said I'd go back," Ellen said with a small, sad smile. "I promised Aunt Rose, and Uncle Dyle..." She blinked back tears at the thought of never seeing her uncle again. "I know it won't be the same as it was. Dyle's gone and Jed's wounded and Peter..." Her breath hitched as she recalled Rose's last letter, that had hinted that Peter was struggling to return to normal life. "I need to go back," she said more firmly, certainty blooming within her like the flowers outside. "I don't know what waits for me there, perhaps nothing, but I need to go back and see." Perhaps then she'd move on with her life; she'd return to Glasgow and take up where she left off. She'd settle and teach and learn to be happy. But first came the island.

The next day, Ellen wrote Fra Newbery, deferring her acceptance of the position at the School of Art for a year, and then with the some of her savings, she booked her passage to New York. Ruby and Dougie would stay in the house while she was gone; Ruby had insisted on paying rent, but Ellen had refused.

"It's enough for me, that you look after it," she told her. "And that I know it's here, if I need it."

Ruby looked anxious at that. "You will come back?"

"I hope so," Ellen answered truthfully. "One day."

"But one day when?" Ruby shook her head, sniffing. "Never mind me. I know you need to do this. I only wish you didn't."

Yes, she did need to do this, even if she had no idea what she'd find at the other end of the journey. Was there a place for her on the island any longer? Could she find or make one? Did she want to?

Ellen stood on the deck of the *SS Athena* as it sailed into New York, just as she had done in 1904, with her da by her side, both of them full of determined optimism. *The fish fair jump into your hand.* She smiled at that, and then remembered how her father had said later how he never really liked fishing. She didn't even know where he was now or if he was alive; she hadn't heard from him since before the war. Yet another ending in her life, but this now was a beginning. At least, she hoped it was.

It was strange to sail past the Statue of Liberty again, with her blank face and raised torch. Fifteen years ago when she'd first arrived, Ellen had been so determined to be happy, to finally find her dreams. She'd had no idea that in just a few short weeks her father would have abandoned her for the railyards of New Mexico, and her Aunt Ruth and Uncle Hamish would have shipped her off to Ontario, to another relative she didn't even know, now-beloved Aunt Rose.

She remembered too how she'd been herded into the Hall of Tears on Ellis Island, and how she'd been separated from her father and examined on her own by a surly inspector; her eyelids had been lifted with a buttonhook to check for trachoma, and a chalk "X" made on her coat because the inspector had decided she was too thin and small. Terrified, she'd rubbed the mark off her coat before joining her father. She'd been a survivor even then.

Now, as a second-class passenger, Ellen bypassed Ellis Island and stepped out onto the streets of Manhattan a free woman, the world spread before her, not touched by war the way Britain was.

She didn't stay in New York, but immediately took a train to Seaton to visit her uncle Hamish before making her way on to Amherst Island. Hamish had retired from working for the Sears Roebuck store in Seaton a few years ago, and now he lived in a set of small rooms above the drugstore where Ellen had first tasted soda pop. He looked far older than Ellen remembered, with a few strands of flyaway hair combed over his head, his cheeks sunken in and his eyes a faded blue, but his smile was ready and warm when she embraced him, and he slipped her a few mint humbugs, just as he'd done when she'd been twelve.

"Ellen, my girl. I didn't know if I'd ever see you again."

"I'm glad to be back, Uncle Hamish."

Hamish popped a humbug into his mouth and sucked it vigorously. "Back for good, then?"

"I don't know. I'm going up to Amherst Island and then I'll see."

"You've done well for yourself back in Scotland, so I've heard. Teaching art, not just learning it!"

Ellen smiled. "I've been happy there. For the most part."

"It's hard to get over war," Hamish said sagely. "But you will, Ellen. In time."

Ellen nodded. She had no external injuries, no scars or missing limbs to learn to accept, simply the emptiness of a life she no longer knew what to do with. But perhaps Hamish was right, and in time she'd be able to move on. She'd find her place. Heaven knew she'd been looking for it long enough.

"But you're well, Uncle Hamish?" she asked. "Here in Seaton?"

"As well as I can be. I'm not getting any younger." His face creased into a smile. "But I'm happy enough. I still miss Ruth, you know, ornery creature that she was. Love of my life, too, she was."

"Yes, I'm sure you do miss her," Ellen answered sadly. "I do, too." Her Aunt Ruth had been a hard woman, but Ellen had known, at least at the end, that she'd loved her, and that had counted for a lot.

"Ah, Ellen." Hamish covered her hand with his own. "I hope you find what you're looking for."

Tears rose unexpectedly in her eyes and she smiled and blinked them back. She thought of Glasgow, and then Amherst Island, and of drawing—something she hadn't done in years—and nursing. She thought of Rose and then Ruby, and then Lucas and Jed. So many conflicting emotions. So many nameless and uncertain hopes.

Ellen leaned over to hug her uncle, breathing in his familiar scent of pipe tobacco and mint humbugs. "So do I, Uncle Hamish," she said. "So do I."

Ellen spent the night at Uncle Hamish's, and in the morning she made her way to the impressive house on Water Street where Louisa's parents lived. She hesitated before knocking on the door, for she didn't know if Louisa was still in Seaton, or if her old friend would want to see her.

As it happened, she didn't get a chance to knock. The door opened and Louisa's mother, Mrs. Hopper, stood there, scowling at Ellen so she nearly took a step back.

"If you're looking for Louisa, she's not here."

"Oh, is she—is she back on the island?" Ellen stammered. "I only wanted to say hello, Mrs. Hopper—"

"She's not back on that wretched island," Mrs. Hopper snapped. "She's gone to New York, to stay with some friends. Her health is delicate now, very delicate. After everything she's been through, her father and I thought she deserved a rest." Mrs. Hopper lifted her chin and glared at Ellen as if daring her to challenge that statement. Ellen realized the woman was ashamed that Louisa had left her husband, and was trying to hide it.

"Of course, of course," Ellen murmured. "If I'd known, perhaps I could have seen her in New York. But maybe I'll see her back on Amherst—"

"I don't know about that." Mrs. Hopper shook her head. "I don't know about that at all."

"I'm sorry for her loss, Mrs. Hopper. And for yours. I never knew Thomas—"

"He was the brightest little boy." Tears glittered in the older woman's eyes and she blinked them back fiercely. "But never mind about that. It's nothing to you."

Ellen knew better than to object; the woman was clearly grieving. After saying goodbye and having the door closed smartly in her face, she went slowly down the stairs, wondering if Louisa would return to the island—and to Jed. Would they get a divorce, as Aunt Rose had suggested? Admittedly, divorce was becoming more and more common, but it would still be a scandal in the small, tightly knit island community. But perhaps Louisa didn't care about that. And yet Ellen recalled how in love Jed and Louisa had seemed at their wedding, how happy they'd been, if only briefly.

No, surely in time Louisa would see sense. She was married, after all. She'd spoken vows. And Jed needed a loving wife by his side, now more than ever. Surely Louisa would see that?

Slowly, her heart burdened by all those cares, Ellen walked down the pavement, away from the Hoppers' house.

The next day, she took a morning train to Ogdensburg, arriving in the late afternoon. She walked to the little ferry landing that would take her to Amherst Island, marveling that she was back; everything looked exactly the same.

It was a warm spring day, a brisk breeze rippling the blue-green waters of Lake Ontario as she stood on the wooden platform and waited for the little boat to make its way across the lake.

Soon she saw it, a distant smudge, and as it came closer, she grinned for, to her amazement, she recognized the boat's captain; he'd been at the helm of the island ferry since Ellen had first been taking it.

"Captain Jonah! I don't know if you remember me—"

"Remember you?" Captain Jonah, white-haired and his face a mass of wrinkles, as old as the ages, spat neatly into the water. "I remember every passenger who ever stepped foot on this boat, missy! It's Ellen Copley, of course, back from Glasgow and France. Are you the la-di-da lady now?"

"No, not at all." Quite suddenly, Ellen felt overwhelmed by emotion—not sorrow, which she'd felt for far too long, but joy. A wild, inexpressible joy. She was home, and she was remembered. "But yes, Captain Jonah, it's me, Ellen Copley."

"Well, come aboard then!" Captain Jonah exclaimed. "Sharpish now, missy. Night's falling, you know, and it gets mighty cold when the sun sets, even in spring."

Twilight was indeed falling by the time they reached the island, now cloaked in soft violet shadows. Ellen had sat in the stern, her face lifted to catch the lake's chilly breeze, the spray from the wake the boat made stinging her face like tears.

"Is someone coming for you?" Captain Jonah asked dubiously, for the little ferry office was shut up tight, and the island's one main street was empty and dark.

Ellen laughed softly, remembering how long ago she'd sat outside the ferry office, a shy, uncertain girl of nearly thirteen, and waited for someone to fetch her. Jed Lyman had come, ungraciously at that, and taken her back to the McCaffertys' farmhouse in his old wagon, where she'd been greeted by five wild and wonderful children.

"No," she told Captain Jonah now. "No one's coming for me. No one knows I'm here. But don't worry, Captain Jonah, I know the way."

"If you're sure…"

"I'm sure," Ellen said firmly. Darkness had settled on the rolling fields of the island, and a whippoorwill called in the distance, its trill familiar and comforting, calling through the ages.

Smiling, Ellen lifted her skirts and stepped off the boat onto the island. Then, with her head held high and her heart so very full, she started walking towards home.

A LETTER FROM KATE

I want to say a huge thank you for choosing to read *Dreams of the Island*. If you enjoyed it, and want to keep up to date with all my latest releases, just sign up at the following link. Your email address will never be shared and you can unsubscribe at any time.

www.bookouture.com/kate-hewitt

Dreams of the Island is the second book in the Amherst Island trilogy, which I first wrote when I was just eighteen, although the story has developed considerably since then! Having loved the *Anne of Green Gables* series with a deep and abiding passion, I wanted to create my own version of the classic orphan story. Diehard Anne fans might be able to spot the occasional homage to L.M. Montgomery in the books.

As I developed Ellen's world, however, her story took on a life of its own, and *Dreams of the Island* travels far from the humble shores of her island home to the streets of Glasgow and the trenches of the First World War, but with Ellen always longing to return to the only place she called home—a place very near where I grew up, actually!

I hope you loved *Dreams of the Island* and if you did, I would be very grateful if you could write a review. I'd love to hear what you think, and it makes such a difference helping new readers to discover one of my books for the first time.

I love hearing from my readers—you can get in touch on Twitter, on my Facebook page, through Goodreads or my website.

Thanks,
Kate

katehewittauthor

www.kate-hewitt.com

@author_kate

Manufactured by Amazon.ca
Acheson, AB